THE PERFECTLY FINE HOUSE

Stephen Kozeniewski
Wile E. Young

Grindhouse Press
PO BOX 521
Dayton, Ohio 45401

Grindhouse Press #063
ISBN-13: 978-1-941918-63-0

Beware the redness!

S. Krzemeski
4/1/23

Meagan
~~To Scruffy~~

Don't believe the
rumors, there is
nothing wrong with
the house!
- Wile E.
Noy
04/01/23

PROLOGUE

IT HAD BEEN TEN EXCRUCIATING minutes since Ms. McIntosh threatened to keep the class behind until they named all six senses. So far they had only been able to come up with four, and aside from taste, which was already on the chalkboard, Bonnie was drawing a blank.

"Anyone? Anyone at all?"

"Smell?" Jane Anderson offered tentatively.

Bonnie was on the edge of her seat. Would this be yet another failed guess along the lines of Sammy Bleeker's "contribution," fashion? To Bonnie's immense relief, Ms. McIntosh nodded and filled in the fifth blank.

"Yes, smell. Very good, Jane. And who knows the last sense?"

They were so close, and yet so very, very far. The piece of chalk waggled back and forth through the air, desperately seeking an up-raised hand. Bonnie scrunched up her brow, racking her memory, but no matter how she tried, she couldn't come up with the last one.

Ms. McIntosh sighed. She probably didn't want to stay late any more than the children did.

"Is there anything in the back of the room that jogs anyone's memory?"

Bonnie looked over her shoulder in unison with her twenty-seven classmates. As they did every day at this time, the kids' great-grandparents had lined up at the back of the room in preparation of taking them all home. Bonnie's Gee-Ga waved at her. She smiled and waved back.

To her, Gee-Ga appeared as crisp and clear as a living person, like her teacher. The other great-grandparents were almost see-through, appearing in different shades of ghostly blacks, whites, and grays. Mrs. Anderson, who she knew from spending many after-noons at Jane's house, was a little clearer, but still not nearly as sharp as her own relative.

"G . . . ghostsense?" Eric Conners volunteered tentatively.

"Very good, Eric," Ms. McIntosh said, "but don't forget to raise your hand."

Eric scowled as Ms. McIntosh wrote a very long word on the board.

"Ghostsense, or mediumship, is the reason you can see your great-grandparents or any other relatives or pets who have passed on. If you . . ."

The bell rang and Bonnie jumped to her feet. Perfect timing. They wouldn't be held behind after all.

She rummaged through her desk, finding her prized train con-ductor's cap and throwing it on her head before joining the stam-pede toward the cubbyholes to grab her bag. Then, as fast as she could, she rushed to the back of the room and took her Gee-Ga's hand to join the line of children and their great-grandparents shuf-fling out of the classroom.

Holding Gee-Ga's hand wasn't like holding Mommy's or Dad-dy's (on the rare occasions they tolerated her doing that). It was a bit like pressing her flesh against a cube of Jell-O, and when Gee-Ga wasn't concentrating, Bonnie sometimes passed through her hand entirely. For now, though, as they started their walk home (or "promenade" as Gee-Ga insisted on calling it) she was pretty solid and Bonnie swung her hand back and forth and skipped.

"How did your matriculation go this fine day, my sweet pea?"

"It was pretty good. We learned about owls."

"Is that a fact? And what did you learn about our fine avian friends?"

"Did you know owls can turn their heads all the way around?"

"I had not the foggiest idea."

A smile crossed Bonnie's lips. Gee-Ga always said that, even though after a hundred years on earth she must have known at least some of the stuff Bonnie told her.

"And sometimes they find the skulls of mice and rats and even bigger animals in their pellets, which is the nice way of saying their . . . their, um . . ."

"Their spoor?"

"No," Bonnie said, feeling her cheeks heat. She lowered her voice as much as possible. "Their . . . poop."

"Oh, their poop. I see now. I had not known that was what an owl pellet was. I would've thought that was a bit like one of the pills I used to have to taken in the morning, or else a handbag."

Bonnie giggled.

"Owls don't have handbags."

"Are you quite certain, my dear?"

Bonnie paused and cradled her chin in her hand.

"I'm not sure."

"Well, I, on the other hand, am quite sure you are correct, seeing as owls do not have hands at all, but rather wings."

"Oh. Yeah, I guess that makes sense."

Bonnie came to a sudden halt. Gee-Ga, who was distracted by their conversation, passed through her and continued floating a few feet before noticing she had lost her. Gee-Ga turned back and gave her a look with a raised eyebrow.

"Have you been stricken by a sudden case of polio, my darling?"

"It's the park," Bonnie said, gesturing at the entrance to Memorial Park, which lay just before them.

"Why, my dear, we pass through this park every day."

"I know."

Bonnie shuffled her feet. She didn't want to tell Gee-Ga about what had happened at recess. Melanie Glass and her mean friends had pulled down Bonnie's pants and laughed at her. It had happened behind the bleachers, so at least it hadn't been a complete public embarrassment, but the other girls were snickering about it all day and making cutting remarks to Bonnie whenever they could get away with it. She could see them from here, hanging out underneath the Mueller statue.

"Hmm," Gee-Ga said. "What if we take the scenic route?"

"Scenic route?"

Gee-Ga nodded. "Come along, little one, I can show you where I grew up."

Now it was Bonnie's turn to give a sidelong glance. "Where you grew up?"

"Indeed. I was your age once, too, you know."

"But that must have been like a million years ago!"

"You know, I'm not too insubstantial to pop you in the mouth, little one."

"You wouldn't, Gee-Ga! Would you?"

Her great-grandmother smiled cryptically and began to float off in the opposite direction of the park. "Keep up!" she called over her shoulder.

Bonnie had to run much of the way to keep up with her Gee-Ga, but she was so excited—both at the prospect of seeing where Gee-Ga had grown up and at the opportunity to avoid Melanie's sneers and taunts—that she didn't feel tired at all. They had never gone this way before, but Gee-Ga floated effortlessly up the dirt paths and into the forest as though she had taken this path every day of her life. She probably had, once upon a time, Bonnie reflected, and it was as familiar to her great-grandmother as the path to and from the elementary school was to her.

After what seemed like an eternity of walking, as the distance finally began to catch up with Bonnie, they finally passed through a copse of trees and into a large clearing overgrown with weeds. The largest house Bonnie had ever seen before sat quietly in the center of the clearing.

The house had to be a hundred years old, at least, if her great-grandmother had grown up there, and it looked like it had been abandoned for almost that long. The windows were nailed shut with boards, and a murder of crows, half living and half spectral, had taken up residence in the gutters. Instead of taking to the air at their advance, the crows stared down at Bonnie and Gee-Ga, their beady eyes sending a shudder through Bonnie's spine. Animals were usually smart enough to run from people if they had any dealings with them. These animals and their ghostly kin hadn't seen people in many, many years.

"Welcome to Jackson Manor," Gee-Ga said. "This would've been your birthright if my nephew Barnabas hadn't been a degenerate gambler."

"What does 'degenerate' mean, Gee-Ga?"

"Never you mind that, right now, my sweet pea. Suffice it to say that some of your relatives were not very smart, and our ancestral home fell out of family hands."

"Who owns it now?"

"The county, I believe, but I haven't looked into the matter in many, many years. This is the first time I've even been here since . . . well, since before you were born."

"Does it have bad memories for you, Gee-Ga?"

Gee-Ga turned, crouched down to about Bonnie's level, and smiled warmly. She ran her airy hand through a strand of Bonnie's hair. Bonnie felt a chill, the ghostly cold a comforting reminder of her great-grandmother's love.

"It's not that so much as I was making more important memories with you, my darling."

Bonnie said, "Yes."

Gee-Ga straightened back up and turned back to her childhood home.

"Is it haunted?" Bonnie asked, tugging on Gee-Ga's dress even as it became insubstantial in her hands.

"It certainly was when I was a young lady. Would you like to go in and see if anyone is still home?"

Bonnie nodded. One of the ghostly crows took to the air as they climbed up onto the porch. The boards creaked beneath her weight.

"Should we knock?"

"I think that would be very polite. Go ahead, little one."

Bonnie stepped forward and reached up to grab hold of a large metal knocker. She had never seen one before, but as soon as she saw it she knew what it was for. She let the weight of the knocker slam one, two, three times, and giggled with each noise as more and more of the crows took wing in alarm.

They waited in silence for a moment.

"Barnabas!" Gee-Ga called out. "Uncle William? It's Lucinda."

Again, there was no response. Bonnie scrunched up her face and looked up at her great-grandmother.

"I thought you said it was haunted, Gee-Ga."

"Well, it certainly *was*. Perhaps the others have moved on."

Gee-Ga held up her hand and the door opened with a slow creak. Bonnie stepped over the threshold. She felt her stomach swim a bit. She wasn't sure what was wrong. Gee-Ga passed over the threshold as well, and as she did so she took on the look of someone drinking sour milk.

"Something's wrong here," Gee-Ga said. "This place used to be filled with spectral bats and insects. It's so quiet now."

"I don't like it here, Gee-Ga," Bonnie said. "I feel funny in my tummy."

"Perhaps we should go, dear."

An ethereal squeak cut through the almost unnatural silence of Jackson Manor. Bonnie zeroed in on the source of the noise. A ghostly mouse sat under a table in the foyer, chittering and staring at her. While she knew her great-grandmother so well she was practically a full-color living person in her sight, the tiny mouse appeared as little more than a chalk outline to her.

"Look, Gee-Ga! A mouse!"

"Perhaps we're letting our imaginations run away with us. Maybe this place isn't so strange after all."

Gee-Ga floated over toward the mouse, and Bonnie followed her.

"Hello, little friend," Gee-Ga said, "is anyone else here?"

Bonnie giggled.

"Mice can't talk, Gee-Ga."

The mouse turned and darted through a door.

"I'll have you know, little one, that everything can talk in its own way. That's the way to the kitchen. He must have good memories from there."

Bonnie wasn't very interested in the kitchen door, though. She had spotted a door that seemed to lead to something underneath the stairs. She walked toward it, mesmerized, and checked the knob. The knob seemed to turn all the way around, but never catch, as though the handle was broken rather than the door locked.

"Gee-Ga, what's through this door?" she asked, turning back around.

Her great-grandmother was staring at the front door with a look of absolute terror on her face. All the color had drained from her ghostly form, and she was no more than a silhouette, just like the mouse. Bonnie had never seen her Gee-Ga that insubstantial before. The closest she had ever come was once, when she had been reminiscing about her lost husband and had dimmed to a bare glow. But now she was practically gone.

Bonnie tried to speak, but her mouth was as dry as a bone. She was rooted to the spot, stricken by a fear like she had never felt before. Gee-Ga turned to look at her.

"Bonnie!" she hissed, her voice like a kettle. "Don't forget me. Please, don't forget me. Don't forget me."

"I won't, Gee-Ga! I won't forget you! Where are you going? I don't want you to go anywhere!"

"Don't forget me! Don't forget me! Please, little one, don't forget me!"

As Gee-Ga continued repeating that same phrase over and over again, Bonnie broke down into tears. She didn't know what was going on and didn't want her great-grandmother to go anywhere.

The ghostly mouse came rocketing out of the kitchen, squeaking up a storm. It stopped a few feet between Gee-Ga and the front door, as though it, too, had spotted the terrifying encroaching thing which had turned Gee-Ga into a barely-there shell of her former self. Then, without so much as a parting squeak, the mouse simply ceased to be there. It was as though it had disappeared, but Bonnie had the sinking feeling that wasn't what had happened at all. The whole time, Gee-Ga never stopped intoning her terrifying new mantra.

"Don't forget me! Don't forget . . ."

Then her great-grandmother promptly vanished. A wolf's howl ushered in the sunset and the cold, lonely night.

1

"YOU SEE, WHAT PEOPLE DON'T understand is: this is what true love looks like."

Donna tried her best to feign interest. She'd been able to successfully plaster a smile on her face and pretend she cared half a million times before, but for some reason listening to the endless story of the endless love between Willie Chang and Lydia dos Santos was intolerable.

"Mmm-hmm."

Donna fiddled with an invoice from last week, double checking all the numbers added up and trying to recall whether she had paid her surrogate for that day yet. She hoped it seemed like she was taking notes about the lovebirds' situation, but in truth she was past caring.

"People think it's strange," Lydia chimed in for what seemed like the first time since the couple had walked in the door, "but are we supposed to live our lives—sorry, Willie—go through our existences based on what people think?"

Lydia was still alive but at a glance might have been mistaken for dead. She had dyed her hair and carefully made up her face in tinctures of black, white, and gray, so she bore a passing resemblance to a ghost. She was a member of the youth subculture which called themselves the Unenlightened (and which most people on both sides of the life gap called ghostfuckers behind their backs). The

Unenlightened made up such a substantial portion of Donna's clients that she had long since grown accustomed to their eccentricities.

"Don't worry about it, snugglebunny," Willie replied, nuzzling the nape of his girlfriend's neck, "it's not the fifties anymore."

Donna nodded with what she hoped was the proper appearance of sympathy. She wanted to tell them she wasn't a shrink, but this was just a part of the surrogacy business. People always wanted her to "understand" why they were seeking a corporeal surrogate. The truth was, as long as their checks cleared, Donna couldn't have cared less about their reasons.

"Is that when you passed away?" Donna asked, pushing aside the invoice and opening her laptop to add a few lines to her budgeting spreadsheet.

Willie nodded.

"It was '57. Not a great time to be Chinese-American. Or a ghost. It was a mess being both."

"I can only imagine."

"Well, things aren't like that anymore," Lydia said, turning and holding up her hand.

The ghost took Lydia's hand and squeezed it. They had only met a half hour before, so Willie was still practically transparent to Donna's eyes. She imagined, for Lydia, he appeared about as substantial as a ghost can get, and his hand would be practically solid as long as he was concentrating—but it was quite simply impossible to concentrate through something as physically and emotionally taxing as sex. That was where Donna and her surrogacy agency came in.

The sign emblazoned on the glass storefront said "We Don't Believe in Unhappy Endings". It was her old partner, Jack Spender's, favorite saying, and in light of all the bad breakups and terminated contracts she'd dealt with over the years, it felt more than a little ironic now. But for new arrivals like Lydia and Willie, the slogan always rang true.

"Well, we have several excellent packages for you to consider," Donna said, pointing at the chart on the wall behind her desk. "I think we should start with your standard overnight package. That's five hundred dollars for eight p.m. to eight a.m."

"Will the surrogate . . . will he look like Willie?"

It was a common question, and she had a canned response.

"All I can promise you is I'll find a handsome young man of

about Willie's age. But the truth is, once Willie possesses him, it won't matter what he looks like. You'll see and feel and hear Willie. You're going to be making love to the person, not the body."

They exchanged a glance, but Donna wasn't worried they'd walk. She had carefully honed that response over her years of doing this work, and nine times out of ten the couple just nodded and continued. The rest of the time she had to wait until they got desperate or broke up, whichever came first.

"This is a little more . . . delicate," Lydia continued, "but what happens to the handsome young man while Willie's inside him? What I mean is . . . where does he go?"

"That's a common question. During possession, the soul of the living person becomes what we call 'pushed aside'. A lot of my surrogates have described it as like being in a half-remembered nightmare. I think it might be a bit like falling into a coma."

"So they're not pushed out? They can't like, float around?" Donna shook her head.

"No, when a spirit is pushed aside he can't manifest as a ghost. Not a lot is known about the phenomenon, really. I guess it's like the hiccups or the common cold. It doesn't really bother anyone enough to solve. Some people think the soul is actually shoved out of the body, but since the person isn't dead, they simply fail to exist. Others think the soul is compressed down, like being locked away in a box. It's a bit uncomfortable, but it's not painful, and I assure you I carefully monitor all of my surrogates for possible long-term ill effects. Nobody's going to die or go crazy or have any permanent issues because you sign up for this service."

They nodded and exchanged a few words. It seemed like they hadn't really been very concerned about that after all, but she'd appropriately cut off their total lack of concern. She waited patiently before finally prompting.

"Any other questions?"

"Have you ever been in love, Ms. Fitzpatrick?"

Donna's hands pressed down on the keyboard, leaving a long, nonsensical string of letters on her spreadsheet. Her mouth worked, as though trying to put together a few words. She didn't know how to respond. No one was interested in a sow like her. It was years since she'd even had a fumbling grope session in the back of a car.

"I meant about the process . . ."

Her office phone began to ring. She smiled sheepishly, but silently thanked the caller for interrupting this awkward conversation.

"Sorry, I have to take this. My receptionist is on vacation. Boy did she need it, too," she said, taking the phone from its cradle. The truth was her receptionist had quit about eighteen months ago due to being overworked, and Donna had yet to replace her. "Fitzpatrick & Spender."

A ghastly voice, dripping with venom and pure malice responded.

"Don't go into the basement."

"Excuse me for just a moment," she said, reaching out and pressing a button to put the call on hold. "Lydia, if you like, there's coffee and danishes."

Donna rose and stepped into the back room, a cluttered, warehouse-like area which she never let the customers see. She picked up the receiver from the landline and jabbed at the blinking button containing her call.

"What do you want, Jack?"

The voice on the other end of the line chuckled and returned to its usual jovial, avuncular state.

"How'd you know it was me?" her partner asked.

"A little bird told me. What do you want?"

"Why, I'm doing very well, thanks for asking, Fitz! How are you doing?"

"Just peachy. How much do you need me to wire you?"

"Have you ever been to India?" Spender didn't wait for a response. "You must. It's incredible here. Tibet? The way they treat the dead? It's incredible."

"I've heard Japan is nice when it comes to that, too," Donna said. "So, you running out of rupees? Need an extension on your credit line?"

There wasn't actually silence on the other end of the line. It sounded like Spender was at a bazaar or something. The chattering of hawkers and livestock in the background continued unabated, but Jack stopped speaking for a moment.

"Credit line?" he replied finally. "What's that supposed to mean?"

"It means I've got a ghostfucker and . . ." Donna looked back toward the office and realized she was shouting way too loudly. She cast a wish to the universe Lydia and Willie hadn't heard her. She lowered her voice substantially and continued. "It means I've got an

Unenlightened and her boyfriend in here and they're not the only ones in line. It means I'm up to my eyeballs in fucking paperwork, and you call once a week, like clockwork, never to help, always to beg for cash."

"Who the hell do you think you are? I built that company from the ground up. I brought you on board. Made you a partner. You wouldn't have anything if it wasn't for me. And you talk about credit lines, like I didn't work myself to death for every penny that business is worth."

Donna pressed at her temple, which was pounding in rhythm with her heartbeat. She couldn't deny any of what Spender was saying. And yet he still came to her, palm upward, looking for handouts from a company he hadn't made a meaningful contribution to since his death two years ago.

"You're right, Jack," she said with a long, drawn-out sigh. "I'm sorry. Let me wire you an advance on your share. Will five hundred do it?"

The sound of smacking lips came through the phone line, making Donna roll her eyes.

"You're beautiful, Fitz. I ever tell you that?"

"I'm about fifty pounds overweight and no man will give me a second look."

"Now, that's not true. You are a handsome woman, and the right guy will come for you. If not now, then maybe you can hook up with a nice young ghostfucker after your big day." After a beat, he added, as an afterthought, "Many, many years from now, of course."

"This is a high-stress industry. I could have a heart attack and die tomorrow the same way . . ."

She trailed off, not adding, "you did".

"Same as me. Well, listen, dying is the best thing that ever happened to me. I'm seeing the world, enjoying my existence, finally, like I never did when I was alive. Listen, here's the account number to send the five hundred."

Spender began rattling off numbers. Donna copied them down directly onto the corkboard, unable to find a loose scrap of paper. She hung up the phone without any pleasantries. She glanced in the mirror and tucked a red lock back. Sometimes she didn't think she looked so bad, from certain angles. But right now she was sweating a storm. She blanched her forehead with a towel, took a deep breath, and walked back out.

"I'm so sorry about that," Donna said, holding out her hand to apologize.

At least, that's what she meant to say. Instead, she collapsed in a heap, feeling the blood rushing to her head and blackness overtaking her vision.

2

"WANT ANOTHER?"

Kyle barely heard the bartender's voice as he stared at the crumbling ziggurat of ashes in front of him. Eugene Sloan had all the qualities Kyle looked for in a bartender: he blended a mighty fine incense, listened sympathetically, and, most importantly of all, was cheaper than a grief counselor.

All part of the reason Kyle continued to come to the pub in his afterlife, good quality service.

The sage embers were still glowing warm in the heavy pewter ashtray. The Arrowhead was the premier hangout for specters like him in Sherman's Forest. The residue of burnt sage hung around the place, inducing a feeling of euphoria for any spirit that walked through the door. But that wasn't the only thing to recommend the Arrowhead. There was the, ah ... well, on second thought, maybe copious amounts of intoxicants were the only thing to recommend the dive.

"Fitz!"

Kyle jumped in the seat, his normal appearance becoming transparent for a split second. He waved a hand.

"No thanks, Eugene. Think I've had it for today."

The bartender shrugged. "Suit yourself."

Kyle swiveled around and tried to ignore the pounding in his head. The old saying "a little goes a long way" flashed through his mind as the effects of the sage coursed through him. For spirits, the burning plant acted like alcohol did for the living, a heady intoxicant that was harmful in large doses.

An excessive amount of sage could banish a ghost from his haunt for a time. It was a horrible experience, one that left a ghost reliving their death until they snapped out of it. Kyle had no idea why it was even still legal, in this day and age, for breathers to even do that.

In his fifteen-year afterlife Kyle had only been cast out with sage once, by an angry ex after a nasty breakup. He had woken up on the side of Interstate 60, the scrapes on the guardrail from his motorcycle still visible despite the passing of time.

A snout brushed under his arm, causing him to wobble on his stool as he looked down in surprise. A dead dog looked up at him with eyes that would have been brown if he couldn't have seen the floor straight through them.

"Well, hi there, boy! How'd you wander in here?"

He scratched the dog under its chin, causing its tail to begin wagging excitedly.

"Ramses!"

Kyle looked up as a girl at the end of the bar stood. Her style of dress was all he needed to identify her as one of the Unenlightened. Under the gray makeup and dress Kyle could see she was attractive and wondered why a girl like her would whittle away her free time fetishizing someone like him. His life wasn't worth fetishizing, that was for damn sure. The dog, Ramses, turned and wandered toward the girl, his form changing from solid (if transparent) to almost an outline like chalk on the blackboard at his childhood school.

Most of the ghost patrons gave the girl a look of distaste as she ushered the dog outside the pub. There was no real way to secure a spectral pet the way breathers had to leash or kennel their living ones. It would either return to her later or it wouldn't, and no one had a bit of say in it excepting the dog. Her duty to restore order to the pub discharged, the girl returned, making a beeline toward Kyle.

"Welcome to my next mistake," Kyle mumbled as he breathed in the last embers of his sage and turned to face the girl.

"Sorry about him. He's curious."

Kyle waved a hand. "No problem. I've always liked dogs."

"I just adopted him. I think he might be a sage addict. He always seems to be snooping around here." She grinned at her own joke.

The girl had colored her hair an ethereal white that was already starting to wash out. Her natural blonde was beginning to shine through, outlining a heart-shaped face that hadn't been ravaged by the passing of years. She couldn't have been more than nineteen.

Kyle snorted to himself at that thought. Age was relative. He was technically thirty-six, but had all the appearance of a twenty-one year-old, his age when the accident had occurred.

"I'm Eileen, by the way."

Kyle snapped out of his thoughts and looked down at the black-painted fingernails of her hand extended in greeting. He tried to focus enough to shake but the sage had done its job too well. His hand drifted right through hers, leaving a wispy trail of mist in its wake.

"Dammit," he muttered as Eileen gave a knowing smile.

"I think that is the coolest thing."

"Get the ghostfucker out of here!"

Eileen winced at the term as Kyle glared at the overweight spirit of Brent Willis.

"Fuck off, mate. Why don't you go eat another triple dipper?"

It was well known how the slovenly redneck had died, a fact Kyle didn't hold back on insulting him with. The fat ghost's face scrunched like a pig trying to squeal and tried to haul himself up, only succeeding in falling to the ground and disapparating in shame.

Kyle had always been skilled at wielding emotions like a knife against others of his kind. Brent was probably reliving his artery-busting death scene at the moment, but he probably wouldn't be out for long. Kyle didn't bother waiting for the man to reappear, instead focusing on guiding Eileen out the door.

"Sorry about that," Kyle said as he took in a deep breath of clean Sherman's Forest air. He felt real, almost alive. It was a common reaction when coming off a sage high. Ramses appeared beneath his hand, licking at it.

"It's all right. I get that a lot." Eileen batted her fake eyelashes that could have looked classy, but only on a hooker. Kyle felt a little sorry for her, but it wasn't like she was the only one with problems. She wasn't even dead yet.

For some reason, tonight, his accident was all he could think about. Maybe he'd had too much sage. He remembered the excruciating pain, but afterward there hadn't been a white light or fire and brimstone, just a brief darkness and then standing up to look at his mangled body, disbelieving the sight.

"My name's Kyle. Kyle Fitzpatrick." This time he solidified enough that Eileen was successful in shaking his hand. Her touch and her smile sent a warm feeling through him.

Haven't felt that in a while.

Eileen looked him up and down as if sizing him up.

"I like your look, Kyle. Really retro."

Kyle couldn't blush but he felt a similar sensation as he looked down at his clothes, that feeling of self-consciousness never going away, alive or dead.

He wore a leather biker jacket adorned with patches he had found interesting looking when he was alive; standard stuff like Metallica and Iron Maiden to be sure, but Kyle had always had an eclectic taste in music that included gems like Celtic Frost and Venom. His dark navy shirt was stained with oil and transmission fluids below the left breast pocket and his blue jeans were ripped. A pair of work boots completed the ensemble. All of his clothing was dark, and his hair was red (a trait he shared with his sister) but until Eileen got to know him better she wouldn't be able to make out his color palette. He wondered if it would be awkward to just tell someone he'd just met.

If this thing with Eileen went well, he wondered if Donna would give him a discount at her surrogacy business.

"I didn't know I was going to die when I did but I at least went out looking as cool as I could."

The joke was lame and Kyle knew it. Donna always said he may have died at twenty-one but his humor had died around the fourth grade.

He was about to ask Eileen if there was someplace she'd like to slip off to when Eugene emerged from the pub.

"Phone call, Fitz."

Eugene waved the phone in his hand like a beacon and Kyle sighed. Eileen rubbed Ramses under his chin and smiled forlornly. "Go ahead and take it. I have to get back to looking for my grandfather anyway. He's been reliving his passing more and more lately."

She began walking away, waving a hand back at him. The ghostly dog followed in her wake.

Kyle began cursing up a storm. He forcibly calmed himself so he could focus enough to grab the cell phone from Eugene. "This better be good or I swear I'll go full poltergeist and smash every mirror you own."

"This is how you answer the phone? What the hell is wrong with you, Kyle?"

It was Donna, all right, but she sounded sickly and rasping, not her usual confident self. His anger disappeared as quickly as it had come.

The obvious question came to him and he weakly asked, "Are you dead?"

She gave an annoyed chuckle, the kind she directed at him every time she thought he was being a little dense. "No such luck. But I am in the hospital."

"Hold on, I'll be right there."

Donna tried to protest but Kyle was already in the current, traveling the connection. Eugene would probably yell at him next time for just dropping the phone, but he didn't care. In what was simultaneously an eon and the blink of an eye, he emerged into the brightly lit hospital room.

Disapparating was an uncomfortable process which Kyle had not yet fully mastered and likely wouldn't for decades, even centuries. It felt like dying all over again, and with all that had been happening lately he would do almost anything to avoid that feeling. If it was anyone else but Donna, he probably would have just taken a leisurely float over.

After disapparating he always suffered from a brief period when he saw the material world in an unpleasant inverse of the way breathers saw the spirit world. The vibrations of Unenlightened were similar enough to ghosts that they were almost visible. Ordinary people were like blobs of light. And Donna had always been like a bright stadium light. Right now, though, her light had dimmed and was disturbingly close to his own.

Kyle hated hospitals. It wasn't that they terrified him, just the way they blended and confused the vibrations of the living and the dead made them seem gray and dismal to his eyes. He wanted to be part of the beautiful, vibrant tapestry, not this confused, cold place.

"You're fading out."

Donna's flat observation yanked him out of his funk. His transparent chest filled with color again, giving him the illusion of life. The world around him came back into focus, like an old-fashioned television set being tuned in. He began to stalk around the room like a caged animal.

"Sorry about that. You know how I get when I disapparate."

"You didn't have to do that. Really, you didn't have to come at all. I'm perfectly fine."

Now that he was himself again, Kyle could read Donna's aura like a book. Her normal red fireball of confidence was displaced by a light blue glow. She was worried.

"What the hell happened to you?"

She said, "Just a fainting spell. It's been a hot summer."

Kyle continued floating around the room in the spectral equivalent of pacing, not saying a word. Silence reigned except for distant nurses hurrying from room to room and the beeping of monitors and alarms.

Occasionally he went right through the hospital bed. Normally it was a grave faux pas (if not a direct slap in the face) for spirits to pass through the living. The Fitzpatrick siblings, though, were close and Donna didn't mind, even welcomed his youthful vitality, while her energy normally calmed him and filled him with confidence. Right now, though, he was getting nothing more than a sickly echo of Donna's usual vibe. He had completed his sixth circuit around the room when Donna gritted her teeth. "Kyle. Stop. Please."

Kyle paused directly inside the hospital bed, staring down at her. He hadn't been fooled by her words, but he was certain after touching her energy. "I'll stop when you tell me the truth."

Donna glared at him. "The only truth is my annoying kid brother never grew up."

Kyle cocked an eyebrow and floated to the end of the bed to snatch the medical chart attached to the end of the frame. Agitated by her evasion, his hand passed right through it.

"Let's see what Dr. Wurmgötter has to say. Panic attack? That's a far cry from a fainting spell, Red."

Donna waved a dismissive hand. When she got annoyed, their family resemblance really shone through. They had the same red hair and fair complexion and though she was a bit more heavyset than he was, he had grudgingly come to admit she was the better looking one. All his life his friends had always told him what a knockout she was, which had caused more than a few schoolyard scraps, and though he didn't fight as much anymore, the sentiment had never really petered out.

Beyond their builds, their most significant difference was their age. By birth, Donna was only a few minutes older than her twin, but since Kyle hadn't aged since his accident, she looked fifteen years older than him. There was something more, though, that he felt like he was only seeing for the first time now. Stress. Her job was aging her prematurely.

"It's nothing. Just a little hiccup. As soon as this quack releases me I'm heading back to the office. I have to finish finalizing the dos Santos arrangement."

Donna began to list the different clients she had to personally validate before the end of the day, the names and procedures rattling around the astral vacuum that was his consciousness. Were he still capable of crying, he would have been bored to tears.

Kyle cut her off by clapping his hands together. "All right, executive decision: you need a vacation."

Donna looked at him like he had just suggested a sexual act and an animal that were completely incompatible. "No way in hell."

He tapped her chart. This time his emotions were enough in check to actually strike it. "Stress-induced panic attack. The facts don't lie. You're wound too tight. Time to relax. How about the beach? See some ghost dolphins?"

She flatly refused, citing the needs of the business and the fact Spender, the freeloading specter, needed his stipend. There was simply too much for her just to up and leave, not to mention the expenses. She yakked on like that for a while.

"Well, you need at least a weekend free of the terrors of the living world. Try living like me, footloose and fancy-free."

Donna snorted "Living like a dead man? That's rich."

Kyle tried to calm himself so he could sit on the edge of her bed. He centered himself enough to hold her hand just for a second before the affection he felt caused her hand to slip back onto the bed.

"Trust me, Donna, if you don't slow down you're going to drive yourself to an early cremation. And as much as I'd love hanging out with you at the Arrowhead, I've got a feeling you're not quite ready for it yet."

Donna stared at him for a long time. Her aura rapidly changed colors as her emotions conflicted with each other before finally settling on a mixture of regret and acceptance.

"Fine. But! I'm going to stay in Sherman's Forest at a B&B or something. And! It will be just for a weekend."

Kyle knew he was lucky even to get this much out of his workaholic sister, but he couldn't resist pushing his luck just a little further.

"And I get to pick the place."

The bitterness in her voice was palpable. "Fine, if it'll shut you up, I'll let you pick the place."

He shot Donna his best devil-may-care grin. "Great! I'm going to pick one without internet."

Donna looked like she was ready to salt, sage, and wind chime him all at once but after a few tense moments she narrowed her eyes.

"Whatever. There's no place in Sherman's Forest without internet access anyway."

"If there is, I'm going to find it."

He floated right through the door before she could protest.

3

DONNA'S THUMBS FLEW WITH A fury she no longer even noticed, let alone appreciated. She paused only to shift her left butt cheek to aid in the cutting of a particularly difficult to deliver fart into the bowl.

"Hello, Eric," her finger spelled out across the tiny square screen of her phone, "I'm so, so sorry you got stuck waiting outside the office for almost 45 (!) minutes. An unexpected family emergency came up Wednesday afternoon. My receptionist was supposed to reschedule all of my appointments, but she's on vacation. I might sack her over this when she gets back, LOL."

Donna paused to run her finger across her chin. She considered admitting what really happened, but only for a second. It was purely a business decision. The sympathy it might elicit from her client could cause him to let her off the hook for missing their meeting, but it would also doubtless cause him to question working with her at all if he knew the real reason for her absence.

"By way of apology, please allow me to take 10% off your final bill. I can certainly understand if you want to work with another agency after this, but I hope you'll give Fitzpatrick & Spender another chance."

That was all bullshit. There wasn't another surrogacy agency in town. Donna served not only Sherman's Forest, but the archipelago of small towns between here and Ganesh City. Spender might've started the business, but after she came on board they had become so good, all their competition had shuttered their doors.

She finished the e-mail by adding a time and date for a new appointment. Her signature block was included automatically, but she still checked it for accuracy, as she always did before sending any sort of correspondence. After she read through the e-mail a second and third time, making no changes, she finally pressed "send" and paused only briefly to attempt to move her bowels before moving on to the next one.

There was no joy in that department. The trip to the hospital and subsequent dehydration had been hell on her already bad constipation problem. She filled a cup from the sink and chugged some water. Five more minutes and she would go for the medicine cabinet for some laxatives, but she hated to resort to that.

"Hey, Red."

Donna gritted her teeth but had long since gotten over being startled by her brother's incessant visits. She glanced up at his visage. They had grown up together, sharing both "a womb and a room" as they often joked, and she knew him better than anyone else on the planet. He should have been as clear as a photograph to her, but right now his appearance was shaky, like a television on the fritz. Kyle had been enjoying sage again.

Without a word, she slammed the bathroom door on him. Kyle didn't even pause before floating right through it. Her bathroom was a tight fit at the best of times, but with her annoying brother inside, insubstantial though he was, it felt like a coffin.

"What do you want, Kyle?"

"You're working," he said, folding his arms as though he had some room to condescend to her in his fifteen-year-old clothes and complete and utter lack of any ability to ever hold down a job more complicated than burger flipper.

She ground her teeth. "I am not," she replied.

"The doc said you could go home under your own recognizance for bed rest. Not to keep working at the job that sent you to the med shed in the first place. You're supposed to be resting. Not working."

"Well, as you can see, right now I'm pooping. Or, at least, trying to."

Kyle reached out and, with a mildly impressive exertion of will, snagged the phone out of her hands.

"Yeah, I suppose this isn't a work e-mail. 'Hi Donna, Thank you so much for meeting with us. We hope you're out of the hospital quickly and doing well. We'd like to schedule an *appointment* as soon as possible.'" The way he said the word "appointment" made it sound like the foulest curse imaginable. "Who's Lydia dos Santos? One of your knitting pals?"

Donna shuffled her pants up her ample thighs. It wasn't like anything was coming of this session with the porcelain monster anyway. She stepped right through Kyle's ghostly form, snatching her phone back on the way. It was normally a faux pas to pass through a ghost, but when it came to Kyle, she had never bothered standing on ceremony. He certainly never had.

She stepped through the door and flopped down on her bed, quickly typing a response to Lydia. Kyle's form bobbed into her bedroom after her.

Donna said, "She's a ghostf . . . she's Unenlightened. I told you about them, I think. The guy's from like the Eisenhower era and she's like fifteen."

"Weird," Kyle said, reclining on the bed perpendicular to how Donna was lying.

She shrugged.

"Eh. Not really."

"Yeah, I guess you must see all kinds of squirrel snacks at that job of yours."

Donna propped herself up on her elbows, the better to glare at him.

"Those people are my clients."

"Those people," he repeated, mimicking her exact tone and cadence, "nearly killed you."

She lay back down and rolled slightly so she could wrap her arms around his legs like she always had when they were young. She hadn't done it in years, and he seemed to notice. It sure wasn't the same. It was like hugging a peanut butter sandwich: soft, squishy, insubstantial at best. He reached down and ran his fingers through her hair. That, at least, was a delight. His touch was so soft it couldn't have been more relaxing.

"It wouldn't be the worst outcome, would it?" she said. "You seem to be doing all right."

Kyle sighed loudly. It was an affectation, considering he hadn't taken a breath in the better part of two decades.

"It's not all peaches and herb, little darling."

The moment of sibling bonding could have lasted for all eternity and she would've been content, but the mood was spoiled when her phone went off.

"That better not be work," Kyle growled.

She checked the caller and shook her head. "It's just the exorcist. I've been meaning to have one in for months but . . ."

". . . this is the first time you've had off?"

She narrowed her eyes and, instead of responding, answered the phone.

"Hello?"

"Yeah, hey there, ma'am, this is Leroy with Associated Smudging and Exorcise. Did you have an appointment for two o'clock?"

Donna glanced at her watch. It was nearly four.

"I did."

"Yeah, sorry, I got held up. Major, major poltergeist infestation at the old Grundon house. Trust me, it was a public health issue that I take care of it."

"It's fine. I'm here all day."

"Okay, good. Well I'm outside if you're ready for me."

"All right. I'll be right down."

She hung up the phone and dropped it back in her pocket. Kyle shot her a sly look.

"You trying to get rid of me, sis?"

She groaned and shook her head. "You remember Mrs. Palladino?"

"No! Is she back?"

"Why do you think I was shitting in the little bathroom?"

"That woman is such a nuisance."

"Hence the exorcist."

Donna struggled to get herself out of bed, lamenting what an elephant she was. As she clambered down the stairs, Kyle ducked into the master bath, presumably to check out Mrs. Palladino's crying act. Were she still alive, the whole upstairs would've been flooded.

Donna opened the door and Kyle apparated next to her, shaking his head and rolling his eyes.

Leroy the exorcist stood on her porch with a clipboard in his hand, furiously scribbling away. He was hairy and sweaty, but not bad-looking, all things considered. Donna never did anything around the house herself (she never had time) so she had long since gotten used to dealing with blue collar guys. The old stereotype of all exorcists having fat guts and their ass cracks hanging out was rarely the case, and definitely not true in this case.

Leroy finally looked up from his clipboard and seemed to do a double-take. Her heart fluttered for a moment, thinking he might have been checking her out, but the little voice in her head quickly straightened her out. In his head he was probably laughing at the manatee he had to work for.

"Hey, Mrs., uh . . ." He checked his clipboard. "Fitzpatrick."

"Miss," she said and instantly didn't know why she did it because it earned her a funny look from both the exorcist and Kyle.

"Right, sorry."

"Donna's fine, really, sorry," she said, holding up her hand as though warding off her past behavior. "Come on in."

She held the screen door open for him and waited as he pulled a pair of plastic covers over his shoes before stepping inside.

"This the specter that's been bothering you?" he asked, making an invisible circle around Kyle with his pencil stub.

Donna giggled and blushed instantly, hating the sound of her own voice.

"Oh, no," she said, "that's my stupid brother. He's welcome. For the moment."

"Hey, I can tell when I'm not welcome." This time, it was Kyle's turn to face the gamut of strange stares from Leroy and Donna. "What?"

Donna rolled her eyes. "Well, usually when someone says that, they disapparate."

Leroy chuckled. She loved the sound of his laughter. Damn it, she had to shake whatever schoolgirl infatuation had gotten into her. This guy was probably eager to finish his work and get home. He certainly wasn't interested in her, so it was pointless even entertaining the thought.

"Oh, no," Kyle said, "you and me gotta talk after this. I'm not going anywhere."

"All right," she said, throwing up her arms in mini-surrender.

"All right, now," Leroy said, "what seems to be the actual problem then?"

"There's some kind of earthbound spirit in the master bathroom. It's an old lady who ODed and then drowned in the toilet. I don't know. She was here when I first moved in, but she was always reasonable and a fine enough haunt-mate, but then a few months ago she reverted back to the toilet, and she's just been a nightmare ever since."

There was a slight delay as Leroy copied down what she assumed was the gist of her story.

"All right," he said. "Can you show me?"

Donna led the way upstairs, cringing with each creak of the steps under her elephant feet. Leroy followed closely behind, right at about butt level. Kyle was already there when they reached the second floor. She opened the door and turned on the light, then scurried out of the way to let the man do his work.

Leroy glanced around the room. Mrs. Palladino was kneeling before the commode with her face inside, wailing and moaning for all she was worth. Occasionally she pulled her head out only to reveal a waterlogged face with red, veiny eyes and stringy hair. Donna had never quite picked up what had been the proximate cause of death, considering it rude to ask, but thought it might have been pills. She knew all kinds of people were drug abusers, but somehow little old Mrs. Palladino had never struck her as the street drug type.

"Yeah, this is pretty bad," Leroy said, glancing at the corners of the room. "I don't think it's the spirit's fault, either. There's, eh, something wonky here. You have an unusual amount of spectral activity in here."

"Do I?"

She looked to Kyle. He shrugged. She furrowed her brow. Why had no one ever told her this before?

"Oh, yeah. You've got an unusual amount of bug spirits in here. Here, take a look."

Leroy reached into his leather tool belt and pulled out a large amethyst amulet on a bit of cord. He held it up to a spot on the wall. A halo of amplified clairvoyance surrounded the crystal. Donna stared into the thusly illuminated area and saw it was indeed crawling with minor spirits.

"These aren't just the local bugs. You're attracting bugs from the surrounding area."

Donna felt flabbergasted. "I guess I just never noticed because I live here."

"Yeah. Happens a lot when people rarely leave the house. Just get used to it."

"What about when they're rarely in the house because they're a workaholic?" Kyle asked.

Donna instantly gave him the death glare and began gesturing for him to disapparate but stopped as soon as Leroy looked toward them.

"Yeah, that can happen too," Leroy said. "You treat your house like nothing but a place to flop and all kinds of stuff can crop up on you. Is there a basement?"

"There's a crawlspace."

"Back down the way we came?"

"You can get to it through the coat closet. I can show you."

"I can find it," Leroy said and turned to head back downstairs.

As soon as the exorcist's back was turned, she mouthed, "Go away!" to Kyle.

He smiled his shit-eating grin at her. Throwing her arms up in frustration, she hurried after the exorcist. She tried to get ahead of him so she could start pulling shoes and coats out of the closet and let him gain access to the crawlspace, but he quickly started helping. When the entrance was clear, he shone a flashlight down.

"Do you need a stepladder or something?" she asked.

"Nah," he replied, "I do this all the time."

With his powerful arms and muscular legs he descended into the dark crevice beneath her house. Suddenly, looking around, she felt like the whole place was off the charts with haunting. Every errant bug or attic squirrel or stray bit of ectoplasm seemed like a massive blemish on the house she had somehow managed to miss for months.

"You want to go down there with him?" Kyle asked.

"Shut up," she hissed. "He's not interested in a cow like me and you know it."

"Cow? What the hell are you talking about?"

She gestured at herself. "You're dead, not blind."

"What? You're a beautiful girl."

She said, "You're my brother. It doesn't mean anything coming from you."

"Actually, it means everything coming from me. Aren't brothers always supposed to call their sisters ugly?"

"I guess."

"Well, then you know how painful it is for me to tell you the truth. My high school friends all dig you. You know that."

"Kyle, that was twenty years ago."

He shook his head.

"They still do. I still keep in touch with Dougie. He asks after you, and he's married. And Tom, don't even get me started on Tom."

Leroy's voice, distant and tinny, drifted upwards. "Yeah, here's your problem right here."

Donna scurried over and stuck her head down in the hold, blowing away an errant cobweb that got stuck in her mouth. By the time she did, Kyle had passed through the floor, and was looking at whatever the exorcist was pointing at, his head turned sideways.

"What am I looking at?" she said.

"Eh, well, it's tough to see if you're not trained. But your home's on a ley line. No wonder your spiritual activity is through the roof." He pointed his chin in Kyle's direction. "You must love it here."

"What do you mean?" Kyle said.

"You feel strong here? Healthy? Sort of like, invigorated? Especially compared to other places?"

Kyle unfolded his arms. "Yeah, I guess I do."

"That's because of this." Leroy stamped the ley line with his foot.

"Well, can we do anything about it?" Donna pursed her lips.

He shook his head. "Not right now we can't. Let me come up. We'll discuss it."

A minute later, as he ran his hands under the sink, Leroy explained further.

"I'll have to kind of map out this ley line. Basically it's this invisible power sink, so I don't know how far it extends or how strong it is. Your friend up there . . . what's happening is, even though she's reached full spiritual maturation from what you've told me, the pull of this place is so strong on her it's reducing her to an earthbound state. Most ghosts, they'll relapse now and then if they're in a state of extreme emotional duress and return to the site of their death and they're unable to realize they're ghosts. Well, you both know all this. If I can drain some power off the ley line, it'll basically free Mrs. Palladino to be herself again."

Donna said, "So how do you do that?"

Leroy scratched the back of his head. "Right, well, I'll have to get some guys out and erect a couple of what's known as obelisks. Standing stones. It's not like we can get rid of the ley line but we can at least drain the power from the part running under your house. I may have to stop by city hall and see if they have any records of how the ley line is situated, and they won't be open until Monday. I may have to do some surveying myself. But once I have a feel for it, we can get those obelisks up in no time."

"And how much is this going to cost me?" she asked.

"That's the big question, yeah. Do you have haunt insurance?"

"Of course."

Leroy seemed genuinely relieved. He said, "Then it shouldn't cost you a dime. In fact, if the previous owner never divulged your property was situated on a ley line, you could probably sue her and make money on it."

Donna shrugged. "I don't want to sue Mrs. Palladino. She's such a nice old lady."

"Well, whatever. In any case, I can't do any more here today. Hang on. I'll run out to the van and get you a couple of Ghost-Away modules."

Leroy headed out to the van.

She glanced at Kyle. "You still here?"

"I told you, we're talking as soon as your new boyfriend heads back to his trailer."

"You're rude."

"So you do like him."

"No, I just don't think you should act like an asshole because someone works with his hands for a living."

Donna's response had to be aborted because Leroy returned with a couple of Ghost-Aways, still in the boxes. He handed them to her, along with his card.

"You can put one in the bathroom and see if it keeps her away, but with that ley line I'm not sure it will. In which case, put it in your bedroom and you should be able to sleep. And there's my card, too. Anything happens over the weekend, anything at all, you call me. I'll come night or day."

"Okay. Thanks, Leroy," she said.

He flashed her a smile. His teeth were so fucking white.

"You're welcome, Donna."

Once he was gone she flopped down on the couch, a Ghost-Away box on either side of her.

"Now what the hell do you want?" she asked Kyle.

"Oh, right. Guess what I found for you." A wicked smile crossed Kyle's lips.

4

KYLE WATCHED DONNA'S EXPRESSION CHANGE
from an astonished deer in the headlights look to a suspicious glare.

"What?" he said. He could see she was in no mood for games, which made it all the better to play around with her patience. "I know how much you hate surprises so I thought I'd spring one on you." He couldn't get too close to her, Exorcist-crack's Ghost-Away boxes working as advertised, but he could at least draw out the fun as long as possible. "For my workaholic sister with the serious body image issue . . . I present . . ."

Kyle concentrated and his voice deepened into a screeching bass. He saw Donna cover her ears as the walls began to vibrate. He mentally smiled to himself as he let loose his inner poltergeist . . .

Kitchen cabinets began to open and shut erratically as the faucet on the kitchen sink erupted in a torrent of brown sludge.

"The greatest gift an apparition could ever bestow on the living . . ."

The television erupted in a field of static that vaguely looked like screaming faces. Kyle watched as the wide mirror hanging over the couch frosted over and Donna hugged her hands to herself and glared daggers at him.

"Will you cut it out!?" Donna half screamed, her teeth chattering. "It's fucking freezing!"

If she called Leroy back for an impromptu exorcising, Kyle

would have considered it a job well done, but at heart he did want Donna to relax, couldn't have her shuffling off the mortal coil and ruining his fun in the afterlife too soon.

He said, "For your stress-free, all-work-suspended pleasure . . . a vacation home right here in Sherman's Forest!"

The cabinets stopped beating, the TV shut off, the water ceased flowing . . . and Donna stared at Kyle with the same skepticism most folks reserved for the people on street corners claiming, with the right prayers or ingredients, you could resurrect the dead.

"Don't discount me so quick, Red. When have I ever let you down?"

There were multiple times but he wasn't going to give her enough time to answer.

"So my friend Tommie Bones heard from his niece about this place in Memorial Park, old mansion or some such that's almost off the grid . . . haunt free."

Donna raised an eyebrow and made a little huffing noise with her throat. "You've been snorting the sage hard if you think I believe somewhere is haunt free."

Kyle had to admit it was a long shot, a very rare phenomenon. The odds of getting hit by a meteor were higher than a building that didn't have some associated spirit attached to it, and everywhere had history . . .

Still, it wasn't unknown to happen but Kyle didn't think he would have seen one within his eternity. If the rumors were true, he wasn't going to let her pass up the opportunity to rest and recuperate somewhere spiritless.

"Tommie and I hit the ether hard, making sure this place was legit and we couldn't find one spirit who had ever set foot inside this building. For such an old place it looks like no one had that much of an attachment to it."

Kyle could see Donna wanted to believe him but he knew she instantly doubted anything vetted by Tommie Bones. In life he'd been a mountain man living up in the Dragon's Backbone and died when his homemade steamer had exploded while trying to deep fry a turkey.

Kyle didn't need to breathe but he put on a sigh for Donna's benefit as he floated across the room and grabbed one of her dining room chairs. He dragged it as slowly as he could and placed it backwards toward Donna, straddling the legs and folding his arms across the back.

"Look, Red, I know you think the best is behind you but trust me life is short . . ." Kyle gestured to himself, his eyes softening, trying to sound as genuine as he could. "And eternity is long. Get out and relax a little before you're drowning in a toilet for the first decade of your afterlife."

Even when he was trying to be comforting he couldn't help but smart off to Donna.

She stared deep into his eyes and Kyle returned the stare. He knew she would break first, after all. He wasn't the one that had to blink.

Donna looked away, Kyle suppressed a triumphant grin as she mumbled bitterly, "You're the most annoying dead brother I've ever had."

"And you're the most anal-retentive sister I've ever had."

Donna gave him a death glare and Kyle stood up with a laugh, shoving the chair as loudly as possible back toward the dinner table. He said, "It's funny because you have constipation."

He heard a noise that sounded like a strangled cat and she came to her feet. She walked toward the door, her face a bright crimson. It occurred to him he might have crossed a line.

"If you don't get the hell out right now and give me some damn peace I'm going right back to work. At least you don't bother me there!"

Kyle headed to the door, levitating through the air and missing the porch steps entirely until he landed on the pavement. He turned around, giving her his best apology smile. "Soooo, let me know when you make the arrangements. I'll come and make sure you're settled in."

Donna said she would, her anger fading away as quickly as it had come. "Don't hit the sage too hard . . ."

"I can't. I have a date."

Donna did a double take as he disapparated.

"Date" might have been stretching the term but he had to get one last jab at pushing Donna's buttons before he left.

He'd put the word out amongst his people to keep a watch for Eileen and her spectral dog; the girl fascinated him, which surprised him. Unenlightened weren't usually his crowd.

Maybe it was due to the fact that fetishizing death usually led to a desire for it.

Suicide was fashionable among the Unenlightened but to the dead it was a dark pollution on the world, like oil slicks on top of the ocean: putrid, foul pustules and shadows that spoke of pain.

Running out of years and dying peacefully was preferable to cutting it short.

Jenny Sutter, who died giving cheap head behind the Arrowhead Pub, had seen Eileen heading toward the park from the police department.

He had appeared in time for her to round the corner. Ramses ran ahead when he caught sight of Kyle and the dog ran in great leaps and bounds down the sidewalk until he barreled into Kyle's legs, rubbing against him and shoving his broad spectral head under Kyle's hands.

"Hey, boy, good to see you too."

"Kyle?"

He looked up as Eileen approached. She wasn't surprised to see him. Confused, maybe, but not surprised.

"What're you doing here?"

Kyle considered telling her he found her intriguing, fascinating . . . for an Unenlightened anyway.

"Well, I had the next thousand years or so free and I thought I'd help you look for your grandfather. You still looking for him?"

She licked her dark black lipstick, smudging it as she looked him up and down before glancing over at Ramses, who wagged his tail and made a boofing noise for attention.

Kyle looked down at the dog. He'd been a stout creature in life, with broad shoulders and a long tongue that lolled out of his mouth when he grinned. Orange eyes, dulled in death to a rusty brown, stared up at Kyle as he stroked the dog's fur. He looked back at Eileen again. "What breed was he? Do you know?"

Eileen shook her head and gave a wry grin. "Not purebred, for sure, but a mix of two massive things."

Kyle had to admit the observation was spot on. The canine apparition came up to his waist.

"He's been a big helper." Eileen knelt next to Ramses and lapsed into the voice everyone who had ever loved a pet indulged in. "Yes, you are. You're such a good helper . . ."

Ramses was too happy and excited to become solid but seemed to enjoy the feeling of a hand waving through his spirit.

"You think I'm attractive?" Eileen was blunt and straight to the point and Kyle couldn't help but grin.

"Well, I'm not getting all hot and bothered, if that's what you're worried about. Drawback of being dead ... no hormones." Kyle chuckled to himself. "Might be a perk for some people."

"That's not what I asked."

Kyle glanced past the red brick archways, dead vines clinging to the aged edifice and into the interior of the park. The sun may have been shining, but to Kyle, it was like someone had slapped a filter over the world, gray light akin to a black-and-white movie seemed to cover everything, a perennial mist taking the beauty from the world.

The bright yellow light that should have brought warmth provided nothing, just a black orb in the sky outlined in white light ... a witness to the dreary world of the afterlife.

There was a dark smudge against the closest tree. Black droplets ran down the bark like tears ... someone had committed suicide there once upon a time.

"Kyle?"

"How did your grandfather die?" He was worried, wondering if they would walk under the tall oak tree and see her family member dangling from the end of a rope.

Eileen seemed taken aback but answered anyway. "He was on a picnic with my grandmother, had a heart attack." She chuckled to herself, her eyes shut as she remembered the day. "I remember when he showed back up on the doorstep talking about how death was the best thing that had happened to him in ages ..."

Ramses shoved his head under her dangling hand, managing to get a solid scratch in before he became so happy he became intangible.

"That's what made me want to become Unenlightened. It seemed like death brought so much more life and freedom than actually living!"

Kyle made a sucking noise, his cheek awash with the memory of a slap as he shook his head. "I'm here to tell you it isn't. It's dreary, boring and ..."

He tried to focus himself and become solid but behind his eyes his mind wasn't standing at the entrance of Memorial Park. No, he was looking down at the crumpled mass of flesh and blood that used to be him on the side of Interstate 60.

"You're starting to outline."

Her voice brought him back and he smiled as the transparent ectoplasm of his being filled back in until he looked almost alive.

"Thanks . . . got lost in my death there for a second." He offered her his arm. "Shall we?"

"So you do think I'm attractive," Eileen said with a smile.

"Intriguing," Kyle corrected.

She laughed as she took his arm. Ramses boofed again and trotted ahead of them as they went into the park, Eileen forgetting her mission and Kyle Fitzpatrick forgetting death.

Kyle couldn't remember the last time he walked through a park with a beautiful girl in tow. In life, he'd been much more comfortable in a pool hall hustling drunkards than outdoors under the hot summer sun.

The grass was beginning to wilt from the lack of rain as they passed through the park. The blades never even wavered as Kyle passed over them but Eileen's heavy footfalls produced a steady crackling.

Specters of deceased park rangers watched them pass from beneath shadowed overhangs, most impassive and some looking angrily at Eileen and the glow of life surrounding her.

Ramses never wavered as he bounded along beside them, happily lost in his afterlife. Kyle envied the dog. Human ghosts had to go to such extreme lengths to obtain the excitement that came naturally to the spirit of the mutt.

Eileen sighed beside him as they walked. Kyle looked her over . . . her pale white makeup was beginning to run in white rivulets down her face as sweat broke out across her brow.

She said, "He always had a thing for this place. He got baptized in that pond behind the trees back there."

Kyle was confused; the term was unfamiliar. "Baptized?"

Eileen grimaced. "Grampa was trying out alternative religions and settled on the Apostles of Jesus the Nazarene."

Kyle tried to hold in his laughter as he asked, "What're they called? Crucians?"

He had heard about them intermittently throughout the years. A fringe cult that believed someone came back from the dead *physically*.

Also, he was the Son of God.

Kyle didn't have anything against religion but facing eternity with nothing but the mundanity of the world he'd always known had left him with skepticism he didn't think he would overcome anytime soon. The closest thing there was to any kind of mainstream religion was reverence of one's ancestors, maintaining their haunts and treating them like the family members they had once been rather than the wraiths they had become.

Crucians were knocking on your door proclaiming mass resurrections of the dead, a promise Kyle heard a million times from snake oil salesmen offering back alley resurrection and escaping with the money from whatever poor schmuck trusted them.

"He's been routinely asking the family to convert, claiming it makes his spirit calm and more in control."

"Now you can't find him . . ."

Eileen nodded with a long, suffering look. "Exactly."

Kyle didn't stop walking but he fixed Eileen with the most serious look he could muster. "Listen here, I've been a ghost a while now and I can tell you . . . no matter how long you've been at this, no matter how much you think you've got it down . . . death hurts and it's always going to bring you back to that moment."

Kyle could feel himself fading away by the moment, the damned spot on Interstate 60 calling him. He took a deep breath to calm himself and put on his most cavalier grin.

"Fear, anger, love . . . everything will bring you hurtling back to death."

Eileen didn't smile but she reached for his hand and Kyle was surprised he could actually feel it.

Eileen said, "Show me where it happened for you someday?"

Kyle promised he would as Ramses began barking and running ahead, the girl and the ghost following. Ramses ran up to a boy dressed in a black shirt painted over like a skeleton with matching paint, another Unenlightened.

"Hey, Joe, what're you doing here?"

Kyle felt a pang of jealousy stab his being, surprising him as he watched the two Unenlightened embrace.

Joe glanced over at Kyle curiously before focusing back on Eileen. "Looking for my mother. Her and Dad came out here a lot before her heart attack . . ." Joe gestured to the woods around him. "It's a big fucking park and Dad can't remember where they had picnicked."

The Unenlightened man saw Kyle giving a disapproving look

41

and pursed his lips into a defiant frown. "Hey, man, she's new, okay? She gets flustered easily and then we have to trek out here to drag her out."

Kyle couldn't judge. There was a time not too long ago where the slightest bit of stress would have sent him tumbling across the damned highway. He held up his hands in a placating gesture.

"I'm just helping the lady find her grandfather."

Eileen gave him a disapproving look before turning back around to Joe. "He liked to wander through here. He got stressed and re-lapsed but he wasn't where he died . . . I think he pulled himself out and went somewhere he liked."

"Yeah, must have . . ."

The living and the dead stood awkwardly in silence for a few moments, neither really saying much else until Joe sighed. "Well, I better get to looking. Good seeing you, Eileen."

"Yeah, you too."

The other Unenlightened left, while Kyle received an earful about how being deceased didn't give him a pass on being rude.

Kyle patted Ramses's ghostly head absentmindedly and smiled the entire time.

5

THE F-150 CAME SHUDDERING TO a sudden halt, sending Donna's papers flying all over the pickup's cab.

"Oh, good grief," she muttered, scrambling to stuff them all back into her briefcase. Then, thinking better of it, she glanced over at the driver's seat. "You all right?" she asked slyly.

Tommie Bones sat there petrified, or something like it. The man could have been Sasquatch's cousin, with his chest-length beard and rippling muscles under a vest that didn't do much to cover the carpet of hair blanketing his chest like a bear.

Half of his face had sloughed off in death, exposing cooked muscle and nerves that dangled like thin strands of web. His arm had exposed bone and shards of metal protruding from where the smoker had exploded. The death wounds gave him a monstrous look, but the truth was Tommie Bones was as happy-go-lucky and joyful as a spiritual dog. All big stories and heart. But right now all of his—distinct, to be kind—features were fading. She didn't know him all that well, so the mountain man appeared fairly gray to her to begin with, but all of the color seemed to be draining out of his form. He was turning halfway into an outline.

She waved her hand in front of Tommie's face. He at least stopped outlining but was otherwise still giving no reaction. This was hardly behavior she wanted to see from someone behind the wheel of a vehicle she was a passenger in. Nor did it set her mind at ease that the entire cab of his 4x4 stank of sage.

"Tommie!" she shouted.

Still nothing. She reached out and attempted to place her hand on his shoulder. She passed through his ethereal form like it was sand, not even the usual gelatin-like consistency of a specter who was focused and paying attention. Passing her hand through his form seemed to get him back on track. He shuddered, but made no comment about the violation of his personal space. He blinked and turned to look at her.

Tommie Bones was a bit older at the time of his death, maybe in his sixties. Still, he had the lithe, fit look of a man who had spent every day of his life outdoors, most of them hunting or fishing. And he had a long, gray beard to rival Santa Claus'. He wasn't unattractive to a certain kind of girl, but he was decidedly not Donna's type. No, Donna's type was more blue-collar: strong, muscular, maybe even a little bald. An exorcist, say.

"Yes'm?"

"Are you all right?"

"Oh."

He seemed flustered. It was a strange look for him. Normally the ghost carried himself with a calm confidence, even if it sometimes veered into an annoying level of arrogance.

"Tommie?"

"Sorry, Kyle's sister, uh, I just feel . . . strange."

Donna hissed through her teeth. She had given up trying to convince the ghost to call her Donna or Ms. Fitzpatrick or Fitz, or goodness, anything. Nope, she was "Kyle's sister" to him and all of Kyle's friends.

"Strange like you can't keep going, or . . ."

"Yeah," he said, putting his hands to his temples. "I don't really know what's wrong with me."

Donna reached into her blouse and pulled out her phone. She checked it. No signal.

"Maybe I should call someone," she said lamely. "I could try the Kevorkian Clinic."

The mountain man shook his head.

"No," he said, "it started when we came out this way. I think I just need to get out of this area. Maybe there's something around here. Something bad for ghosts."

"Oh! Oh, yes. My friend . . . I mean, that is to say, my exorcist

... I mean, this exorcist I know was just telling me about that. There are these ley lines of great spiritual energy that crisscross the earth affecting ghosts. It reduced my haunt-mate to a complete wreck, like she'd never been away from her site of death before."

"That must be it," he agreed, "a ley line or something."

"How far is it to the mansion?"

The specter pointed one slowly discoloring finger east. "It's only about a hundred yards that way. You can see it from here."

She perked up. "Oh, is that all? Well, I can make it that far myself."

"Are you sure, Kyle's sister? I promised him I'd take you out here. I really should go the rest of the way."

But she was already out of the truck and pulling her suitcases out of the rear. She came back to Tommie's window and pressed a few bills into his cup holder.

"Oh, no," he said, holding up his hands, "I'm not supposed to—"

"Tommie," she said, cutting him off, "I've only known you a short time. But based on this trip and what Kyle's told me about you: take the fucking money."

"I guess I *was* sort of hoping you'd offer."

"How did I guess? Now get out of here. Head back to the Arrowhead or wherever. And if you don't feel better, promise me you'll make straight for the clinic."

He made no such promise and she didn't stop to wait for one.

Donna cursed every step, wondering why she insisted on bringing a hair dryer and summer clothes, not to mention her laptop, when she wouldn't even have Wi-Fi. For that matter, why had Kyle's buddy been too messed up to simply drive her to the front door? She never would have agreed to ride with that throwback if her car battery hadn't died. Kyle was exultant at the idea of Tommie driving her.

"Good. That means you won't be able to leave and swing by the office. It'll be a real vacation," Kyle had said.

Now she was gritting her teeth. Come to think of it, killing her car battery was the sort of poltergeist bullshit Kyle would have reveled in. She wouldn't be surprised if it was working just fine when she got home.

She didn't have long to dwell on her half-formed suspicions, though. Her stomach began to lurch as soon as she reached the estate grounds. When she passed over the threshold, she nearly blacked out. Damn bags. She dropped to her knees, clutching her head, and focused on breathing. The world swirled around her. An athlete she was not, but was she really this out of shape?

No. She was probably having another panic attack. But why now? Just from the stress of carrying her bags from the car?

Or was she so absolutely deranged that the idea of being out of touch, even for just a few days, was causing her physical symptoms? That had to be it. This was getting out of control. Kyle was a shithead, but he was still her brother, and he cared about her. This whole thing seemed silly and pointless, but if she was really this screwed up from working herself to the bone, then something had to give.

She vowed then and there she'd give this vacation nonsense a real college try. If she was such a workaholic, surely she could devote herself to reading a book, cooking a meal that didn't come out of a box in the freezer, and maybe even (sky above forbid) getting some fresh air and relaxing.

The agency wouldn't survive anyway if she killed herself. She had to focus on being a healthy person. Maybe losing some damn weight. Then and only then would she be a good worker, which was what she wanted. And with that, the weird woozy emptiness began to subside. She left the bags in the doorway and took her valise inside. She went up to the master bedroom and threw herself onto the four-poster, breathing heavily.

A few hours later her eyes opened, seemingly of their own accord, and she was startled into wakefulness. It took her a moment to get her bearings. She checked her phone, but there was no signal. Already it was darkling outside. She couldn't believe she'd been so exhausted she'd passed out. Normally she was so hepped up on coffee and candy bars and worrying about her cases she could barely sleep at night. No doubt that contributed to the anxiety problem.

She turned on the bedside lamp, which was covered in an inch of dust. It lit up, so there was power at least. Whether that meant somebody was paying the electric bill during all its years of disuse or if the owner had turned it back on just for her was hard to say.

She didn't know the Jacksons personally, but remembered their story from the news. It was a very strange case a few years back, still unsolved as far as Donna knew, and all anybody in Sherman's Forest could discuss for about a month. Lucinda Jackson, deceased, had been walking her great-granddaughter Bonnie home from school.

For some reason they stopped by the old family estate and the ghost simply vanished.

The cops checked all of her usual haunts and even cordoned off the place of her death. It was unusual for a specter who'd been around that long to have a relapse, but it did happen from time to time. Lucinda Jackson never turned up, though. For about a week, all of Sherman's Forest was in a tizzy, combing through the woods and all the old abandoned houses. The ghosts turned over every stone, checking the Arrowhead and all the hangouts in Ghosttown. But Lucinda had seemingly disappeared.

While it was rare, especially while kids were still growing up, ancestors did occasionally jet off somewhere, sort of the ghostly equivalent of a mid-life crisis. Lucinda Jackson was probably on a beach in Maui or somewhere, enjoying the good death, having decided she'd given enough of her time to her family.

Bonnie's parents were left reeling. Who had time to look after their own kids, after all? No one was supposed to have to worry about childrearing until they'd been long dead and seen their kids' kids have kids. Donna, like most of the rest of the town, had chipped in a few bucks so the two-parent home could make a go of it. She stood up from bed, feeling much better than earlier, but still a little off. The closest comparison she could think of was when she had gotten an inner ear infection from swimming as a kid. She stretched her arms back and yawned. Actually, she felt well rested. Maybe it was the fresh air. Maybe it was being away from it all.

She opened her valise and started shuffling through some of the paperwork she brought with her. She glanced at some disclosures from Willie Chang and Lydia dos Santos and then stopped herself.

"No," she said.

She straightened out her papers so all the corners were even, then placed them back in her valise. Gamely, she pulled out a paperback novel and tried to flip through it but couldn't concentrate. She pinched the bridge of her nose.

"There really is something wrong with me, isn't there?"

Climbing down the stairs, she glanced over at the bags, still sitting by the doorway. The fastidious business owner in her wanted to go over, drag them each upstairs one by one, empty them out, and arrange them in her new bedroom like she would have at home. She took three steps toward the door before stopping.

"Nope," she said out loud.

Her voice echoed throughout the house. She reached up and rubbed her arms with her hands. It was chilly. She snapped her fingers.

"That's what's off. I don't think I've seen a ghost since I got here. Did Kyle say this place wasn't haunted?"

She walked over to what she guessed was the door to the basement, opened it, and peered inside. A set of creaky wooden steps led down into absolute darkness. A lot of people died in their basements from gas leaks, floods, or trips and falls. If there was company here, maybe it was hiding downstairs.

"Hello?" she called out. "Is anybody down there?" She suddenly had a perverse thought. "Lucinda?"

Naturally, no response came. Beyond the beam of light that shone from the parlor's light source, around the bottom of the steps, the basement was like a great, gnawing blackness. She searched for a light switch but couldn't find one.

"Eh . . . flashlight," she muttered.

She rummaged through a nearby bureau and, sure enough, found a flashlight within. She tried to turn it on, but the batteries were dead.

"Well . . . there must be a light down there."

She slowly climbed down the stairs, gripping the rail and babying her feet as she went. It'd be her luck to trip and break a hip or something when she couldn't reach anybody. At a minimum she'd be stuck there until Kyle swung by to visit later tonight, and then he would torment her mercilessly about it.

When she reached the last step, she discovered the basement floor was poured concrete. She found herself utterly unable to see and felt twice as disoriented as before.

"This is a dumb idea," she said under her breath before yelling again. "Hello? I'm vacationing upstairs and wanted to introduce myself."

She moved forward into the encroaching darkness, her left hand on the wall, feeling along it for a light switch, her right hand up, searching for the cord to a naked bulb. She slowly pushed one foot out, shuffled it in a slight circular motion to make sure she wasn't going to bump into something, took a step, then repeated the process.

Any ghost worth their salt would have been making low, strange noises at this point. More damaged ones would have been exhaling ice-cold air on her neck. Hell, even an animal would have been chittering away in the corner. But there was nothing. The quiet was so complete it registered almost like a whooshing in her ears. She couldn't remember the last time she'd encountered silence so absolute. Maybe never.

Her right hand touched something. A cobweb? No. That was the string she was searching for. It had a tiny conical metal tip dangling from the end. She pulled on it gently. Once on, the naked bulb flickered like it hadn't been used in a while but didn't mysteriously go out. Nor did it fill with blood, explode, or burn so bright that looking at it would blind a person.

"What is going on here?"

Her words echoed back to her, sounding naked and alone.

She glanced around the basement. It wasn't finished; just a dank place where the Jacksons had kept their washing machine and dryer, now united almost as one by a thick network of cobwebs. A rusty pipe seemed to be leaking very slowly. That could be a sign of spectral activity. Or of nothing, really. She checked it and noticed it wasn't an actual leak. It was a slow drip from condensation. Probably not ideal, but nothing to get upset about. The closest thing to scary in the whole basement was the water heater because it vaguely resembled a grinning mask. But no matter how close she pressed her nose to it, nothing ghastly leapt out to attempt to frighten her.

She began the endless climb back up the stairs. She checked around. The kitchen was empty. A few old cans were hiding in the cabinets, but no spooky faces or boiling eggs or skeletal hands. She even pulled down the folding ladder and climbed up into the attic. The attic was . . . an attic. Expired paint cans lined one wall and boxes of long disused holiday decorations were scattered around the bare plywood floor. She returned to her room and sat down on the bed.

"This place is fucking bizarre," she said, furrowing her brow.

In the basement there hadn't been a rat or even a cricket. In the attic there hadn't been the spirit of a bat or a squirrel. And come to think of it, she hadn't seen so much as a spectral bug since she'd set foot on the property. And then there was Tommie's unexplained headache on the drive up. Could ghosts even get headaches? She supposed they could interact with things like sage and salt, so it must have been at least theoretically possible.

Kyle said this place wasn't haunted, but was there something wrong with it? Could ghosts not come here?

She thought about asking Leroy if that was even possible. Were some houses . . . unhaunted? Was that even a word? Thinking about Leroy made her sigh. She wondered if he had noticed her. She had probably been another jerkoff customer in his eyes. But she, on the other hand, couldn't get him out of her mind. Her hand strayed tentatively toward her crotch. She was on vacation, after all.

Her tummy growled at her. Maslow's Hierarchy triumphed again. She picked the grocery sack out from her pile o' stuff. She shouldn't have left the perishables out while she was sleeping. The gallon of milk was room temperature to the touch, but she figured it would be okay. She headed to the kitchen and started putting the food away.

That finished, she poured a little olive oil in a pan and started cracking eggs. She was about halfway through making breakfast for dinner when something clattered outside. Maybe there was a ghost on the grounds after all. She rushed to the kitchen window and peered out. A light breeze ruffled the trees, but otherwise she couldn't see anything. Then she heard a groan, a definite groan, coming from the front of the house.

Turning the stove down to low, she hurried out the front door, drying her hands with a dishtowel as she went. She stepped onto the porch and squinted into the cresting darkness.

There!

She spotted a gray, ghostly figure in the distance, doubled over in what looked almost like pain.

"Oh, shit," she said, realizing who it was, then shouted, "Kyle!" She waved to him, but he didn't look up.

"Kyle?" she repeated a moment later, more tentative. Kyle looked up at her, but shook his head.

"What's wrong? Come up here."

Her twin didn't move. He seemed to be losing color. Worried, she hurried off the porch and toward him, breaking into a run as he groaned again. Before she could reach him, he disapparated.

6

PAIN . . .

It was all Kyle felt as he lay on his back, staring up at the sky and wondering why it was turning red.

He remembered a truck braking in front of him, then the guard-rail as he tried to avoid it.

Flying . . .

The scraping asphalt and metal crushed his organs and tore his skin from his chest. His motorcycle skidded away as he tumbled.

Kyle came to a halt facedown. Coughing and struggling to breathe, he heard the screech of protesting tires and then more pain as his legs were crushed under two tons of onrushing Honda.

He stared at the sky, raggedly breathing bloody coughs and wondering why the beautiful tapestry of blue sky and white clouds was turning red.

He was biking down I-60 again. There was a truck, pain, flying, red sky . . .

Kyle Fitzpatrick experienced his death on endless repeat, free of charge.

Then, like a beam of fresh air, Donna's face appeared through that red void and he heard her muffled voice from far away. "Kyle . . . *Kyle!*"

A distant car horn sounded and Kyle came back to himself, nearly hyperventilating as he tried to shove the memories down into whatever ethereal void contained his mind. The realization hit him with all the weight of the Honda that had taken his legs before the end.

He had relapsed.

Damn it. He ran his hand through his hair. He could almost feel the panic sweat, though he hadn't actually sweated in a decade and a half.

"Are you okay? Kyle, look at me!"

He waved a hand at her. She stood next to him with her arms crossed and the slightly puffy look she got in her face when she worried. Which was pretty much all the time.

Kyle gritted his teeth, trying to keep himself solid until the spectral memories of pain passed from him and the calm embrace of ectoplasmic eternity embraced his spirit again.

"I'd haunt a park bathroom for some sage," he muttered as he stood up.

Kyle was surprised when he saw the darkness surrounding him. The sun was shining brightly only a moment ago. He had gone by the Jackson place to check on Donna and . . .

"What time is it?"

Donna, silhouetted by her car's headlights, gestured around. "It's the middle of the damn night. What time do you think it is?"

I-60 was a busy highway no matter the time of day but none of the cars paid them any mind as they passed. The Dragon's Backbone and Sherman's Forest were distant landmarks on the horizon compared to the nearby lights of Ganesh City. Skyscrapers, suburbs, and industrial districts twinkled like glowing stars fallen to Earth.

"I'm sorry, Red. I haven't had a relapse this bad in years."

The memory of his death was still rattling around in his head. As he stared with sunken eyes in the direction of Ganesh City, Donna's anger seemed to fade away. From the look on his twin's face—which he had learned over the years to read almost like a book—he could guess his form was flickering like a staticky TV.

"Come on, let's get in the car before some asshole hits me. It's weird. You know, the battery's working fine. All of a sudden."

He grimaced and tried to think of something smartass to say, but his trademark wit and sarcasm were gone, replaced by a haunted feeling as he remembered what he had seen at Jackson Manor . . . or more accurately tried not to remember.

For the first five minutes she badgered him about having to get a taxi from the vacation home back to her place in the middle of the night (she described the exorbitant rates in detail) in order to pick up her car so she could go looking for him, and all the other petty logistical minutia she always obsessed about. But when she finally shut up, she shut up for good. It was at least another hour and a half back to Sherman's Forest and for at least an hour they rode in silence, even though Kyle could see Donna's aura swirling in a mixture of frustration and worry.

"Have you been doing anything that could have caused this?" she asked finally.

Kyle glanced at Donna like she had slapped him. "What?"

Donna didn't meet his gaze, looking resolutely ahead. Her lips tightened as she reiterated, "Have you been doing anything to hurt your consistency? How much sage have you done this week?"

Kyle tried to keep the sudden burst of rage that flickered through him from causing the engine to stall. Relapsing had left him badly shaken. Poltergeisting now, without being able to control it, would be a ticket right back to the side of the road. And nothing terrified him more right now than the thought of that reddening sky.

"I'm not a fucking addict," he said, forcing a calmness into his voice that wasn't genuine.

Donna bit the bottom of her lip in a way that suggested she was trying hard to hold back what she really wanted to say. "You're irresponsible and always have been. After Mom and Dad died and moved to Hawaii, who worked to pay the bills? And who went wherever he wanted, did whatever he wanted . . . and then crashed his damn motorcycle!"

Kyle looked out the window. The glass was crystal clear due to his lack of a reflection. The dark trees and streetlights were almost hypnotic. All he wanted to do was tune Donna and her accusations out.

"Stop ignoring me!"

He felt uncomfortable, like someone who stood up too quickly and got lightheaded. Turning, he saw Donna waving her hand inside his face, swirling the spectral material that made up his spirit.

"Will you cut it out? It wasn't like I wanted to relapse."

Donna turned her eyes back to the road. "I know you didn't mean to but you did. And that matters."

He shook his head. "No, it wasn't . . . I mean, I haven't relapsed in years. This was different. It wasn't prompted by emotion or trauma."

Kyle didn't want to think, much less speak, about what *had* caused the relapse but she was persistent. The question she'd clearly been dying to ask tumbled out as they hit the Sherman's Forest city limits.

"It was the mansion, wasn't it?"

Kyle licked his lips, a tic driven by memory rather than need. He nodded.

"What's wrong with it?" she prompted.

Kyle thought about the house. He could feel it like a hole in his being. The miles flew past. They crossed Leary Bridge with the river churning underneath, heading northeast down Salter Street toward the manor.

"It's nothing, Donna. Nothing's wrong with it."

Bow Avenue passed outside, houses and restaurants dark except for a few ghosts haunting the streets.

"I don't understand. Your buddy Tommie wouldn't even get near it. And when you did you looked like a breather who'd eaten raw chicken. I've never seen a ghost fake discomfort."

That was because there was no way for a ghost to fake pain. Real feelings and stimuli happened so rarely there was no bluffing your way through it. Sage was real. Wind chimes were real. Occasionally heartbreak was real.

What he had seen at the house, though . . .

He stared out at the passing Milk Bar with its veneer of civility and class for the living. A contrast with the Arrowhead a few blocks down, decrepit and fading like the haunts it catered to.

"Tell me, Kyle." She gritted her teeth. "Please."

Memorial Park, where he'd been with Eileen hours ago, passed by and Kyle opened his mouth. "It was . . . it was like . . ." He gritted his teeth and tried to strain the words out. His eyes widening, he could feel himself returning to the side of I-60 as his vision turned red.

"Kyle!"

Startled by her shout, he came back to himself as they turned up the road to the mansion. He felt queasy. That was also a feeling a ghost couldn't fake.

"Donna, stop."

"I'm not stopping. Maybe it's a psychological thing. It isn't haunted so it freaks spirits out or . . ."

Kyle began to feel panic as they rounded the corner in the treeline and the mansion came into view. The mansion, along with that thing no words would let him express.

"Stop. Please?" Kyle said.

"I mean, it isn't like you can die again. So you need to pull up your big boy britches and . . ."

"*Stop!*"

The car died as his shout echoed through the trees around him. He stared in pure, undisguised terror at what lay before him.

"Donna, it's nothing, nothing, nothing, nothing . . ."

He continued to repeat himself, his voice rising in pitch until it was nearly a screech. The repetition didn't subside until Donna drove him away from the manor.

The fear never subsided.

7

DONNA DANGLED HER FEET OVER the side of the gutter. She took another bite of her apple and glanced down at her book. It was a non-fiction piece about rare religious sects. She was in the middle of a chapter about the Crucians, a funny little group that believed in a creator deity and the resurrection of the flesh on some indeterminate date in the future. Pockets of active practitioners survived to this day, mostly in the Middle East.

She flipped back and forth between the demographic information graphic of the current chapter and the last. The two sects had about the same number of adherents, though the Zoroastrians were about a millennium and a half older. She'd forgotten her bookmark, and being utterly repulsed by the idea of dogearing a book, she memorized the page number she was on and put it aside.

Taking another bite of the apple, she leaned back and stared up at the sky. She hadn't crawled out on a roof like this since she was a kid. Halfway through she'd started to worry she would fall through the shingles, leaving a great big hole like a cartoon character. But it had all turned out fine. She ran her finger along the seam between the shingles. This place was so strange. First there was Lucinda Jackson's disappearance years ago, then Tommie's weird reaction to it, and finally Kyle's relapse. Both of the ghosts had acted like they were practically unable to come onto the grounds. And worse, Kyle was unable (or unwilling) to explain what he had seen.

The place was wrong. For ghosts, at least. She wished she knew an expert on paranormal matters, someone who could let her know what this "nothing" Kyle had seen was. It was unlike anything she'd ever heard of before.

Suddenly she paused, losing her grip on the apple and watching it roll down the roof, jump the gutter like a skateboarder, and splatter all over the pavement below. Her stomach fluttered as she reached into her wallet and pulled out Leroy's card. She ran her fingers over the embossing.

"Leroy Tate. Psychic Medium. Licensed and bonded exorcist. Expert in paranormal affairs."

She did know an expert after all. One she was desperately looking for an excuse to call. And now she had just such an excuse. No, not just an excuse, a reason. A great big, compelling reason. And yet somehow she was as terrified as a schoolgirl to actually pick up the phone.

It was two hours later, two almost solid hours of staring at the lone landline telephone in Jackson Manor before she finally took the receiver off the hook. It was another fifteen minutes of hanging up every time she heard the dial tone before she could finally bring herself to put finger to keypad.

That, though, was less on account of her childish crush and more on account of how unnerving it was hearing a dial tone. She'd never picked up a telephone before without hearing the moans of half a dozen apparitions. Not here on the Jackson grounds, though. There was nothing.

"Associated Exorcism and Smudging," someone said on the line.

Donna nearly jumped out of her skin. She hadn't realized she'd actually dialed the number on the card. She looked down at her fingers, wondering if they'd been possessed. Maybe this place wasn't so empty of haunting after all.

"Uh . . . hi. Is this Leroy?"

"Yes, ma'am. How can I help you today?"

"Um, yeah, I don't know if you remember me but my name is Donna Fitzpatrick. I had you out to my home when my local haunt started relapsing. You said there was a ley line under my house."

"Of course, of course, Mrs. Fitz. Of course I remember you." Her heart fluttered in her ribcage. "Well, I've got everything set up to get the obelisk erected tomorrow. City Hall was a breeze and the boys are available."

"Good, good. That's good to hear."

"How's everything else going? Are those Ghost-Away modules working out for you?"

"Oh. Well, actually I'm calling about something else."

"Oh?" he replied.

Was it her imagination or had his voice taken on a husky tone? Shit! She suddenly felt panicked and wanted to hang up the phone. He thought she was asking him on a date.

"It, uh . . . I, uh . . . well, you see, my brother . . . I'm staying in . . . do you know the old Jackson place?"

"Oh, ah, sure. Yeah, I remember it from the news a while back. You're staying there? I didn't mean for you to incur any expense. Will you let me pay for the rooms?"

"Oh, no, it's not like that. This was a pre-planned vacation. I was going to come anyway. Please, don't, ah, you don't owe me a dime."

"All right. So what seems to be the trouble?"

Donna looked down at her hand to see she'd twisted the phone cord around her finger. Another girlish behavior she hadn't gotten up to in ages. She quickly extricated her hand from the mess.

"This might sound strange but have you ever encountered a . . . like a . . . sort of a ghost no-man's-land? Like a no-go zone? I mean, even with the Ghost-Away modules or burning sage, a really determined specter can enter the area, right? They just hate it."

"Yeah," Leroy agreed, "that's true. That stuff is more of a deterrent than a strict repellant. But I think I've heard something along the lines of what you're talking about. I talk to a lot of spirits in this business, and more than a few of them believe there's something off about the Jackson place."

"Really? I couldn't get my brother to say a word about it. All he would say is it was nothing. And he had this friend, too, and he got sort of . . . sick? I know that's not the right word for a ghost, but—"

"Yeah. Yeah, they don't talk about whatever it is that goes on there. It's strange. Sort of a third rail for them, I guess."

"Huh. Well, I'm glad I'm not crazy."

"Nope, not crazy. Is it causing *you* issues, though?"

"Well, I mean I felt a little woozy when I crossed the threshold but I thought it was, um, lightheadedness. Mostly it's weird. Lonely. Almost like . . . you know when there's a storm coming and you can sense it in the air? Smell it, almost?"

"Sure. You want me to come out and take a look?"

"That'd be great. I don't think I have my checkbook, but you take plastic, right?"

"Oh, I'm not going to charge you, Mrs. Fitz. Honestly, I've been raring for an excuse to check that place out. Let's call it professional education. I can write it off on my taxes anyway."

"Oh, ha ha," she said, without actually laughing, "great. But, ah, you can call me Donna."

"Sure thing, Donna. I'll be right over. I just have to finish up this call. Give me . . . an hour and a half?"

"Okay."

She hung up the phone and started fanning herself with her hand. An hour and a half? Oh no! She had to make something. And she was a terrible cook. She also didn't want it to look like she hadn't been putting something together to impress him. It had to be big enough for two in case he wanted to stay, but small enough she could pass it off as only her supper if he decided not to stay.

Shit. Shit shit shit. And it wasn't even like she was in her own place. There were the groceries she had brought with her. She rifled through them with a fury.

Spaghetti. Perfect. As always, Italian food was the savior. She could make some spaghetti and sauce out of a can, maybe spice it up a little. Except, damn, she hadn't brought any spices with her, not even thinking of it. Well, canned would probably be fine.

She could make up some sausages. Oh, but shit, what if he was a vegetarian? She couldn't put the sausage in the sauce then. But that was how she made her sauce savory. Maybe she could make two pots: one for vegetarian sauce and one for meat sauce. Then he could just pick whichever he liked. Or neither, since he almost certainly wasn't going to stay for dinner anyway.

An hour later a knock came at the door and she realized she was hip deep in making a pasta dish and her guest was early. She turned down all the burners to low, rinsed her hands off, and quickly hurried to the door, hoping she wasn't waddling like a walrus. Her blood pressure felt like one of those strongman mallet-swinging devices at the carnival shooting up to the very top as she opened the door.

Leroy was standing there, a pendulum in his hand, looking around the porch.

"Hi," she said.

"Hey, Mrs. . . . sorry, Donna. This place is nuts!"

"Is it? I'm glad I'm not crazy, then."

"No, not crazy at all. I get it now, what you said before about feeling woozy or lightheaded or something. My alarm bells started going off as soon as I reached the property, but now that I'm on the porch, it's like I could almost fall over."

"I know, right?"

Donna watched as he moved from spot to spot on the porch, pointing his crystals in every corner and cranny, shaking his head, occasionally muttering under his breath, and generally ignoring her. She waited, wringing her hands, until he stopped, pinching his temples. He looked like he was in genuine pain.

"Are you okay?" she asked.

"It feels like going up in an airplane. You know how you don't even realize something's wrong until your ears pop?"

"Do you have any idea what it is?"

He shrugged. Then he sniffed the air, and a look of pleasure crossed his face.

"Did I catch you at dinner?"

Donna looked back into the house. "Oh, yes, I forgot all about that," she lied. "Are you hungry?"

Almost as if on cue, Leroy's stomach grumbled. He clutched at it.

"Well, actually, I haven't eaten all day."

"Do you like spaghetti?"

Leroy held out his hand and tapped his wrist, as if checking for vital signs. She furrowed her brow.

"What are you doing?"

"Oh, sorry, I was just checking to see if I still had blood in my veins."

Donna giggled, and suddenly regretted it, worrying it had sounded foolish.

"Okay, I get it. How about sausage?"

Leroy's eyes looked like they were about to bug out of his head.

"A nice, sweet Italian sausage?"

"Sure."

"*Si, me gusta mucho!*"

"Isn't that Spanish?"

"Spanish is all the Italian I know."

The smile never left her face. "You really kind of lit up there for a minute."

"My ex-girlfriend didn't eat pork or red meat," he explained, "so to be supportive I didn't either. It was all turkey and chicken and vegetarian food for a year or so and I guess I sort of forgot to get out of the habit."

"So you love sausage but you haven't had it in a year?"

He nodded.

She said, "Well, in that case I insist you join me. And . . . you did say ex-girlfriend, right?"

He smiled. "I did."

He followed her into the house. As soon as he passed the threshold, he stopped in mid-stride and grabbed his head again.

"What is it?" she asked, hoping the alarm wasn't too evident in her voice.

"It's even more extreme inside, isn't it?"

"Is it?" she asked. "I know I've been here for a few days so I must be used to it, but I don't remember it being bad after the initial attack."

"Well, you know, I became an exorcist because my sixth sense is a little stronger than the average bear's. Plus, I've been doing this for so long my senses are a bit more attuned to it. If there are pockets of different influences, I'd be more sensitive to them than you would."

"A sensitive man. Every woman's dream."

"I can fix a car, too."

"Well, there you go, then."

He followed her into the kitchen and looked around.

"You're making enough food for an army! Are you sure I'm not the first guy coming by tonight?"

"Stop it. First and only."

"Good. Can I do anything to help?"

She shook her head, turning the burners back up and blending the sausage sauce with the regular sauce now that she knew he didn't have any dietary restrictions.

"No, I've got things pretty much under control here. Well, you could set the table."

He puttered around, searching for cutlery and dishes. She didn't have to point out much. When she'd arrived, the kitchen had been untouched for years, but was otherwise fully stocked. She'd scrubbed off the few dishes she'd used and left them in the drying rack. Leroy went immediately to those. He set the table as she pulled apart a loaf of bread, buttered it, and threw it in the oven. Everything else was pretty much ready.

"Mmmm. My mouth is watering. That sausage smells incredible," he said.

"And here I was worried you were vegetarian."

He shot her a sly smile. "So you'd been meaning to invite me to dinner all along, eh?"

She blushed. "Oh, uh ... I, uh ... I mean, the thought had crossed my mind."

He waved it off. "I'm joshing you."

As they sat down and started to eat, Donna was astonished at how well they hit it off. He laughed at her jokes, told some of his own, and seemed genuinely interested in what she had to say. Eventually, the conversation turned to the house and its strange nature.

"What do you think is going on with this place?" she asked.

"Well, I don't know."

"Illuminating."

He chuckled. "What I mean is, in all my fifteen years in this business, I've never seen anything like it. Everywhere I've ever been is haunted to one extent or another. Every house has a ghost or two. Public buildings usually have a half dozen or more. Plus, ghosts flitter around, checking out various places. Even out in the woods, where you would think there might be no otherworldly activity, there are going to be spectral squirrels and raccoons and deer. This place, if I had to qualify it, it's like ... the place is perfectly normal. No apparitions at all." He gestured around. "No cats, no dogs, no rats, not even a cockroach. It's unheard of."

"Well, remember how you said my house was particularly afflicted because it was on a ley line?"

He nodded.

She said, "Is it possible this lies on like, a reverse ley line? Or maybe as far as possible from all the ley lines that it's like a zone of complete normalcy?"

He twirled a few strands of spaghetti onto his fork against his spoon. "It's possible. I'll have to do some research. Call some friends in the field. I'd do it now, but, you know ..." He pointed upward.

"No reception," she said, completing the thought for him.

He bent his head over to slurp up some of his spaghetti, but when it came back up, strands hanging from his mouth, his eyes looked like saucers. For a moment she was worried he was choking, but he wasn't spasming.

"What? What is it?"

Unceremoniously, he opened his mouth and let the spaghetti fall back to the plate. It was a childish, repulsive gesture, yet somehow she was more turned on than she'd ever been. There was an obvious passion in his eyes.

"No reception," he repeated.

"Right. No Wi-Fi, no—"

"No, I mean, what if . . ." He paused, struggling to articulate the words. "I mean, we know a lot about ghosts. They exist on a different wavelength of energy from us. They vibrate at a different frequency than we do. So if ghosts are a form of energy which takes on a shape and appears a certain way, how is that different from, say, a television, or a radio, or a cell phone signal?"

She shrugged. She knew a bit about the paranormal world too, but hers was mostly a customer service industry. The nuts and bolts of it she mostly left to, well, specialists like Leroy.

"I don't know. It makes sense what you're saying," she said.

He formed a small globe by bringing his hands mostly together. "We've always presumed the world is, uh, essentially, a haunted place. There are spikes of energy, flows of it, like the ley line under your house. But what if we're wrong about that? What if Earth is like a television set, receiving a signal, and those signals are ghosts? We could have areas where the signal breaks. You know, you drive out into the country and the radio stations all start to fade until it's one loon asking for money. Then even he goes away."

"So this might be like a spot of normality? An area where ghosts just can't . . . transmit?"

He shrugged and took a sip of his wine. "It would be kind of a radical idea. Hell, it would turn everything we know about the spirit world on its head. Open up whole new fields of research. I mean, off the top of my head, imagine if we could strengthen the signal somehow? We could reach out and touch, really touch our loved ones who crossed over."

"That would put me out of a job."

He cocked his head. "My goodness, I've been so rude. What do you do?"

"I run a surrogacy agency."

"We might put you out of business. But don't worry, you'd be making billions on the lecture circuit. Imagine it: The Lady Who Discovered a Place With No Haunts."

"I'm sure we could come up with a sexier term."

He looked her up and down. She suddenly felt her breath catch in her throat.

"I couldn't imagine a sexier subject, though," he said.

She leaned in toward him, hopeful, but she didn't have to wait long. He reached out and took her firmly by the neck, kissing her deeply and passionately.

8

KYLE FELT LIKE HE'D HITCHED a ride on a comet hurtling into the deepest void in space.

It was quiet here in the expanse of pure undiluted silence, a peace he hadn't known in the pain of death. No bland afterlife, no painful relapse, just simple peace as he floated.

When the sage hit ended it all came crashing back, reality and its assorted woes.

The Arrowhead Pub abounded with spirits that morning but all of them were giving Kyle a wide berth. He didn't blame them. His form flickered from the tide of unwanted emotions as he tried to keep himself from relapsing.

He stared at the mirror behind the bar and the telltale image of a red road flickered across the reflection.

The bar went tense, as though a static charge were building in the air. Small cracks began to form on the mirror as Kyle's rage washed over the building like a tide.

Ghosts shot him looks of complete disgust as his anger brought them out of their own highs. Kyle didn't care. The rage focused him, making him feel nearly alive. Solid, almost.

He grabbed the plate of burning sage, vapors wafting up from it. He felt the discomfort. The sage had a stronger effect the more solid and alive he felt. He wanted to go back to the peaceful void.

He wouldn't relapse again.

A strong, living hand grabbed the bowl from the bar top in front of him. Kyle stared up in undisguised anger at Eugene, who stared him down without an ounce of fear or trepidation.

"You've had enough, Fitz."

"Give it back."

The portly bartender shook his head, a mixture of pity and frustration washing across his face. "Tommie, make sure he gets home."

Kyle was vaguely aware of his friend behind him. Tommie's face was morose and worried, something Kyle knew was reflected on his own features. He turned back to Eugene and dug his hands into the bar.

The wood of the bar chipped under the weight of his fury. He focused all of his frustration on the bartender. Kyle's face distorted as his mouth dropped open far longer than a human jaw physically could. Bloody tears ran from his eye sockets, and a scream that was half cat, half television static built in his throat.

"I . . . want . . . my . . . sage," Kyle said, accentuating each word with a hint of promised violence.

Eugene snorted. "Give me a break. You think you can scare me? Did you forget what I do for a living? I've dealt with violent spirits ten times your age." He pulled a wind chime from behind the bar top and stared down the desperate, angry spirit in front of him. "Go home and get sober. This isn't healthy."

"What the fuck do I care about my health? I'm already fucking dead!"

It might have been the sage high or the memory of what happened at Jackson Manor making him reckless, but Kyle reached out, stretching distorted limbs toward the wind chime in Eugene's hand as Tommie shrank away.

But he was too slow. Eugene tapped the chime with his index finger. The sound scratched at his mind, pain racing through his spectral form. The ectoplasmic energy that made up his spirit fuzzed like a T.V. with bad reception and he struggled to stay coherent. Kyle clutched his ears and fell backwards, screaming in agony as he writhed, hovering over the floor.

The other spirits in the bar began disapparating, quietly cursing Kyle's name as the sage highs they had come to indulge in were ruined by the pain of the ringing wind chime.

"You calm now or do I need to ring it again?"

Kyle grumpily waved him off. Eugene looked around the near-empty bar.

"Well, you happy now? You scared off all my customers."

"Ah, you did that yourself," Kyle said, glaring at him.

"Watch it," Eugene warned. "The only reason I'm not banning you is because we're friends and I know you relapsed recently." The white fire of pain slowly subsided in Kyle's being. The bartender looked at him with supreme pity. "Pull yourself together and then you can come back. Why don't you spend some time with that pretty little ghostfucker you've been hanging out with?"

The memory of blood running cold hit Kyle at the mention of Eileen. He looked at the clock hanging over the bar. He was supposed to be on a date with her right now. The plan was to meet at the park an hour ago.

Kyle was borderline desperate as he hurried through the park. It seemed more deserted than usual. The disc golf course should have been bustling with half a dozen college kids home for the weekend and indulging in the pleasant coolness of the day, but Kyle passed hole after hole and only saw the baskets of chains clicking in the wind. Of the few people he saw running along the trails, none had seen the pale girl or her spectral dog.

A breeze caused the water to lap against the shore of the pond off to his left. He floated down a dirt incline to reach the trail running around the perimeter of the water. He followed it to a flat area where people liked to picnic.

In life, Kyle had brought many a date to that area. The oak and pine trees surrounded it in thick foliage, a barricade to all but the most dedicated of explorers. Kyle could have easily passed through the cover, but if Eileen had sought privacy, the trail would offer a good view of his approach.

Aside from the fact the spot was a good place for dogs like Ramses to chase balls into the water, he wasn't sure why he thought Eileen would be there. Maybe it was a longing or intuition, or maybe he hoped to repeat something from his living days that didn't involve tumbling over asphalt.

A spectral duck quacked at him, causing him to smile. As the ghostly bird went about its business, he spotted Eileen. At first, it was a moment of triumph. He could have sworn the dead center of his ectoplasm beat with life once again. But one look at Eileen's distraught face threw any manner of joy out the window as he floated along the path.

The pale girl didn't even look up at Kyle's approach. She stared intently at the pond. Lapping waves of brown water barely tickled her toes as she dangled them over the edge. Her white dress was stained a light shade of green from sitting on the grass and her gray makeup had distorted from the light sheen of sweat. Kyle thought she had a natural beauty that surpassed any faux ghost look.

"Hey, E, sorry I'm late." The girl didn't respond. She stared determinedly out at the pond, her pupils like pinpoints of darkness. "I was at the sage bar and lost track of time."

She wasn't responding and he could see why. She was angry and confused, her aura a swirling tide like a whirlpool. He put on his best devil-may-care smile and gave her an overexaggerated shrug of his shoulders.

"Oh well, guess Ramses and I will have fun all by ourselves."

He whistled as loud as he could and called the ghost dog's name. Kyle expected the big oaf to come running out of the woods with his tail wagging, big dog grin plastered on his face as his tongue lolled out of the side of his mouth.

The woods were silent except for the chirping of distant birds and the ever-present breeze.

Dumb dog is probably chasing a dead squirrel.

He cupped his hands to his lips and called again, "Ramses!"

Nothing.

"He's not coming. He's . . . gone." Eileen's voice was deadpan and her eyes hadn't left the pond.

"What?"

"He went to fetch the ball and he's gone now."

Kyle was unsure what she meant. "Well, which direction did he go?"

The Unenlightened girl held up a limp hand, pointing out toward the middle of the pond. Kyle followed her gaze and felt himself beginning to regress again as the bottom fell out of the world.

It was there, in the center of the pond, like it had been at Jackson Manor with Donna.

It was smaller than the one at the mansion, less all-consuming, but staring at it still caused a sharp spike of fear to shoot through his spirit.

"Kyle, what is it?" she said.

Eileen came out of her funk, clambering to her feet and hovering close without touching him. Her voice had that deep, throaty quality of someone who was barely keeping their emotions from overwhelming them.

"It's . . ." Kyle tried not to let his fear show as he put on the fakest smirk he could muster. "It's nothing. Come on, let's look around for Ramses."

Eileen didn't move. She pointed a finger. "He swam out to the middle of the pond and disappeared."

Out of the corner of his eye he saw the spectral duck that had quacked at him in annoyance float too close to the center. Then it was gone.

"Do you know something? Where's Ramses?" Eileen asked.

Kyle shook his head and opened his mouth, desperately trying to tell her exactly what he saw at the center of that pond, but the words wouldn't come. They were like claws raking down the back of his throat and sending sharp spikes of pain through his sense of being.

Describing something shouldn't have been painful to him. He was dead and pain was a feeling of the living, something he could only fleetingly touch.

But the thing in the center of the pond let him feel all the worst things no one would have wanted to hold onto. Panic, despair, pain . . . fear.

"You're lying to me, Kyle Fitzpatrick."

He gulped guiltily, a holdover from his days amongst the living, and nodded. "Yeah, but it isn't what you think."

"Please!"

Eileen's eyes were full of tears and her teeth were clenched as the truth began to dawn on her. This kind of thing was unheard of but nothing was impossible. Through the pain that wracked him he tried to find an analogue, something Eileen could understand, words that wouldn't tear him to pieces while he spoke.

"It's . . . it's like a hole in the world," he said.

Eileen looked at him and then at the center of the pond which didn't look out of the ordinary to her.

Kyle added, "It's gnawing. Gnawing and getting bigger and Ramses fell into it."

His voice rose in a panic now as Eileen's eyes filled to the brim with tears of confusion and pain. "He can't be gone. He's not gone. Why are you saying this!?"

Kyle looked away in shame as red began to tint his vision. The thing at the center of the pond was the same color. "Because it's the truth."

Something inside Eileen broke and she sank to her knees, her face paint running from the flowing tears. He could already see the asphalt and two lanes of Interstate 60 stretching into view all around him. Maybe Donna would come to rescue him again.

His sister . . .

His mind flashed to Donna, alone in Jackson Manor, unaware of what was around her. He never should have let her go back there, but he was so stubborn about her taking a vacation. All it would take was another panic attack.

And Donna would be gone, too.

"E?" Kyle managed to gasp out through his clenched teeth. "Babe, do you have your cell phone on you?"

The Unenlightened girl glared daggers at him. "Okay, sure. My dog is missing, but whatever. What other favors can I do for you? Want a blowjob?"

He crouched beside her, arms wide, trying his best to comfort her. "I'm sorry. I don't mean to be insensitive. I care about Ramses. A lot. But it's my sister. She's in trouble from this same thing. Please?"

Her glare didn't fade, but he must have been convincing because she handed him the phone. He focused with all of his willpower, shoving away the pain to punch in Donna's number one slow digit at a time.

"The number you are trying to reach is unavailable—"

Kyle snarled and ended the call. He handed the phone back to Eileen, who practically snatched it from him. While he was still focused, still mostly solid, Kyle leaned down and brought Eileen into an embrace. She tried to fight it at first before she cried against his chest.

For a moment he felt like they were a real couple going through their first heartache. Then the trickle of tears passed through him, small wisps of ectoplasmic mist forming and disappearing just as quickly, reminding him they would never be normal.

"I've got to check on my sister. Why don't you head home and I'll meet you there shortly?"

The temporary warmth and comfort between them disappeared, as if she left him completely. Her aura of vulnerability and openness was replaced with her usual cold, suicidal veneer. No one should have been so eager to join the dead.

Eileen took a deep shuddering breath, wordlessly passed straight through him, and walked determinedly down the path. As good as a middle finger to a ghost.

He despised disapparating in the best of conditions, and right now he was not in the best of conditions. There was only one person who was worth taking the risk for. He concentrated on Donna and felt himself fading, riding the ethereal lightning to get her away from Jackson Manor.

Kyle reappeared, feeling his spirit pulled back together like letting go of an overstretched spring. When his vision became clear again he screamed and fell back, scrambling across the dirt to get away.

It was barely a foot from him. The mansion was farther up the drive, but the effect that branded his senses and sent fear rocketing through him had become so much larger, encompassing the whole manor grounds.

If he had decided to reappear a bit closer . . .

Any thoughts of hypotheticals were sent screaming from his mind as he looked at the red glowing horror before him. His mind fled and he felt himself physically fall back, screaming a melody of madness and despair.

Then he was tumbling down the side of Interstate 60 wondering why the sky was turning red.

9

DONNA LIFTED TWO OF THE Venetian blinds and peered out. The night was quiet and peaceful.

"What are you doing?"

Startled, she grabbed her heart and whirled around. Leroy had been dozing gently, but not anymore, apparently.

"I could have sworn I heard my brother out there last night."

He was naked. So was she. This wasn't a movie, after all, where hands and sheets casually cover breasts and lovers walk around in bras or bathrobes post-coitus.

"Wouldn't this phenomenon prevent that?" he said.

"Which phenomenon are you referring to?" she asked, crawling back into bed, as much like a cat as she could muster.

He furrowed his brow, unsure what she was talking about. Then he felt it.

"Well, there seems to be a *phenomenon* causing the strange hardening of certain entities in my groinal area."

She giggled, too much like a schoolgirl for her tastes. "And what do you think is causing this . . . phenomenon?" He leaned in and pressed his forehead to hers. "A very beautiful girl by the name of Donna Fitzpatrick."

"Beautiful?" she asked, crossing her arms over her breasts. "I think you need to have your eyes examined."

He shook his head. "Went to the optometrist a month ago.

Clean bill of health. Dentist the month before that. Perfect choppers, too."

He bit at the air, as if demonstrating.

"When was the last time you saw a pneumatologist?"

He chuckled. "I've got to see one at least once a year to stay licensed as a psychic medium."

"Really? I don't think I've been to one since high school."

He shrugged. "As long as your third eye isn't developing cataracts, no reason you should. I, on the other hand, need to know my secret peeper is in perfect condition on the regular."

He leaned back and patted the pillow next to him. She crawled up and snuggled into the crook of his arm.

"You really think I'm beautiful?"

"Yes."

She shook her head in wonder. "What's wrong with you?"

"What's wrong with you, more like. How have you made it this far in life without realizing some people see the world differently? You seem to think because you're not supermodel skinny nobody could ever find you attractive. What a ridiculous notion. I've known girls who thought I was repulsive because of my baldness. My ex-wife sure thought so."

She ran her hands over his head.

"I think it's great," she said. "Can I rub it for luck?"

"I'm suddenly finding you unattractive again."

She scowled and rolled over to turn her back to him. Laughing, he shook her, but she folded her arms and refused to turn back around. They were halfway to wrestling—and whatever that might lead to—when a distant voice called out.

"Hello!"

"What was that?" she asked.

"I don't know," he said.

"Is it a ghost?"

He nodded. She had a feeling the sound was coming from a spirit, but couldn't necessarily tell by listening. Leroy, who was much more experienced in such matters, could. They jumped out of bed and began pulling their clothes on. Leroy had pulled his crystal out and was waving it around wildly as he was tugging one of his trouser legs up. She giggled.

"What?" he asked, looking up at her.

She reached down and clasped the crystal in both hands.

"One thing at a time," she said.

The 'hello'-ing continued as they looked around the house on their way down the stairs. When they reached the first floor she glanced toward the basement, but Leroy shook his head no.

"I'm still not seeing so much as a mouse inside," he muttered.

It was too much to hope for. They both turned and headed out onto the porch. Scanning the horizon, she couldn't see anything, but a moment later, Leroy pointed off into the forest. What easily could have been a shrub, she now saw was a pale, shimmering ghostly figure. He had the look of a staticky television set and was almost doubled over in pain.

Leroy tucked his crystal back into his pocket. "Well, he's clearly outside of this no-ghost zone."

Another low moan echoed through the early morning stillness. A few live crows flew overhead. It was almost bizarre to see a flock of the black animals without at least a few of their passed-on compatriots with them. The birds themselves even seemed a bit shocked by the lack of their spectral brethren, if shock could really be attributed to them and Donna wasn't simply projecting onto the dumb animals. They seemed to be looking around and closing ranks as though birds were missing.

Together they walked out into the woods, passing beyond the cold, dewy, overgrown grass of the lawn and into the weedier, rockier soil of the woodland area. Donna cursed herself for not putting on shoes before undertaking this journey, but now she was so far out that it would take too long to go back for them.

She felt woozy when she crossed over the barrier of the strange effect. Her ghostsense returned slowly to her, and she could spot sparse crickets and frogs of the spiritual variety off in the woods. Leroy seemed to take the change much harder, stopping to grab his head.

"This is . . ."

He shook his head, unable to express his thoughts in words. She patted his arm and then took it. Together they steadied themselves and, like sailors setting out to sea rediscovering their sealegs, they felt the sense of the spiritual returning all around them.

They approached the crouching figure.

"Oh, shit," Donna said, covering her mouth.

"What is it? You know him?"

She looked down at Willie Chang. She knelt by the greaser, who was still crackling with static.

"Willie," she whispered.

"Donna," he replied, "you've gotta . . . ugh, I hurt."

"Come with me." She reached out and tried to grab him, but passed right through his body. "Dammit. He's too ethereal."

Leroy lowered himself to join them.

"What'd you say his name was? Willie?"

"Willie Chang."

Leroy put his crystal round his neck, kissed it, and closed his eyes. He controlled his breathing and concentrated, muttering a mantra under his breath for a few seconds.

Donna watched, fascinated. She'd never really paid attention to exorcism work, having never considered it particularly interesting. But now, suddenly, she found everything Leroy did fascinating.

Leroy reached out with his fingertips, eyes pinched closed, and didn't quite touch Willie's shimmering form. "Willie Chang, can you hear me?"

Willie stopped crackling and looked up at Leroy. The exorcist seemed to have lent him some of his strength.

"Yes," Willie choked out.

"Can you disapparate?"

"I'm . . . trying."

Willie's words were pained and clipped. Leroy breathed deeply and concentrated harder until a bead of sweat formed on his forehead. Instead of gathering his powers to cast a spirit out, he was doing the exact opposite, granting Willie strength and purpose.

"Can you now?"

"No, I still don't think so. There's something weighing on me, like a great big rock on my shoulders."

Willie's words were at least coming smoother and faster.

"I need you to move farther away from the house. That direction." Leroy pointed. "Can you move?"

Willie nodded and moved slowly, almost agonizingly slow, slower than she had ever seen a ghost move before. He started to float in the opposite direction from Jackson Manor. He bobbed through the air, seeming to gain color and strength until he was finally bobbing along like a regular, happy-go-lucky spirit, albeit a bit more chalk outlinish than usual.

They followed along behind him and soon reached what looked like a disused fire pit. The center was hard-packed with old ash, mixed to an almost concrete-like consistency by the rain. The weeds and undergrowth had crept very close to it over the years in the absence of the actual lick of flames.

Donna sat down on the circle of bricks and patted the area next to her. Willie sat next to her while Leroy remained standing. He was still whispering his mantra, concentrating, albeit far less than when Willie had been in near-existential crisis mode.

"You doing all right?" Donna asked.

"No," Willie said, notional tears running down his face, dripping off, and evaporating in the air like puffs of smoke.

Leroy seemed surprised. "Are you still in pain from the house?"

Willie waved his hand through the air. "No, it's not that. Thank you for your help with that. It's . . . it's Lydia."

"Lydia?" Leroy prompted.

"His girlfriend. Or, sorry, fiancée," Donna said.

"Not anymore!" Willie began blubbering into his hands.

His despairing attitude stood in stark contrast with the badass greaser outfit he affected. It was a bizarre juxtaposition. Leroy and Donna exchanged a look of cynicism.

"One of your clients, I take it?"

Donna reached over and tried to pat Willie on the back, but despite Leroy's ministrations he was still recovering from the effects of being so near the house and had barely any substance.

"What happened, Willie?" Donna said.

"Roderick Ellington happened."

He said the name with such scorn, Donna almost instantly guessed what had happened. The broad strokes of it, at least. The sort of people she serviced talked about eternity and forever love, but at the end of the day they broke up as often as regular flesh-and-blood couples.

It was quite common in her line of work, actually. So much so, in fact, that Spender had instituted a small fee for cancellations. She hadn't fought him on it for ages and eventually had to give in.

"Who's Roderick Ellington?" she prompted.

"I know him, actually," Leroy said. "One of those hoity-toity Victorian-era specters. A family hired me to kick him out of the apartment where he'd hanged himself. He gave me the whole song and dance about 'I was here first' and 'Don't you have any respect?'"

"That's him!" Willie agreed. "He's about as interesting as dryer lint, too. All he does is write that depressing, make-you-want-to-kill-yourself poetry and the girls all swoon over him. 'There once was a man from Nantucket and I hanged myself standing on a bucket.' You get the gist. Lydia fell for his horseshit hook, line, and sinker."

Donna pinched the sinuses of her nasal passages. This sort of thing happened a lot, too. With the Unenlightened, old and dour wasn't a bug in a lover, it was a feature. And the older and dourer the better. She'd probably end up trading Roderick in for some Colonial-era headless horseman in a few weeks.

"Well, I'm sorry to hear that, Willie. And I don't want to be rude, but I'm on vacation right now."

"I know! I know! I'm sorry. I really didn't mean to . . . I didn't want to screw up your time off. I didn't know where else to go. I talked to your friend Tommie at the Arrowhead, and he told me you'd come up here. I thought maybe you could talk some sense into Lydia. Remind her what we had. I mean, most people don't . . . get it. But you know what real love is. You probably see fakers walking in and out of your door every day. But what we had, it was special. I could tell you got it. I saw it in your eyes. And I thought maybe if there was an impartial third party that told Lydia what she was throwing away, she'd at least reconsider it."

Donna sighed. She got down on one knee and reached out to clasp Willie's hands in her own. He was still largely insubstantial, but he came to solidity a bit under her touch.

"Willie, I'm so sorry this happened to you. It's cruel and it's unfair. But it's not really my place to get involved in the love lives of my clients. In fact, ethically, I'm obliged not to. If I meddled and pushed people to be with one another when they shouldn't be, I could benefit financially from that. And that's pretty close to fraud. At least, it's a gray area. I wish you the best and I'm sorry you're hurting, but I really have to stay neutral in this."

Willie's features sagged, and his hands returned to complete insubstantiality under her grasp. She returned to her seat next to him.

"I guess that makes sense. I should've known. Stupid, stupid, stupid!" Willie knocked on his forehead three times in succession.

"Now," she said, "you're not stupid. You're heartbroken."

"And I'm messing up your vacation, too!"

"You didn't," she soothed, but he was already continuing on.

"I thought I'd be out of your hair in five minutes, but first I tried to apparate into the mansion, and I couldn't. I've never encountered anything like that before. So I apparated as close as I could and started floating over here. But then I hit that . . . wall. What is wrong with this place?"

"Nothing," Leroy said. "It's perfectly fine. There's just no haunting. Not a single ghost. But what does it look like to you?"

Willie glanced back in the direction of the Jackson place, with a look on his face that suggested if he still had a spine, a shiver would have run down it.

"I-I . . ."

He sputtered, his mouth almost unable to move. Donna and Leroy exchanged a worried glance. She grabbed Leroy by the lapel and whispered in his ear. "This is what happened to my brother. It made him relapse."

"Willie, relax," Leroy said. "Breathe. I know you don't have lungs anymore, but your spirit will remember it fondly. Remember what it's like to breathe."

Willie closed his eyes and forced his chest in and out. Donna watched the exchange, fascinated. She had heard of exorcist tricks like this, but this was the first time she'd seen any in person. Leroy clutched his crystal closely, whispering his mantra under his breath. Donna leaned in to try to hear what it was. All she could make out was "dark."

"Focus," Leroy said in a calm, soothing tone. Not a condescending one like people might use with a pet or someone else's unruly child, but a calm, pleasing tone someone might use with a lover. "Focus on me. Willie Chang, can you hear me?"

Leroy was invoking Willie's name. It was the oldest trick in the book, but it was working. There was power in naming ghosts.

At college Donna had once taken a course on nameless ghosts. There were a few dark, ancient beings who had survived millennia haunting Mesopotamia, the African grasslands, and other places where mankind had its deepest roots. Some had names impossible to pronounce or even guess at this late date and others pre-dated the idea of names or maybe even language itself, her professor had theorized. They were monsters, a menace to their haunting grounds.

Willie, though, was no ancient near-deity and they very much knew his real and only name. Leroy was able to invoke it, over and over again, stabilizing Willie's presence and giving him strength and lending him some of his willpower.

"Yes," Willie replied, "I'm still here."

"What do you see around the manor? Is it like a bubble?"

Donna's head turned from man to man, amazed at what she was watching. Leroy almost seemed to be dominating Willie, like a stage hypnotist's trick.

"It's . . . red. But . . . also . . . not red."

Leroy pursed his lips. Not exactly helpful.

"What else can you tell me?"

"It's like . . . there's nothing there. I've never seen or felt anything like it. Like an emptiness. A nothing. Almost a . . . hole in the world."

Leroy paused and put his fingers to his lips. "Not a presence but an absence?"

Willie started to shake and flicker like a guttering candle. "I-I-I can't be here anymore. I can't! It's . . . it's growing!"

By the last word, Willie was shrieking. Donna and Leroy both whirled around but they couldn't see what Willie could. When they turned back, Willie was on his feet, floating a few inches off the ground. "I need to go. I need to go now."

"Did you say it's growing?" Leroy asked.

"Please, please, mister, let me go."

Leroy looked to Donna for confirmation. All she could do was shrug.

"You're the exorcist," she said.

Leroy said, "Go, Willie. Go head back home."

Before the words were out of his mouth, Willie had disapparated. Leroy reached out and entwined his fingers with Donna's.

"Curiouser and curiouser," Leroy said, clucking his tongue.

"Will he be all right?"

"Ectoplasmically? Yeah, he'll be fine. Not sure what can be done about the broken heart, though."

Donna said, "He'll recover. He has all eternity to. I'll talk to him when I'm back on the clock, maybe."

"Well, shall we head back?"

"Yes, let's. But can I ask one small favor?"

"Name it."

"Will you carry me?" she asked.

He grinned. "Why's that?"

She pointed down at her bare feet. They'd been aching this whole time, minus the minutes she'd been sitting around the fire pit.

"I'd love to," he said. "I'd love to sweep you off your feet, but—"

"I'm too fat," she concluded with a scowl.

"No," he said. "I'm not wearing shoes either."

Glancing down, she saw Leroy had indeed rushed out in a hurry as she had. She sighed, overloud and overlong.

"Very well, then. I'll carry my own bulk. But you owe me, mister."

"A debt I intend to repay."

They started to walk back toward the mansion. The feeling of disorientation struck them, but now, having experienced it already, its effects were somewhat dampened. Even so, due to his sensitivity, Leroy was still grasping his thighs and breathing heavily by the time Donna had recovered.

"Notice anything?" he asked. She shook her head. "Look where we are."

She looked around. All she saw were trees and undergrowth. "I don't see anything special."

"Last night, when I arrived, I didn't get hit by it until I was on the porch. Then when we came out this morning, we recovered around the property line. Now we're hitting the effect and we're still in the woods."

She felt her heart sink. "When I first came here I didn't experience it until I was already inside the house."

"Willie said the effect was growing. This could be . . . bad. I need to talk to some people I know. We might need to issue a warning to the town."

"Maybe it's not growing, per se. Maybe it's just shifting."

"Even so, a rogue no-haunt zone, or whatever we're calling this thing, would be like a boulder rolling down a hill if it moves into town. And if it is growing it would be like a volcano. Maybe we should ask the mayor to evacuate all specters to be safe."

She shrugged. "If you don't think it's overkill."

His silence was more telling than a verbal response would have been. As soon as they were back on the porch, Donna shrieked as she felt her legs swept out from under her. She smiled as Leroy carried her across the threshold. The mood was successfully lightened.

"Isn't this a bit premature?" she asked, biting her lower lip.

"Oh, geez," he said, stumbling to put her back on her feet.

"Don't drop me!"

"I won't!" He lowered her gently down. "I didn't mean . . . I . . . you said the thing before about carrying you, and—"

She kissed him on the nose. "I know what you meant, you big dope."

He rubbed his hands down his sides. "Well, I really should get back to town. I hate to break away but this—whatever it is—we really should tell some people."

"Okay," she agreed. "My time here's up this evening, but I might head back now anyway. I at least want to call Willie and make sure he's all right."

A few minutes later, both dressed, they stood in the foyer, neither wanting to part just yet.

"Well, I should probably get to packing," Donna said finally.

"Okay. I'll, um, I'll call you later."

"You'd better. If I find out your nickname's 'Love 'Em and Leave 'Em Tate,' I'm going to come by your shop and slash the tires of your van."

"Oh, skies above. You took it right to that level, huh? There's no fuck around in you, is there?"

"Not an ounce of it." He leaned in and kissed her one last time. "Can I ask you something?"

"You can ask."

"What's the mantra you're always saying? I can't quite make it out."

He blushed and turned away. "You're not supposed to."

"Oh, I'm sorry," she said. "I didn't realize that was a personal question. I don't meet a lot of exorcists."

"No, no," he said, dismissing her concerns with a wave of his hand, "it's not really a personal question. I'm embarrassed by the story behind mine. But I'll tell you what it is. I like to say, 'All dark, all the time.'"

She furrowed her brow.

"Oh. What's the story behind that?"

"Now *that* is a personal question. But maybe I'll tell you. One day."

10

KYLE HAD NEARLY PULLED HIMSELF out of his spiral when Tommie Bones appeared next to him.

He watched the morning sun wrench a place for itself out of the sky as its orange rays penetrated the veil of red and pain that was his existence.

He was dead. In fact, he'd been dead for years. What he was experiencing wasn't real. Or, at least, it wasn't taking place presently. Kyle had been trying to convince himself that was true for most of the night while he relived his death *ad infinitum*.

Tommie didn't interfere, a courtesy amongst the deceased. When a specter relapsed, a breather might try to help, but the dead would let him handle his own business without pity.

What the sight of his friend did give him, though, was that extra push. The pain and confusion faded and Kyle groaned as he wearily rose to his feet. He felt like he had gone on a cross-town sage binge, his ectoplasm throbbing in protest as he gestured for Tommie to help him.

Strong hands that more than likely had wrestled bears in life steadied Kyle as both of them stared at the sea of light and life that was Ganesh City. Kyle watched the dead and the living going about their business as they had since time immemorial: moms and dads pursuing their dreams while their children romped with great-grandparents baffled by the latest electronics. Cars honked, angry poltergeists played havoc with the electricity, and the city moved along, oblivious to Kyle Fitzpatrick and his friend.

"It really is beautiful, isn't it?" Kyle whispered.

Tommie grunted in reply. "Let's go home."

Tommie disapparated. Kyle considered following suit for a moment, but his relapse was too fresh on his mind. He began floating home.

Kyle hung up the phone at the gas station. Donna was safe and back from her vacation. She'd discovered the weirdness and promised him it was all in hand. His attempt to rush to the rescue had turned out to be pointless. Worse than pointless, since it had led to his relapse.

He was blue. He decided to look for Eileen.

She hadn't wanted to bring Kyle home to meet her family yet. They were still reeling from the fact she had become an Unenlightened.

When Kyle couldn't find Eileen at her apartment in Meadowbrook, he headed over to 4th Avenue where her parents lived. He wasn't used to the fear gathering in his gut and wanted to check if they knew where she could possibly be.

The houses on 4th Avenue were high class. Donna made a comfortable living but the people who lived here breathed wealth through every fiber of their spirits. All the houses looked the same to Kyle's eyes, three story affairs with iron railings running up to the front doors and tangles of ivy running up the aged edifices in glorious spouts of green. Wood and brick mixed together to create homes that spoke of rich histories and power. Kyle could see lanterns burning behind high windows, a glimpse of families clustered around their dinner tables laughing brilliantly as their ancestors floated overhead.

No wonder Eileen hadn't wanted him to meet her family. The only work he'd done lately was filling in for Eugene's regular bouncer now and then at the Arrowhead.

Kyle had appeared at the head of the street but when he saw what the road passed through, he stopped himself and cursed under his breath. Headstones lined both sides of the street.

Cemeteries and graveyards were for the rich and the elite, the people who wanted their bodies to disappear slowly beneath the ground while their beautiful monuments would remain for all time, proclaiming they had lived once.

Rich specters would gather round, burn sage, and discuss who had the best headstone, while grave robbers would constantly try to unearth and steal their remains for a sweet ransom. To have your bones stolen was the height of gauche in high society. There was money to be made in graveyard security, but regular blue-collar ghosts disdained such work, so the wealthy usually swallowed their customary disdain and hired breathers.

Kyle licked his lips on reflex as the memories of his long dead nerves fired. He took a hesitant step forward, trying to ignore the pointed looks of the spirits hanging around the graves beside him. He knew he didn't belong. His clothing signaled poverty at worst and lower class at best, and his inability to change it showed he was still young for a ghost. But instead of turning away in shame, he strode forward.

The wind picked up and blew through the oak trees lining side-walks on either side of him. He could poltergeist with the best of them, and he dared any of those rich bastards to stop him as he crossed onto 4th Avenue.

Dead brown leaves blew across the pavement. An old Cadillac driven by a man in a suit drove right through him as if he wasn't even there. Kyle didn't bother giving the man a middle finger as he moved over to the sidewalk and stared around. He tried to focus, looking for familiar aura trails in the ether, places that echoed of Eileen.

He found her.

Kyle sprinted toward the brilliant white glow and looked up at the three-story historical home. A white picket fence divided the immaculate lawn from the sidewalk. The woodwork was painted a deep black and the curtains were equally as heavy. A crimson door with a decorative wreath prevented him from seeing inside. To the living it would have been just another wealthy family's home, but it told the dead a different story.

He could sense pain, sadness, and worry, all of it recent. Happi-ness had dwelled here, but had been reduced to tattered scraps on the stone path.

Eileen was here, though. Kyle was sure of it.

He focused himself and unlatched the gate. The dregs of happy feelings evaporated into nothing as Kyle floated past the ethereal leftovers. The crimson door drew closer and Kyle breathed deeply, though it wasn't necessary. He wasn't afraid. He was in love.

He focused on his hand and reached for a brass knocker in an ornate lion's mouth. The metal ring rapped hard against the wood and Kyle felt nervous as the last impact echoed off the other houses.

The door opened slowly and whatever bravado Kyle was trying to muster faded when he was face-to-face with the stern-looking older woman on the other side. She was dressed like a woman from the twenties, with short made-up hair and a bright sequined dress that flickered with every turn. A long, black cigarette holder dangled between her middle and index fingers. Instead of tobacco, a small quantity of fresh sage burned at the end.

The woman's face flickered from a youthful glow to elderly wrinkles almost as if she couldn't tell how she wanted to present herself. It was harder to see in the aged version of her face, but Kyle had no doubt this woman was related to Eileen, probably her grandmother or great-grandmother.

"Can I help you, sir?"

Her voice had an airy quality of refined southern charm that spoke of a classical upbringing. No doubt that brought its own ingrained sensibilities with it. It must have been agonizing for this woman to know her descendent was a member of the Unenlightened. Social movements of change had never been popular with the living elite, much less those who had passed on and become set in their ways.

Kyle gave his most winning smile and asked hesitantly, "Is Eileen here?"

He looked over the woman's shoulder, hoping he could catch a glimpse of the beautiful girl craning to see who was at the door, like in the movies. She wasn't there and the woman's choice of face had finally settled on crone. Her wrinkles deepened and her eyes grew dark. A powerful gust of wind began to blow down 4th Avenue.

"Eileen is indisposed at the moment, young man, and will be for the foreseeable future. Now would you kindly vacate our—"

Kyle focused hard and elbowed his way past the much older spirit and into the house. He was thoroughly prepared to be dragged off by the angry relatives protecting Eileen but he wasn't leaving until he made sure she was all right.

"Now hold on, young man! You are not welcome here!"

Kyle ignored the older specter's protestations as he floated from room to room shouting, "Eileen!"

The interior of the home was quite modern, as though the imposing façade of the outside melted away to reveal a heartless interior. From the tile to the furniture, everything was painted a sterile white. Dead animal furs as dark as the night sky lined the pillows.

A television spat a news report at a group of gathered ghosts sitting around the box. The news wasn't focused on the hole or void or whatever it was that had taken Ramses. Didn't they know what was out there? No, of course they didn't. The world was continuing on, television awash with the newest celebrity gossip.

"World's First Ghostranaut" flashed across the screen in a large font. A freak accident had apparently killed Lieutenant Commander Lucas Tremblay aboard the ISS. A vacuum lock hadn't cycled correctly and, sans spacesuit, Tremblay was now enjoying fame at the expense of shuffling off the mortal coil. It was news to be sure, but news Kyle didn't have time to indulge in.

The audience of ghosts turned away from the television to look at Kyle with a mixture of shock and revulsion. They seemed offended a spirit of such obvious poverty would dare enter their home. Then again, they might have just been offended he was trespassing.

"*Someone get the chimes!*"

Kyle ignored the threat and shouts of alarm as he glanced into the kitchen, which was all black granite countertops, gray appliances, and an island. The stairs to the upper floors were past the kitchen. Kyle dashed through and raced up the steps, his deathly constitution propelling him faster than any living runner.

On the second floor there was a door with fake cobwebs and a small blackboard decorating the outside. The slate was scribbled with chalk drawings and words Kyle couldn't understand. He recognized it as Eileen's handwriting only when he saw the word *Ramses* amongst the rest of the scribbles and nonsense.

Kyle focused and turned the door knob as her family reached the top of the stairs.

"Stop," someone shouted, "you can't—"

Kyle ignored them and floated in. He looked around the room for the woman he cared for more than he wanted to admit.

The room was dark. A candle burned low on the other side of the room, casting flickering shadows everywhere. A low, brown dresser stretched across the opposite wall while hanging black book cases adorned the other walls. Posters from famous ghost bands

Kyle only heard of in passing were plastered against every piece of available wall space.

Pale clothes littered the floor: socks, underwear, and dresses. Black lipstick scribbled across the walls drifted in and out of view as the candle flickered on the other side of the room.

Words like *Gone*, *Hopeless*, *Ramses*, and, perhaps most upsetting, *Kyle's Fault* were drawn all over the wall in overlapping pigments of black and red. Kyle felt the world drop out from under him as he looked for Eileen, whispering her name even as his heart broke.

The girl was huddled in the center of the room on the other side of her bed. Kyle passed straight through the mattress, his lower legs disappearing beneath the unkempt and tangled sheets.

"Eileen?"

The black eye shadow and mascara had run across her face. Her formerly gray dress was torn and dirty as though she had run through the woods and rolled around in the dirt. The white carpet under her bed was stained a worrying shade of red. Dark maroon cuts littered her arms. The wounds had clotted, but the damage was done. The girl's teeth had matching red stains, the lipstick smudges around a cut on her arm indicating she had been sucking on the wound.

"Sweetheart? It's . . . Kyle." He was reluctant to say his own name.

Her hands were wrapped around her legs and she stared absently at a candle burning on her nightstand, her eyes never leaving the flickering candle.

"Eileen?"

He tried to reach out and place a hand on her shoulder but her mouth dropped open in a loud, piercing shriek. She didn't stop screaming until Kyle pulled away from her. He suddenly felt sick, something he was unprepared for. The intense wave of grief hit him and the world began to fade to red.

He had to sit down. He couldn't . . .

Kyle struggled to emerge from the mattress, sinking to the floor and staring at Eileen. She smiled like a madwoman at the flickering candle.

"She's been like that ever since she came home."

Kyle turned and saw the woman who had answered the door bobbing hesitantly at the entrance to the bedroom. The rest of the family clustered behind her, heads craning to see what was going on.

"You must be the young man she was going on and on about." The old spirit's face shifted again, becoming younger as she saw Kyle's distress. "Don't relapse on me, young man. We have business to discuss."

She was attempting to sound stern, but she couldn't keep a certain inner decency out of her voice. Kyle was in a bad way and the woman could see it. If he could have cried hot tears he would have, but the tears wouldn't come. The dead didn't cry, they suffered. And the pain he was feeling now made him long for the redness of the road.

"My name is Marie. Eileen is my great-granddaughter."

Kyle looked up at the woman and tried to make his mouth work, finally managing to stammer out his name. The older spirit regarded him a bit longer before turning around and addressing the rest of her extended family.

"Will the rest of you kindly give us a moment?"

The ghost of an older man with a three-piece suit and monocle looked startled as his great belly rumbled. His voice came like train cars charging down a railway, "Marie, I'm not so sure that's a good—"

"I'll brook no argument, Phineas! Give the boy and I a moment."

Apparently Phineas knew better than to provoke an argument with the matriarch. He turned around and began herding the rest of the family spirits back down the stairs. Marie took a hit of the sage cigarette she still held, fading slightly as her outline contrasted against the walls. The older ghost carefully lowered herself onto the edge of the bed and stared hard at Kyle. Her piercing eyes bored into him like green specks of light in a white ocean. He did his best to meet her gaze without fear.

Eileen ignored them both, continuing to stare at the candle and occasionally giggling.

"Tell me, Kyle, what was my great-granddaughter to you?"

Without hesitation he replied, "She *is* someone I care about."

Marie nodded slightly, accepting Kyle's words. "But if you cared about her so much, why is she like this? And where were you when it happened to her?"

The questions hit Kyle like twin bullets and his anger rose, his inner poltergeist threatening to emerge and trash the house, down to the foundations if necessary. Objects began to clatter on the shelves, Eileen's knick-knacks beginning to move as Kyle's anger manifested.

Marie watched it all with the cool practice of someone who was absolutely unintimidated by theatrics or emotion. Kyle would answer her questions at the end of the day.

He tried to get his anger under control and not look at Eileen for fear of losing himself all over again. His outline solidified until he was panting.

"I was helping her look for Ramses, her dog." Marie continued to stare at him, her eyes pressing for more details. "There's some . . . thing at the old Jackson house. Something terrible. And it's spread to the lake."

The older ghost looked unconcerned as she blew a ring of sage. "What is this terrible thing, then?"

Kyle shook his head. Even thinking about it sent his spirit into nausea. "I really can't say. It's like nothing I've ever heard of before. It's hard to believe it's even real."

"Except you saw it," Marie pointed out, "and so did my beautiful girl. Are you saying this 'terrible thing' left her in this state?"

Kyle shook his head. "She couldn't see it. I think only ghosts can see it. But she watched Ramses wander into it and he was . . ." Kyle tried to think of the appropriate phrase before settling on the easiest to understand. ". . . he was gone."

Marie breathed in more of the sage and bluntly replied, "I see." They sat in silence for a few more moments before Marie spoke, her voice steely and cool. "I believe you."

Kyle was startled but tried to keep his head about him. "I think she's in shock. Nothing like this has ever happened before. Here's what I think you should do—"

"I've had quite enough of your opinions, Mr. Fitzpatrick. I believe your story but that doesn't suddenly mean you're a trusted family member." The older ghost rose and Kyle followed suit. It seemed their brief détente was at an end. "Until she becomes well again, I would ask you not to come by here again. If you do, I *will* call the authorities. I'm prepared to forgive your trespassing once, in light of your feelings for my descendant."

Kyle wanted to protest but Eileen's great-grandmother looked like she was ready to kick his spirit up and down 4th Avenue if he protested. Everyone seemed to blame him for Eileen's condition. Why wouldn't she?

If this was his last opportunity, he decided he'd better take another shot or regret it forever.

"Eileen, look at me."

The Unenlightened girl's stare never wavered.

"Mr. Fitzpatrick . . ." Marie warned.

"Eileen, please!" His voice was pleading.

"*Mr. Fitzpatrick!*"

"*Eileen!*" He sobbed the name.

"Leave. Now."

The old woman's voice was like a roar and Kyle suddenly found himself rebounding out of the room and smacking through the opposite wall. He'd never been poltergeisted with such sheer strength of will before. He felt like he couldn't breathe, even though he hadn't had to for fifteen years. He fought hard to keep himself together as his vision turned red.

Kyle barely had a chance to calm down before he felt his specter tighten like a giant fist was encircling him. It flung him down the stairs, past cheering family members, and finally out the door. He tumbled across 4th Avenue, coming to a rest as the crimson red door, still hanging open from his earlier intrusion, slammed shut.

Pain. So much pain. Clearly, Eileen's great-grandmother was not a specter to be trifled with.

He stared up at the window with the flickering candlelight he knew was Eileen's. Marie was standing there. When they locked eyes, she blasted the curtains shut.

11

"SEE, WHAT I DON'T THINK people get—what people miss, really—is this is what true love looks like."

Donna listened. Lisa Vasquez and Walter Channing were the seventh set of avatars of true love to walk into her office so far this morning. And she could not stand listening to them. Something had changed in her since going on enforced vacation.

Or maybe it was meeting Leroy. Certainly she couldn't get his face out of her mind. Or maybe it was both.

Reluctantly, though, she had to admit Kyle was right. Seeing Leroy was probably what was making her feel better in the long run, but going away had put her in the right frame of mind to start seeing someone in the first place. She was feeling better about herself and when she glanced over at the mirror, someone who didn't look fat anymore was staring back at her.

"Can I interrupt you, Walter?" Donna said.

Walter, who happened to be the warm body in this coupling, seemed taken aback, but nodded docilely.

"I think you two are about the cutest couple I've ever seen. Now I'm coming real close to crossing a professional ethical line saying this, but I would be lying if I said absolutely anything else right now." They both smiled, then turned to stare into each other's eyes. Donna continued. "We could keep talking for the rest of the day, but I want to get you two taken care of *tout suite*. Now, I can offer you a package—"

The bell on the door jingled. Donna looked up to ask the incoming couple to take a seat but was struck dumb when she saw Steven Hager float through the door, his unmistakable goat-like beard trailing behind him.

Donna's mom had gone to high school with Steven, but now he was the sheriff of Sherman's Forest. He'd been elected in a landslide about six years ago. The aneurysm had taken his life twenty years before. He was young for an elected politician, but not an unheard of age.

Donna remembered thinking at the time of the election his opponent was far better qualified, but, of course, it had come down to identity politics. The other candidate was a breather, and ghosts were an almost monolithic bloc of voters. Donna sometimes held out hope someday America would elect its first living president, but she'd probably be dead by then and would vote against him.

It wasn't exactly as though the living were second-class citizens, but it often felt like the dead patronized them. She imagined it was similar to the way women were treated a hundred years ago, before suffrage. Sherman's Forest wasn't really that bad, being as they were in the New World and the town had only been founded a few hundred years ago. A place like Damascus, though, which had been occupied for millennia and where spectral politics had become deeply entrenched, was a veritable city of the dead.

She and Steven were familiar but never exactly close. Steven certainly wasn't wearing a face that said he was stopping by to rekindle their old acquaintanceship. He took the Smokey the Bear hat from atop his head and clutched it in his hands, waiting expectantly.

"Um, excuse me for a moment," Donna said.

"Is everything all right?" Walter said.

"Yes, fine, I think."

Donna rose and approached the sheriff. "Something I can help you with?"

His expression was dour. "I think you'd better shut down the office and come with me."

Donna's heart sank into her stomach. She didn't know what was going on—Kyle must've been up to no good—but she knew her business was going to suffer badly due to the first early close this week. Twice was only going to exacerbate the situation.

"I, uh—"

"Everything's all right, folks," Steven said, addressing Lisa and Walter. "I need Ms. Fitzpatrick's expertise on an investigation. She's doing the town a favor."

"Oh, okay," Walter said, rising from his chair.

The lovebirds walked out the door and Donna locked it, flipping the sign from "open" to "closed." She glanced at the slogan on the window. "We don't believe in unhappy endings." She was starting to hope that would turn out to be true of her own story.

"What's going on, Steven?"

The ghost sighed, obviously an affectation for one of his ilk. But his face said it all. Something terrible was afoot.

"My brother?"

Steven cocked his head. "Your brother? No. A couple of your clients, I believe."

Donna furrowed her brow. "My clients? There's some trouble?"

"Yeah. I'm hoping you can talk them down off the ledge, so to speak. Lydia dos Santos and . . ." Steven flipped through his notebook.

"Willie Chang." Donna supplied the second name before he could find it himself.

Steven tucked the notebook back into its place. The notebook, gun, and badge were physical objects. Donna imagined it took him a great deal of willpower to carry those around with him, but being unarmed against human perps was a dangerous risk. A ghost could attempt to poltergeist and scare the shit out of someone living, but that was about the most that could be hoped for.

Donna climbed into the passenger seat of Steven's Crown Vic. As she'd expected, the dead man put his few physical possessions down on the dash. For a ghost, it would be tough enough controlling the vehicle without also carrying something. With them it would be akin to a human drunk driving.

They started driving toward the park.

"How's your mom doing?" Steven asked toward the beginning of the trip.

"Um, I don't hear from her much. Pretty typical relationship, I guess."

That was the extent of their conversation. Donna was on the edge of her seat the whole trip, but also terrified to ask what happened. Willie had seemed far worse than unhinged the last time she'd seen him. She'd hoped he would've shaken it off by now, but it wasn't exactly her job to make sure every jilted lover who canceled a contract with her wasn't going to run off and do something stupid. She'd do nothing else with her time.

A few of Steven's deputies had set up a barricade near the duck pond, and half the town seemed to have turned out to attempt to push their way through it. Donna paused, though, because something felt off. She realized all of the spectral spectators were farther back, well behind the barricade.

Lydia dos Santos was standing on the bank of the duck pond. She looked completely unlike herself, and it wasn't the absence of her usual Unenlightened-style makeup. The crowd parted grudgingly for Steven's car as he flashed the lights a few times and sounded the siren. The deputies opened the barricade for him.

Steven slammed on the brakes suddenly, sending Donna lurching. If she hadn't been wearing her seatbelt she would've smashed her teeth to splinters on the dashboard.

"What the hell?" Donna asked, turning to look at him with alarm.

"It's . . ."

Steven's eyes were wide. Donna recognized that look. She'd seen it in Tommie, then later in Kyle, then Willie Chang. It was the look of perverse, profound, almost confused distress that struck specters when they encountered the Jackson effect.

She turned toward the duck pond. The grounds of Jackson Manor lay on the other side. Was it possible the effect had spread this far?

"Nothing?" Donna prompted. "A great red nothingness?"

Steven's eyes widened more. He maneuvered the car into a less panic-inducing position before taking up the conversation again. "You know something about this? We were thinking it's a strange meteorological phenomenon. Like the northern lights or something."

"Maybe," Donna replied. "I don't know if I know much more about it than you do."

Steven's Smokey hat reappeared around his head. "Well, let's put a pin in it for now. We're in kind of a crisis situation here and we could use your help."

Donna said, "I understand."

She stepped out of the Crown Vic. Steven's deputies, the spectral ones at least, were giving the phenomenon a wide berth. The living seemed mostly unaffected, but Donna recognized the head-ache and disorienting effect of the phenomenon reflected in pained and uncomfortable expressions on various faces.

Only one person out of uniform stood, or rather floated, on the same side of the barricade as her. He had a dry, sunken face and wore an ascot and some decidedly out-of-style clothes. He must have been a severe dipsomaniac in life to appear so sallow and miserable in death.

"You must be Rodney Ellington," Donna guessed.

The 19th-century specter perked up.

"Roderick," he replied, his voice almost exactly as nonchalantly pompous as she would have expected. "Are we acquainted, madam?"

She shook her head. Steven floated toward them both, his thumbs tucked into his belt.

"I guess you're familiar with the situation?" the sheriff asked.

"Situation?" Ellington jumped in, looking as though he might faint dead away, despite being centuries dead. "Is that all having my heart wrenched out of my chest is to you, Constable? Is that all the bitter fruits of life rotting on the vine are worth?"

"I didn't mean any offense by it, sir," Steven said, with the restrained tone cops sometimes got when dealing with someone odious but unavoidable, "just that Ms. Fitzpatrick is familiar with all the particulars and wherefores. Now, Ms. Fitz, if you'll walk this way and see if you can convince Willie to step away from the meteorological phenomenon."

"Willie?" Donna asked, glancing over toward the mud bank.

All she saw was Lydia. Disheveled. Out of sorts. Not herself. Donna realized with a sinking feeling what happened.

"He's possessed her."

There were grave consequences for illegal possession. Being deliberately reduced to a relapsed state, a la Mrs. Palladino, was one of them. It was torture for a specter, sometimes enforced for years. There was not much she could promise Willie to get him to release Lydia's body, and he, in all likelihood, knew it. This was most likely a fool's errand, but she understood Steven had to exhaust all possible options.

"And you already talked to him?"

"Yes, and Mr. Ellington. And we tried to get Willie's great grandparents to talk to him, but they're in China right now and we can't get them on the line. I've got a call in to Ganesh City for a hostage negotiator, but in the meantime we're doing whatever we can to keep him calm and present. He mentioned you."

Wow. He had exhausted about every option before coming to her.

"Calm and present?" Donna asked. "Why, what's he threatening?"

"Avoid bringing that up, if possible."

One of Steven's living deputies, Paulos according to his name-tag, approached and threw a salt-filled vest over Donna's torso. She struggled to fit into it, and Deputy Paulos helped her Velcro it in place. If Willie attempted to poltergeist or otherwise inflict damage on her, the vest would help protect her, the deputy explained. Yeah, right. About as much as a rain slicker would protect her from nuclear fallout.

Once that was complete, she sighed. Everyone was staring at her expectantly, perhaps the glassy-eyed former Lydia most of all. She walked toward the pond bank.

"Hi, Willie," she said.

"H-. . . hi, Donna."

It was strange hearing Willie's voice coming out of the girl's mouth, or as close an approximation as Lydia's vocal cords could make. Donna tucked her thumbs into the armpits of the vest.

"What are we doing here, Willie?"

"I'm just . . . I'm . . ."

He looked down at Lydia's feet in shame. They were shoeless. It looked like he had possessed her when she was asleep. Her hair was disheveled and she was half-dressed, and it seemingly hadn't even occurred to him to finish dressing her.

It suddenly struck her what he was planning.

"Willie, why don't you come here and take my hand. Aren't you cold?"

Lydia's body shivered, as if at her suggestion, and he ran her hands up and down her arms.

"Yes," he sputtered, "freezing."

"Well, I can see why," she said. "You're barely dressed and you're up to your ankles in wet mud. Here, why don't you come on away from the pond and we'll get you some hot coffee or . . ."

"No! No no no no no."

Lydia's head shook rapidly back and forth. Donna grimaced.

One trick she had learned from her trade, at least, was ghosts were so unused to being cold or hungry or tired while occupying someone else's body that sometimes they had to be reminded what they were feeling. She had hoped a little insight would have taken her further with Willie than it had.

She said quietly, "I think you'd better vacate Lydia's body."

Lydia's head bobbed back up and, this time, instead of glassy, her eyes looked crazed.

"We're in love. You know it. You saw it. You told me as much yourself."

Donna held up her hands. "I didn't say that. You pressed me on it, a couple of times, in fact, and I refused to say anything, remember? And do you know why?"

"Professional ethics," he spat back, venomous as a pit viper.

"That's part of it," she agreed, "but part of it, too, is love is . . . mercurial. Two people fall in love and then one falls out, but maybe not the other. Or maybe they drift apart. Or maybe one falls deeper in love and the other stays the same. Love isn't a static state. It's a journey. It's all over the map."

He paused, almost seeming to believe her, but then shook his head. "No. Ours was a romance for the ages. Like Romeo and Juliet. Or Tristan and Isolde."

"And what happened to them?"

He turned away from her and toward the hole in the world.

"No, no, no, Willie, look at me. Don't look out there. Look at me."

"Lydia and I can be together forever, though. I realized what this thing is. It's like a portal. To another plane of existence."

"You don't know that."

He pounded Lydia's heart with her fist. "I believe it. Right here. I'll take her into it and we'll be all each other has."

"Is that really what you want? Even if that's true, and I don't know that it is—for all I know, you could go into that thing and disappear from existence—but even if you're right, do you want Lydia to be with you because she had no choice? Because there's nobody left but you and her?"

"That wouldn't be why. She would be so advanced, so far beyond this human form that she would understand, I mean really understand what I feel. We'll be like one."

"I haven't seen anything point to that being true. I think if you go in there you'll cease to exist."

"It is true! It is! And I'll prove it! I'll prove it to all of you."

"No, wait!"

Willie made for the water. Steven and the other deputies started rushing toward them, but only the breathers could make it past a certain halo of the effect, and even as they did so, they clutched their heads, dizzy. Willie must have been wracked with confusion and pain, being as far past the halo as he was. Only being in Lydia's body, perhaps, was keeping him cemented to reality.

"Please listen to me," Donna said, grasping for some words, any, really, to keep Willie talking. "There's something beautiful in being chosen. There's something special about somebody, out of all the billions of people and trillions of souls out there, choosing you, just you. But the flip side is sometimes you're not chosen. Or sometimes the choice changes. It's the power and danger of free will. Without the tails, there's no heads. Without the shadow, there's no light. She chose you, and it was nice for a while, but then she chose somebody else. She chose Roderick."

"Roderick," he sneered, glancing at the dandy, who looked nearly panicked, but couldn't come any closer to the effect than he already was.

Willie-cum-Lydia spat on the ground in Roderick's direction. The Victorian ghost looked hurt, betrayed, then angry, remembering it wasn't actually Lydia who had spat at him.

"Yes, Roderick. I know you don't like him. He's unlikeable. Damn unlikeable. Not like you. You've got it all. Prospects. Looks. Money. Who knows why she chose that fancy clown over you. But she did. And you have to let them try to be happy together. Maybe at the end of it she'll come back to you. Maybe not. But if you really care for her, and I know you do—"

"I do."

"Then you have to trust her. You even have to trust her to make her own mistakes."

Through Lydia's eyes, Willie looked back, at Roderick, at Steven, at the gathered crowd. He was hurting all right. Deranged, probably. But mostly she saw a young, hurting man, still somehow immature even at half a dozen decades old.

"You're wrong," he said quietly, and she recognized the calmness in his voice as coming from having made a decision, "but you'll see I was right."

He turned and splashed out into the pond. Donna stumbled after him, her feet sinking into the wet mud and squishing as she pulled them out, minus one shoe. She tried to dive into the water after him, but she wasn't quick enough.

Lydia dos Santos lay face down in the water, bobbing along in the waves. Nothing animated her anymore, neither Willie's soul nor her own.

Donna sat down miserably in the mud as the living deputies quickly outstripped her feeble attempts to catch up and hauled the body back to shore. She glanced over, but they weren't doing CPR. Lydia was still alive. Technically. Her chest rose in the rhythm of ordinary breathing, but her eyes were rolled into the back of her head. No matter whether the medic shone a light into them, clapped her on the cheek, or anything else, she wouldn't respond.

Slowly Donna extricated herself from the mess of the riverbank and sloshed back to where Steven waited.

"Did you see that?" one of the spectral deputies was saying to another.

"What?"

"The effect? When she went into it?"

"Yeah," the second deputy agreed, "it shrank."

12

THE NEWS HAD SPREAD, THE secret was out, and all the dead could talk about was the end.

Spectral tourists from Ganesh City became a regular sight, and more were pouring in from ever more distant locales every day. Just last night Kyle had shared sage with a visitor whose accent he found impossible to place. It turned out he had come from the tiny village of Kraighten, Ireland.

Most came to see the phenomenon and then left. Seeing the afterlife missing from over the duck pond and Jackson Manor sounded fascinating, but in practice it was horrifying.

Kyle was wandering aimlessly through Sherman's Forest, trying to avoid thinking, and feeling nothing but cold despair. He had never suffered from clinical depression in life but could imagine this was how it felt: trauma and then endless hopelessness.

He'd been fortunate not to regress since the time Tommie had picked him up. In a perverse way, he almost would have preferred it. At least it would have been an escape from this torturous melancholia.

He was making his way down Old Sutter Road, the early afternoon sun bathing the world in deep shadows. The lights from the surrounding restaurants began blinking to life, reminding Kyle of the ghosts of fireflies cavorting around a weeping willow with their living kin.

Kyle didn't know how much longer he could go on like this, without her. He had tried sage (of course) but it only made the sorrow and unending darkness worse. He was beginning to get desperate, looking for anything that would alleviate his pain.

That was why he had decided to find someone to possess.

This neighborhood on Old Sutter was a byword for gentrification. The new owners had driven out all the undesirables—spirits and living alike—and fortified heavily against their return.

Eileen had told him all about how trendy the area had become for the Unenlightened. Restaurants, coffee bars, and even a small bookstore were all themed to appeal to the youth, both living and dead. Plenty of haunts prowled the area, eagerly soliciting their souls for people looking to have a little illegal thrill.

It was a dangerous gamble in any case. He may not have been possessing someone against their will, but unvetted possessions were still illegal. There'd be plenty of trouble if someone found out after the fact. Sheriff Hager came down particularly hard on rogue specters that tried to experience unsanctioned possessions. Still, he was desperate to experience something other than what he was feeling now.

Kyle lurked in the shadows of an alleyway, for all any passerby could tell just another dead bum sitting beside the dumpster, blank eyes focused on something only he could see. The living and dead passing by paid him no attention.

Kyle watched on with a predatory gaze, eyes like fading stars, malevolent against the shadows. A group of girls with lattes, a kid on his cell phone oblivious to the sidewalk, two ghosts walking hand in hand enjoying their eternal afterlife . . .

None of them suited his purposes.

Then Kyle saw her. She had pale white hair and wore threadbare gray clothing, but her aura sparked and fizzed like an exposed power line, all anger and fire, a hurricane of emotion.

Kyle smiled like a shark and floated up to introduce himself.

The girl saw him coming and looked around anxiously, unsure of what this raggedy spirit with the too-wide grin wanted from her.

Kyle introduced himself, "Hey, looking for a good ride?"

The girl stopped in her tracks, eyes jumping with excitement. "Maybe. Are you offering?" Her eyes were storm clouds of worry. "Are you safe?"

Kyle nodded emphatically, floating around her in a slow circle.

"Just looking for a little something real. It's been a hell of a day."

The girl's smile was weary, promising she sympathized. "I understand that. My grandparents tell me I need to fixate on the living instead of the dead. They told me possessions are only between people with deep bonds." She sighed, dramatic and petulant. "My friends are doing it all the time and it hasn't hurt them yet."

Normally, Kyle would have listened to her story, commiserated, seen if they had a connection. But this night, he wanted to feel. "Well, if it's your first time, I promise you that you could do worse."

The girl seemed to think on his words. It took everything for Kyle to sit there, patiently waiting for a temporary pass at life.

Finally, the girl smiled. "Fuck it, let's do it."

Kyle began preparing for the intricate process of shoving aside her soul so he could take residence. He could see the cracks in her aura, fissures leaking black smoke where the girl felt weakest. Body issues, insecurity, anxiety, and fear were the chief chinks in her spiritual armor.

The girl's eyes were closed, but he heard her whisper, "What's your name?"

Kyle didn't answer as he reached for the largest crack that hissed welcoming black mist like the memory of a sauna he had once frequented. Already he could feel something again: anticipation.

Then there was sharp pain and he stumbled backwards as the note of a single wind chime rent the air. He turned around, looking for the source, when the chime sounded again.

The Unenlightened girl hurried away, only glancing back once as Donna stepped out of a car across the street. Kyle glared at her and the chime in her hand.

"Is that really necessary?" He tried to put on his best shit-eating grin but Donna's eyes were hard granite.

She rang the chime again.

The sound was like a nail being driven down his ear canal. Kyle clutched his ears as his features faded, clothing turning to gray mist that drifted off and was lost in the late evening breeze. His vision started to fade to red but softened as the initial note dissipated.

"How could you be so stupid?" Donna spat the words like venom.

Kyle looked down at the street, unwilling to meet his twin's gaze.

"Do you want to end up locked up in a salt cell? You know, there are worse punishments, too."

"I know!" he snapped.

He didn't need to be reminded about enforced relapse. He'd been thinking about it the whole time out here. Donna just thought she was so damn clever.

"Let me guess: you don't care what happens to you."

He shrugged. She pounded on her own chest and he could tell she was riled up.

"What about me? Did you even think about me? How this would destroy my business? My reputation?" Her voice never wavered but Kyle could hear the pain behind it. "How alone I would feel without you?"

"You have Leroy now." Even to his ears the excuse sounded empty, an attempt to shift the blame off himself and what he had intended to do.

Donna nearly crushed the wind chime in her trembling hand. "If I could slap you, I would."

Kyle raised himself up. He didn't say anything. The initial shame was beginning to fade, replaced by the ennui which had settled over his existence.

"Ring it again, Red. At least pain is something."

Kyle watched Donna's eyes widen in shock as he stretched his arms out like a crucified scarecrow. A dead smile, containing no joy or happiness, was plastered on his face.

Donna shook her head slowly, her mouth hanging open in the way Kyle knew meant she was fed up with him. He had grown up encouraging it, died knowing it, and now saw it almost daily.

Kyle looked at her pleadingly. "I'll relapse if I don't feel something soon."

Donna pocketed the chime. "What happened to that girl you told me about? Eileen?"

Kyle's silence wouldn't have been enough for the average person to interpret, but his twin immediately recognized the kind of pain he was dealing with. She probably couldn't pick up on the specifics, but recognized this was no mere breakup. Strong emotions hit the dead harder than they did the living.

"What happened? Coma?"

He shrugged and shoved his hands into his pockets. "Sort of. Worse, really. She's like a brain damage patient or something. Like an infant, almost."

Donna tenderly put a hand on his shoulder. He was heartened to be firm enough to receive the loving gesture.

"I understand you're hurting. But this is not the solution. And trust me, you do not want Steven Hager hauling you in for any form of unlawful possession after what happened today."

Kyle cocked his head. The twin thing kind of worked both ways. He could tell she wasn't talking about anything ordinary, either. She didn't wait for Kyle to ask and detailed exactly what had transpired between Willie Chang and Lydia. Kyle felt his ennui slip away when Donna had described the comatose girl, the dissipation of her relationship, and the murder of her soul.

"Jesus, Donna. When they find Willie they're going to charge him with first-degree possession and who knows what else. He'll be regressed for a couple of centuries."

"I don't think they are going to find him," she said.

Kyle stared silently at the setting sun.

She said, "So I make the mistake of turning over this whole fucking town looking for my brother to make sure he's okay, to make sure he's safe, and what is he trying to do when I find him?"

Kyle winced as Donna accentuated every word with a poke to his translucent sternum.

"*The. Exact. Same. Fucking. Thing!*"

Silence reigned after that, the living and the dead both giving the warring siblings a wide berth as the sun dipped below the horizon, its light replaced by the neon signs of Old Sutter Road.

"She was . . ." Kyle struggled to find the word. ". . . special."

Donna's gaze softened. "They're all special until they're not. You've got all of eternity. She won't be the last."

Kyle's features hardened, becoming more real. "It's different this time."

Donna smiled. "Listen, if you want a body that bad, there are legal ways to do it. How about instead of shacking up with some back-alley reprobate with every psychic problem in the book, why don't I call up one of my shift workers for a small, two-hour possession and you and I can talk about it over dinner."

Kyle perked up and suddenly felt a small twinge of joy pierce the gray sorrow. "Thanks. How much will I owe you?"

Donna waved her hand but fixed Kyle with the best death glare she could muster. "You want to pay me back? Never try this again. Swear to me."

Kyle wasn't sure if he meant it or not but he promised to be a good little ghost.

"Good. Where do you want to eat?"

Kyle had wanted to try a new diner on 5th Eileen had spoken of in hushed tones, the breakfast-for-dinner options apparently sublime. It had been so damned long since Kyle had eaten breakfast or dinner that Eileen's descriptions practically left him salivating.

He watched as Donna called one of her contractors, a man named Royce, to meet them at the diner. She was promising him copious amounts of overtime pay.

She said, "Darrell will be pissed I gave this one to someone else, but that's what he gets for not answering his phone."

Kyle didn't know or care a bit about her internal office politics, but nodded eagerly in agreement with her assessment.

"So where is this joint?" Donna asked.

Kyle shrugged his shoulder back toward the alley. "Through there and a few blocks down."

Kyle wasn't focused enough to take Donna's arm but they walked as close together as they could, heading for the alley as Donna looked down at her stomach.

"Great," she said. "Of course greasy diner shit would be your choice. I was beginning to feel like a normal-sized human again too."

Kyle said, "I keep telling you, no one thinks you're overweight but—"

He stopped as they turned the corner to the alley. Staring hard down the path, his eyes focused and then widened as he suddenly became intensely solid and began tugging on Donna's arm. "Let's go a different way."

Donna's brow furrowed, her face a mask of irritation. "I don't have time for your stupid . . ."

Kyle sort of wanted to keep it from her, but also sort of wanted her to realize what he was seeing. He watched as Donna's eyes widened and she turned to look down the abandoned alleyway.

It was wedged between a pizzeria and a clothing store that were shuttered for the night. A green dumpster with flies hovering around it, hoping to eat the cheesy leftovers from the day's customers. A drainage pipe dripped water onto the pitted and chipped concrete, creating a glum pool of grimy water in the shadows.

The only light was a buzzing bug zapper that had definitely seen better days. Kyle doubted it could have handled a gnat, much less a fly. Everything about it seemed normal, more urban grime that wouldn't have looked out of place in any other American town, but little things about it would've sent chill bumps racing up his arms and turned his stomach if he'd still possessed either arms or stomach.

The shadows were longer, almost cloying. The flies buzzing around the garbage drowned out the drone from the bug zapper. The water seemed thick with muck. Then there was the absence. Something should have been occupying this narrow concrete path but wasn't.

Donna turned around and Kyle watched the realization hit her. "It's down there, isn't it?"

Kyle stared directly at it. It was smaller than the other two he had seen but equally as terrifying as it squatted at the other end of the alley. There was something wrong about it. Wrong and calling out to his despair, "Jump in and end it!"

Kyle blinked and broke his gaze. He looked at Donna and gestured back toward the well-lit Old Sutter Road. She didn't have to be asked a third time before they hurried away, the living and dead patrons of the neighborhood parting before them, then looking back at the alley to see what caused the commotion. Kyle shouted a warning as the spirit of a young man from the sixties, all hairspray and confidence, swaggered into the alleyway.

There was a shout of alarm, a moment of silence, then panic. The ghosts were shouting, disapparating, and relapsing as the reality of what lay at the end of the alley became apparent.

The rumors were true.

The secret was out.

The living and the dead looked at Kyle, murder, confusion, and blame in their eyes.

"Come on!" Donna shouted.

Kyle followed her to her SUV, trying not to let the red at the edge of his vision consume his world.

13

DONNA BROUGHT THE CAR TO a halt outside of town at a truck stop on I-60. For the entirety of the trip, silence had lain over the interior of the SUV like a shroud.

"I'm going home," Kyle said, leaning forward.

Donna put her hand on his chest as though it were solid and he were a child straining to escape his seatbelt. "The hell you are."

"The hell I'm not. You can't—"

"Where do you live?"

He scowled. "Ghosttown."

"Who do you live with?"

He didn't respond.

"Why don't you stay with me tonight and in the morning we'll get a feel for how bad this thing is?"

"I don't need you to babysit me."

Without missing a beat, she ratcheted the tempo of the conversation up to 11.

"Apparently you do! What the hell was that back there? No. You know what? We're not going to rehash it."

"It was . . . a moment of weakness."

"Oh, a moment of weakness. Well, I'm sure that should hold up fine in court. 'Counselor, why did your client rape that girl?' 'Oh, it was a moment of weakness, Your Honor.' 'Oh, well, case dismissed then. What's next on the docket?' 'Oh, three murderers and Kyle

Fitzpatrick for soliciting unlicensed possession?' 'Well, I'm sure they all had moments of weakness, so . . .'''

"Stop, stop."

Unable to face her, Kyle turned away to stare out the window. Suddenly the guilt chilled her blood like venom from a snakebite. Maybe he was a stupid, immature bastard, but this wasn't helping.

"Kyle, I—"

Someone started tapping on Donna's window and she nearly jumped out of her skin. She put her hand over her breast, but breathed a sigh of relief when she realized it was Royce. She rolled the window down. "You nearly gave me a heart attack!"

"You'd better have, like, two hundred bucks for me," her most dependable freelancer said in a near-monotone deadpan.

He stuck his hand in the window, itching at his palm.

"I'm not in the mood anymore," Kyle growled.

"Even better," Royce grumbled. "I'll take my money home and microwave the lobster and filet I took home in a doggy bag from my favorite restaurant, you know, in order to take this call, this so-called emergency, this I'll-pay-you-no-matter-what-Royce, once-in-a-lifetime, middle-of-the-night-on-a-Sunday-night, oh-by-the-way-meet-me-outside-of-town-at-some-filthy-truckstop-instead-of-on-Old-Sutter-Road-like-I-promised—"

"Okay, okay, fine," Kyle said, worn down by Royce's never-ending sentence. "Would you just pay the man, Donna?"

Donna slapped a fat wad of cash she could ill afford into Royce's hand. He riffled through it far too quickly to count it, but seemed satisfied and stuffed it into his pocket. Donna thought she'd be rid of him then, but he seemed conflicted for a moment, as though the gruff, "I-got-out-of-bed-for-this-shit" attitude was belied by an actual heart underneath. That always seemed to be Royce's M.O.

"You know, not for nothing, Donna's brother, but I feel like you could use the two hours incognito, if nothing else."

"Huh? What do you mean?"

"Your picture's all over the news."

Royce pointed through a window to the interior of the truck stop. Televisions tuned to all the different cable news networks were nevertheless all displaying the same thing: a picture of Kyle's mug from his mourning portrait. The noise was inaudible, but it didn't need to be. They were all discussing Kyle's status as the apparent discoverer of the duck pond/Jackson Manor phenomenon. The Fitzpatrick twins exchanged a chagrined look.

"Don't tell me you enjoy having these non-breathing mouth breathers all staring at you," Royce continued, glancing at the back of his fingernails.

The inhabitants of the truck stop (mostly, but not exclusively, of the ethereal extraction) were by-and-large pointing at Kyle and whispering pointedly to each other. Donna attempted to deny it and reassure Kyle they were both being paranoid, but the words withered on her tongue. She was shamed into silence by the transparency of her lie.

Royce leaned inside the window, practically ignoring Donna in the driver's seat.

"Like I said, I'd love nothing better than to go home right now. But I'm an honest son of a bitch, if still a son of a bitch. Since you already paid, why not at least wear me as a disguise for two hours and have a malt? You look like you could use one."

"What I could use is a slug of tequila."

"Sorry, kid, tequila's sunrise ain't happening in my body."

"No booze," Donna clarified.

"Milkshakes are all right. Well, not all right. I have to use the elliptical for two hours every morning to keep the pounds off from this job, but you get the idea."

"Why don't you two go around back," Donna said, "and I'll get us a table?"

Grumbling, Kyle slipped through the car door and floated alongside Royce to a more secluded spot behind the truck stop. To get through her days, she couldn't let herself fall into the trap of thinking of her job as a dirty business. But at times like this she couldn't overlook the underlying seediness of it. In a way, was what she did so different from what she had chewed out Kyle for trying to do?

She walked into the truck stop and all eyes locked on her. The place consisted of two large lavatories, a convenience store adjacent to the fuel pumps outside, a fast food joint, and an all-night coffee shop. She grabbed a table at the coffee shop. It seemed like a chain, but not one she recognized.

There was no server, so she figured she'd wait for Kyle before she went up to the counter. There was no telling what he would want. On the rare occasions he clambered into a body, he was worse than a pregnant woman.

Sometimes he was all over the map. For all she knew, he might go hog wild on a case of beef jerky from the convenience store. He might as likely have a sudden hankering for diet soda, which, as far as she could recall, he had never drank in life.

Ghosts and hosts had a weird, almost alchemical bonding during possession, and she had long since given up guessing what the blending of a particular spirit and a particular physical body would turn out to be like, even if she knew both very well, as she did in this case.

"That guy's with you, isn't he? That Fitzsimmons guy?"

She looked up. The teenage barista was staring at her, elbows on the counter, head in her hands, loudly cracking a piece of gum.

"I don't know what you mean," Donna said, searching desperately for something at her table to concentrate on.

The counter girl rolled her eyes. "All right, lady. I hope he gets a big old six-figure book deal."

A snort drew both their pairs of eyes to a custodian who was wringing out his mop into a mobile bucket.

"Something to say, Whitey?" the counter girl asked.

The custodian didn't raise his eyes from his appointed mopping, but he spoke clearly enough for them to both hear.

"Yeah, well, don't kill Whitey for saying this, but they ought to relapse that boy for the rest of time. Ghosts disappearing. It's a crime, I tell you."

"How can it be a crime if it's never happened before?"

The door opened and Kyle entered in his Royce-skin suit, looking a bit flustered and fiddling with Royce's shirtsleeves. Donna stood up and took Kyle's arm to steady him, leaving behind the two bickering late-night employees of the truck stop.

"You want coffee?" he asked, Kyle's telltale cadences sounding strange coming out of Royce's mouth.

"Nah, I suddenly lost my taste for that joint," she said.

She shelled out some cash for a bag of Twizzlers and a half gallon of unsweetened tea at the convenience store. She'd never seen Kyle eat licorice in his life, and she distinctly remembered him putting sugar in all of his iced tea. Yet another weird ghost/host combination, it seemed. They stepped outside, where there were a few open-air tables. After wolfing down half of his bag of plasticky sugar, Kyle stopped and leaned back.

"This is bad, isn't it?" Kyle said.

"Yeah, it's shit. It's just corn syrup."

He stared at her, something unmistakably Kyle-like in the pits of Royce's eyes.

"That's not what I meant," he replied testily.

"Oh. Yeah. It's pretty bad," she agreed.

"What am I supposed to do? Go on the lam? Disapparate to Phoenix? Or to New Delhi like your friend? Get half a world away from this?" An unexpected shiver roiled Royce's body at the mention of disapparation. She knew how much Kyle hated doing it, especially lately.

"Maybe you should talk to Sheriff Hager. He could probably put you in protective custody or something."

"Sit in a circle of salt down at the BFPD? I'd feel like a circus animal on display."

"Well, it doesn't have to be that, necessarily. I mean, maybe he'll put some officers outside your apartment for protection."

Kyle shook Royce's head. "Don't be dumb. You make it sound like Steven's going to bend over backwards to get me help. But he's a ghost and he answers to the ghost community. And from what I can tell the rest of the ghosts want me relapsed and lying in that wreck on the side of the road and . . ."

Kyle shivered, though it was a dark, warm night. Donna reached out and tentatively put her hands on his. It was strange to be touching Royce and feeling her brother—sort of.

"Hager is not going to railroad you. This is a public health issue, like a gas leak or a poltergeist infestation. They can't nail you to the wall for discovering it. Hell, I'm the one who really discovered it."

"Lucinda Jackson's the one who *really* discovered it, I'll wager," Kyle muttered darkly.

"Regardless, whatever's going on, you didn't do it. You're not responsible. I'll get Leroy and the whole damn Exorcists Union to testify to that if I have to."

"Yeah, sure," Kyle agreed bitterly. "It's not like the court of public opinion ever determined someone guilty without due process, right?"

Tentatively, Donna reached up and put her hand on Royce's cheek. It was Kyle that was looking at her, though, and Kyle who felt her touch.

"It's not going to go that far. They'll stop dragging your name through the mud in a few days. Leroy's working to figure out what's going on. Once he does, we'll fix it. It'll all turn out to be a tempest in a teapot. You'll see."

"You have an awful lot of faith in Leroy, considering he's someone you just met."

Donna ran her teeth against each other.

"I'm in love. I know it sounds stupid and premature and—"

Kyle held up his hands, and his signature roguish smile played across Royce's face almost flawlessly. "Say no more. When it comes to stupid and impetuous, who do you think you're talking to?"

"The master," she admitted.

"That's right: the master."

The lights from a tractor trailer shone in their eyes before it pulled past into the diesel fueling area.

"Hell of a romantic spot you've picked for us," he said.

"Want to go back to town? Back to . . ."

She trailed off. She'd almost been about to bring up 4th Avenue and the phenomenon's unprecedented and seemingly unchecked expansion. Kyle rose, not acknowledging the faux pas. He tossed their empties into a trash can and belched loudly, a distinctly un-Royce-like gesture. He held up his finger for a second, before regaining his composure.

"We could do your house," he said. "It's on the other side of town. I mean . . . if that's all right with you."

"Yes, of course. You'd better leave Royce's body here, though."

"Is he going to be disoriented? Do we have to stay? Because I'd rather not."

She shook her head. "Royce is very experienced. He won't even be dizzy, I bet."

"Then let's beat feet."

The same trucker who had nearly blinded them blasted his air horn as he pulled out of the filling station. A few other trucks responded in kind. The result was a miniature cacophony of horn blasts.

"You know, there's something I've always wondered about," Kyle said, unexpectedly.

Her keys already in her hands, Donna stopped. "What's that?"

"Well, you remember Paranormal Studies class in high school? The spirit world is on a different vibration wavelength from the physical. Wind chimes make a noise that's closer to that vibration, salt's crystalline composition seems to exist in both worlds, and the disintegration of sage distorts the vibrations." He ticked off the three objects on Royce's fingers. "Those are the three basic physical components that can affect the spirit world: salt, burning sage, and the sound of chimes."

"Yeah, but you didn't remember that from PS 101 class," Donna said. "That's what the guy on the Ghost-Away commercials always says."

Kyle laughed, a weird blend of Royce's voice and his own. "Yeah, you're right. What's his name? Billy . . . something."

"Buster. Buster Beats."

"That's it. 'Ghost-Away. The Fourth Physical Component,'" he said, mimicking the famous pitchman's signature style, before dropping back into his own voice. "Guess I discovered a fifth."

14

ROYCE'S MUSCLES SPASMED AND A light sheen of ecto-plasmic mist drifted from the man's shoulders, eyes, and mouth as Kyle left the man's body. Maybe he should've bought him a cigarette for the one-night ride.

Kyle left Royce in the small picnic area behind the store, where the gum-encrusted cement gave way to rolling green grass leading into the low-lying hills and forests that met the mountains in the distance. On the rare occasions he dabbled in possession, he always found the most awkward part to be leaving an unconscious man to the tender mercies of their fellow man. Donna always insisted it was fine and part of the job, and Kyle supposed, when he thought about it, most people he knew, living or dead, gave the recently dispossessed a wide berth. It was one of those things people did, like not stepping on a ladybug.

The stars twinkling in the darkness were gorgeous. They weren't even really stars, at least not to Kyle. They were holes into the spirit world, showing the living that sometimes there were brief spots of light in the dim gloom of death. Kyle didn't think he'd been particularly poetic before he died but now everything seemed amplified, as though the host body had sharpened all the feelings and desires in his spirit to a scalpel. He loved this feeling and didn't want it to leave.

"You give good life, buddy boy," Kyle whispered to the unconscious Royce.

He patted the top of his head and left his body. Kyle had only taken possession a few times in his afterlife, always of the opinion that holding onto something you couldn't have led spirits to addiction and dangerous levels of desperation and anger.

He was determined not to be one of those.

Floating up into the night air, he became coherent again and let the wind take him for a spell. He drifted back down into the parking lot where Donna was waiting anxiously behind the wheel of the car, fingers fidgeting as she shot wary glares at anyone who seemed to recognize her. Kyle hurried and passed through the roof of the car into his seat, hoping some passing spirit from a dead trucker or lot lizard didn't spot them.

"Want me to take the long way home?" she asked with a grin.

He didn't answer.

The irony of a ghost who was scared to disapparate and had to be driven around wasn't lost on him, but his time on the road back into town gave him some desperately needed time to think. Donna was quiet, probably thinking about her new beau with the exorcist's butt crack. Semi-young and in love, 'til death do they possibly part.

Kyle hadn't wanted to be a celebrity. He was more of a below-the-radar delinquent. It was easier to carouse around town if your face wasn't plastered on every TV screen.

He wasn't sure how anything could go back to normal after this.

Donna's housing complex was an upscale place only well-off breathers could afford. Ghosttown, where Kyle lived, was a mixed bag, packed to the gills with the dead from all walks of history and all sorts of financial levels. But this place catered exclusively to individuals of the living persuasion.

Donna cut off the ignition and Kyle floated through the door, looking around at the bright lights and hard angles of the architecture. Well-manicured lawns that saw daily doses of sprinkler water, landscape meticulously maintained, stairwells with ironwork full of artistic flourishes and crafted metal all seemed to conspire to make this a far cry from the dive room he occasionally haunted.

Donna saw his face and smiled. "You look like you've never been here before."

He shook his head, trying to clear out the cobwebs. "Some residual Royce, I guess. He must be really into landscaping or something. I never realized how nice your joint was before."

She shrugged. "It isn't much, but it's home."

"Hate to see what you think is excessive."

Their walk-and-banter was cut short when Kyle caught sight of the Channel 12 news van parked directly in front of Donna's townhouse. He didn't have enough time to tell Donna to head back to the car before the reporters spotted him.

"There he is!" the cameraman shouted, pointing a fat finger at the Fitzpatrick siblings.

The woman who was obviously his boss hurried over, shoving a microphone into their faces and hastily shouting out her required spiel hoping for a quote. "Sparrow Thames, Channel 12. Can you tell us anything about the Jackson phenomenon and how you discovered it?"

Kyle put on a carefree smile and prepared to shout his trademark, "Fuck off," hoping only a little bit the cameras were live, but Donna quickly moved to smooth things over and prevent his name from getting dragged any further through the mud.

"Hi, Sparrow, Donna Fitzpatrick. My brother has been through a harrowing ordeal and is on the verge of relapse. I'm afraid your line of questioning is going to push him over the edge . . ."

Donna trailed off with a shrug. She shot him a pointed look and Kyle did his best to wipe the smug grin off his face and play the part of traumatized specter. It was a routine he was all too familiar with, having conned their grandparents countless times during childhood, before Donna had become an old stick in the mud.

Kyle said, "Donna? Why is the sky red? There was a truck . . . Why are you here, sis?"

The reporter with the tangled hair bun and the cameraman verging on his first double bypass backed off swiftly. Causing a ghost to relapse intentionally was a misdemeanor that could take a hefty chunk out of either of their paychecks. With three witnesses, no judge in the country would rule against him.

Donna guided him up the stairs of her porch, the catchphrases and bywords the instructors taught the living to keep ghosts grounded if they were in danger of relapsing rattling out of her lips. Most breathers spouted those words like they were magic, but Kyle knew that was a load of horseshit. The intensity of the emotional connection, the deepness of their personal bond, these things kept spirits grounded much more effectively than meaningless words. In that sense, Donna was a better choice than most to keep him from relapsing.

Still, Kyle played along until they were out of sight of the news van and he focused himself again to shake off the red at the edge of his vision. Maybe he'd taken the pretend freak-out too far. "Fucking vultures," he said.

Donna gave him a disapproving look that he shrugged off. Here it came. Breathers always defended their own kind.

"Don't be too hard on them. They're trying to earn a living. You said it yourself: you discovered the fifth physical component. You can't blame people for being interested."

He didn't bother to mention a sprinkle of salt or a puff of sage was hardly as permanent as the holes that seemed to be gobbling up spirits.

Donna opened the door and walked in, dropping her keys and bag on the small wooden table next to the door. Kyle glided in afterward, the dim illumination provided by the landing light, doing little to alleviate the gloom.

"Hold on a second," Donna muttered before the lights in the townhouse blazed on with tungsten brilliance.

The townhouse was virtually new and the architect's choices had leaned toward new age rather than a more classic style. A kitchen, all black marble and stained oak, was off to the left past the entryway. Modest furniture on smooth wooden floors adorned the living room that led out onto the back porch with a full view of the distant mountains.

Not for the first time he was struck by the above-modest lifestyle she led. Their family had never been super-wealthy, but they had always been comfortable. Donna, though, had managed to spin her opportunities into a life that would have made most people jealous, despite her misgivings about her profession.

Kyle sighed, the regret of his short life filling him and transforming into envy. He hadn't done much with his life or afterlife and now . . .

Now people thought he knew something they didn't about this thing that devoured spirits.

"I'm not one to condone your bad habits but you can burn some sage out on the back porch if you'd like."

Kyle appreciated Donna's concern but he was in no mood to lose himself with smudging. Oddly, he had never felt more awake, more focused, than now. This maudlin afterglow was probably one of the many reasons he rarely indulged in bodily possession.

His thoughts and misgivings were interrupted by a polite knock at the door.

Donna urged him to stay out of sight as she answered the door. Kyle phased through the nearest wall, halfway into the guest room, and listened intently for whomever had found them now, eager for a story.

"Kyle!" Donna's voice was calm, maybe even a little warm, and he emerged from the wall.

Donna was standing next to a woman who, while matronly, hadn't lost her looks to the ravages of age yet. Kyle could see her aura, a calm and confident red that flickered like dancing flame against the backdrop of gray. She was concerned, not curious. The woman took a step forward, hand palm up, toward Kyle, who involuntarily took a step back.

"Fitz's brother! I've heard a lot about you."

"Yeah, lady, I'm apparently all over the news." The woman kept advancing. "Could you not do that please?"

Something about the woman was off-putting. He looked to Donna for help and glowered as he saw her trying not to laugh her head off.

"Kyle, this is my neighbor, Angela Abbott. She's a medium."

Ugh. The last thing he needed right now was a therapy session. Breathers always thought they knew more about what it was like to be dead than the actual dead. But unless he wanted to float through the wall and back to where the news van was parked, there wasn't anywhere to go. He gritted his teeth as Angela approached with that upraised hand. She looked commandingly at Kyle, who reached out and placed his hand in her own.

Her dark black hair was halfway to gray and her dark brown skin was crisscrossed with telltale wrinkles that accentuated rather than detracted from her beauty.

"Eileen," she said.

Kyle stiffened at the name as the woman searched through his spirit.

"You don't have to hide your pain. People that care will be there for you."

What the hell would you know? Kyle thought as he took his hand away from the woman.

She smiled gently. "I know you blame yourself. I know this thing scares you. It'll be all right in the end, though."

Kyle glared as the medium woman turned and walked into Donna's kitchen.

"Sorry," Angela said. "Didn't mean to throw you into the deep end of the couch. How about I get something on the stove and you two tell me all about this thing?"

Donna glanced at Kyle before joining her friend in the kitchen. Kyle didn't feel like contributing. Instead he settled on the couch and turned on the TV, which, of course, was playing a news story about the phenomenon.

Kyle glowered at the screen. The dead lined the streets, eager to get a look at the alleyway containing the effect. Sheriff Hager and his deputies were firmly keeping the lookie-loos back. All it would take was one to commit the ghostly equivalent of suicide by rushing toward the alleyway and there'd be a riot.

He had known Steven Hager a long time. His mother had gone to school with him or something, but Kyle had developed his own quasi-adversarial relationship with the man over the course of being busted a few times for general poltergeist mischief. Whether out of respect for his mother or just being his way, Steven had always let Kyle off with one of his trademark stern warnings.

Kyle couldn't remember a time when he had seen the sheriff look this stressed. His form was barely there, the details fuzzy and transparent. Kyle turned up the volume.

". . . we can't confirm anything yet but it does appear the phenomenon reported in this alley has disappeared."

15

DONNA STARED AT THE CONTENTS of her refrigerator, which consisted of a variety of takeout containers and an extra-large box of baking soda. She fingered her chin in a staccato tapping motion.

"I want you," she whispered, laying her hand on a full-sized cardboard box which contained precisely two slices of Panucci's meat lover's with extra vermicelli. "But I probably shouldn't have you."

Instead of the mouthwatering pizza, she pulled out a box of mostly peapods and tiny corncobs in brown sauce, then another of white rice. She grabbed the butter dish, glanced back at her butt, wiggling it a little in her bathrobe, then put the butter back and grabbed the olive oil dispenser instead.

"For Leroy," she intoned reverently.

Leroy had, naturally, never said a word about her weight. Basically she decided to get into shape for him. In fact, she wanted to get into shape for herself, and Leroy was a convenient excuse. Eating the less unhealthy leftovers for breakfast was hardly what anyone would call a strict new diet, but it was a start.

She grabbed a pan from the dish rack, one that had been sitting there for days but was at least clean, and threw it on the stove. She dumped her perfect rhombus of rice into the pan and poured some olive oil over it.

Kyle passed through the wall of the guest bedroom. "Thank crap you're up. I'm going stir-crazy in here."

He picked up an apple from her wax fruit display and began tossing it from hand to hand.

"Good morning, brohim," she said, barely covering a yawn with her hand.

"Yeah yeah yeah. Don't you have anything to *do* here?"

She shrugged. "There's a TV in—"

"No! No TV! Never again. In fact, I'm going to break this damn TV."

He floated over to her dusty, rarely used 85-inch flatscreen and started to half-assedly attempt to pull it off the wall. Luckily, it was heavy and well-installed, and Kyle was too finicky and agitated to manipulate much of anything.

"Stop it," she said. "If you don't want to see yourself on TV, then don't turn it on. Don't break it."

He pantomimed ripping his hair out. "What am I supposed to *do* here?"

"Can you really not stand to be creeping around the streets of Sherman's Forest for even a few hours?"

"Can you not? Can we not right now? I'm feeling cooped up in here. I'm going nuts."

"All right, look. I wouldn't normally support your debauchery, but I think your old lava lamp is in the game closet somewhere."

Kyle perked up. "Smoke a little sage, power up the lava lamp . . . them's the makings of a good morning."

"There, I thought so. Take your mind off of the, uh . . . business."

A series of sizzling noises began sounding from behind her.

Kyle said, "Your, uh . . . popcorn's popping."

"Shit," she groaned, rushing over to the stove to pull the rice off. The bottom of the rhombus was completely black and the rest of it was starting to tumble into a pile. She grabbed a spatula and began scraping the scorched mass off the pan. She dumped the brown sauce in, deciding, fuck it, it could become a breakfast soup instead of a discrete dish on a bed of rice.

When she finally sat down at the breakfast bar to eat her marginally healthy, gruel-like mash, Kyle floated past with the lava lamp nestled on top of a copy of Trivial Pursuit. He put those down on the coffee table before grabbing the bowl she had set out on the back porch the night before for him to use as an ashtray.

"Want to play?" he asked in his best teasing voice.

She sighed. "No. I've got to go to work today."

Kyle made a sour face. "It's Sunday! Your office is closed. Who goes in when the storefront is closed? Spender's idea, probably."

She narrowed her eyes, irritated because he was right about Spender fighting her about having a day off a week and only winning because he was the senior partner.

"I took off all of last week. You insisted. This week I had to shut down for another day while two of my clients committed some kind of weird, nihilistic murder-suicide. None of this is going to be good for business. My agency is—"

"Hanging by a thread? Were . . . were you going to say, 'My agency is hanging by a thread?' Was 'hanging by a thread' going to be the next four words out of your mouth?"

All Donna wanted to do was pull her spoon back like a catapult and launch a volley of brown gunk in his direction, but it would pass harmlessly through her jackass of a brother and end up spattering on her floor. Which she would have to clean later.

"I have to get caught up," she asserted flatly.

"All right," he said, lounging back on her couch, "but don't blame me if I happen to peruse all of the Trivial Pursuit cards and then school your ass later."

Leave it to Kyle to spend a perfectly good day burning sage, watching glowing bubbles, and trying to cheat at a children's game. In fact, he was lighting up a bundle as she watched.

"No no no!" she shouted, jumping out from behind the bar and moving faster than she had since high school track. "Outside! Outside!"

"What do you care? Didn't old Mrs. Palladino take off after your boyfriend fixed the ley line?"

Donna planted her fists on her hips. "I don't want my house to smell like Woodstock."

Kyle rose grudgingly from the couch and looked out toward the porch. He stood there for almost thirty seconds. "Eh . . . on second thought . . . maybe not."

Donna's left eyebrow attempted to crawl up her forehead and fly off her face. As much as she disliked Kyle's addiction, it did make his behavior . . . predictable, and she had never seen him turn down a smudging before.

"What's with you?" she said.

"Eh . . . nothing. I need to cut back. You know."

Then it dawned on her. He didn't want to go outside. "You're still worried about the news trucks, aren't you?"

"Uh . . . yeah. The news trucks."

Kyle was being shiftier than usual. Donna grabbed the remote and knew something was up even before Kyle came flying at her. Of course, he passed right through. He was too agitated to even knock the remote out of her hand.

". . . with my own two eyes."

Roderick Ellington was on the news, his eyes looking wetter and beadier than usual. The chyron described him as a local poet.

"Oh, this fucking guy," Kyle moaned.

"When my paramour disappeared into that . . . inexplicable anomaly, it shrank. Shrank, yes! It was in the alleyway, and then it receded. Clearly it feeds upon spiritual beings. If it's my opinion you're seeking, I believe that roustabout Kyle Fitzpatrick should be found and fed to it."

Donna's jaw dropped. She turned to look at Kyle, who was sulking in the corner. Another ghost came on screen, repeating a sentiment similar to Roderick's. A knock at the door startled them both.

"I thought you said the reporters couldn't come in here uninvited," Kyle said.

"It's trespassing if they do," she said.

Left unsaid was the more obvious issue. Journalists might have to respect the law, but an angry mob didn't. Even for a ghost he looked a little green in the gills.

"Don't you relapse," she warned, "but be ready to disapparate to . . . is there someone you can trust?"

He hissed between his teeth, obviously not even interested in disapparating for an emergency. "Tommie?"

"You can't go to Ghosttown."

The knocking sounded again. Donna walked and peered through the eyehole. She breathed a sigh of relief when she saw who it was.

"Leroy," she mouthed to Kyle, who looked like he was ready to disappear, health be damned.

He relaxed. Donna quickly opened the door and then practically yanked Leroy inside. As she slammed it back shut, flashes went off and dozens of questions were shouted.

"I love it when you touch me like that," Leroy said with a grin that made her want to climb on top of him.

"You remember my brother, Kyle," she said, before the flirting got out of control.

"The man of the hour," Leroy said, walking up to Kyle and sticking out his hand.

"Thanks," Kyle said, grimacing and taking it, though, by the looks of it, he was still mostly insubstantial.

"I've never met a celebrity before!"

"All right, all right, crystal monkey."

Leroy turned to look at Donna. "He's sensitive," she mouthed. Leroy shrugged.

"Well, ah, what are your plans for today, Donna?" Leroy asked.

"The office is closed today but I was going to go in and get caught up on some paperwork."

"Good. Cancel them."

Leroy reached into his pocket and pulled out a crumpled, quartered sheet of 8.5 x 11 paper. It was a printout of what looked like a spa coupon.

"Extrasensory deprivation?" she asked, reading the coupon.

"Research," he said, tapping the printout to his forehead. "I asked around with some of my peers. They're all atwitter about the phenomenon, especially since the news broke wide. Nobody's ever come across anything like this before, but a few friends I trust said it reminded them of one of these salt therapy rooms. It's this room, lined from wall to wall with pink Himalayan salt. Totally relaxing, therapeutic, and it's like a ghost no-go zone. I figure we can go, see what it's like, maybe ask the staff a few questions. Plus it makes for a relaxing date."

"There's the real reason," Kyle scoffed.

Donna cast daggers at him before turning back to her . . . was boyfriend the right word? Was it too soon? Whatever. His offer was tempting, but she absolutely had to get to the office.

"Leroy, that's sweet, but I have to do some work."

"Her agency is hanging by a thread," Kyle said.

"Kyle!"

Leroy smiled beatifically. "It's an hour. Maybe another hour to drive there and get the tour. Surely you can break away from work for two hours? To see your boyfriend? Who's been working all kinds of hours off the clock to help you?"

He looked like a puppy dog standing there. She looked back at

Kyle. "Well . . . but my brother . . ."

"What," Kyle said, "like you weren't going to leave me alone here all day anyway? Go. Enjoy. Or work. Whatever."

"Well, I just got out of the shower, but let me pull something on. And I guess I'd better finish my breakfast."

"Or we could grab something on the way?"

She leaned in and kissed him. "Bless you, Leroy Tate. Kyle, you'll really be okay alone?"

"Yeah, sure," he said, trying to sound confident, though she could always read between the lines with him.

She hurried back to her bedroom and pulled a dress on as quickly as possible. She supposed for a spa day she could get away with no makeup. A moment later she rejoined Leroy, who put his arm out for her to take, like they were a couple in Victorian London or somewhere. They stepped outside and the flashes and shouted questions began immediately.

"Maybe we'll be famous ourselves before this is over," Leroy said. "Donna Fitzpatrick and companion."

She poked him in the ribs. "More like world-famous exorcist Leroy Tate and local woman."

Leroy started to lead her down the steps, but she stopped short. She hadn't noticed it in the brief moment she had opened the door to let Leroy in, but on the outer perimeter of the news vans, a veritable army of spirits was lurking. Roderick Ellington was there, looking dour, and his dozens of compatriots didn't look any happier. Kyle's lynch mob. They seemed to be hanging back on account of the media, so for now Kyle was probably safe.

"Hold on a minute, would you?" she said.

She stepped back inside. Kyle was already lighting a bit of sage, and was quickly and shoddily trying to hide his transgression as Donna re-entered. She didn't really care, not with so much else going on.

"Roderick's out there."

"Oh, that prick!"

"He's got friends with him."

"Ah, fuck." Kyle tossed an imaginary rock, as though skipping it across a pond.

"For once in your life, be cautious. At the first sign of trouble, disapparate. Go to Japan if you have to. Nowhere's too far to be safe."

"I'm not looking forward to it, but you don't have to tell me twice."

She went to the door. For some reason, she turned back one last time. "I love you, Kyle."

"I love you, too, Red."

16

THE FAMILIAR BUZZ OF SAGE filled his essence as he floated, concentrating on the bubbling green lumps of the lava lamp. The blobs traveled up and down, down and up, filling him up with a sense of contentment absent the past few days.

Green globs of goo floated through the ether.

Lazy things like him drifted through their afterlives.

Roustabout, Ellington had called him. Kyle liked that. Fitzpatrick the Roustabout. It sounded dashing, a good counterpoint to the accusations the pompous windbag had been throwing his way.

His thoughts drifted toward Donna and her new boy toy. Despite the insults and jabs he threw her way, it had surprised him when she professed her sisterly love.

Maybe he should have rethought smudging inside her townhouse after all.

Guilt killed his buzz faster than anything else and he reluctantly put out the burning sage.

He didn't know what he would do for the rest of the day. He couldn't go home, the media vultures had seen to that. He was trapped like a rat in Donna's townhouse.

Something a roustabout would never stand for.

Straightening his jacket he decided it was time for Roderick Ellington to undergo a good afterlife ass kicking.

Kyle knew he was going to get a good tongue lashing from

Donna for doing what he was planning, but he also knew it would bring those ghosts with their itchy trigger fingers running.

He began to concentrate, focusing his rage against the poet and every other damn idiot spirit who'd taken his side until the lights were flickering in irregular patterns. A faint moan echoed through the townhouse, and outside the spirits hanging around the outskirts of the housing complex took up a collective cry of alarm.

The first few began appearing in the townhouse a few seconds later.

Kyle smiled a devilish grin at the gasbag spirit of Ellington as he appeared, screeching, "*Find him now!*"

"Don't have to look far, mate." The dead had gathered. Kyle had set the stage. Time to vent some anger. "I believe it's trespassing to apparate into someone's home uninvited."

Roderick Ellington sputtered about the impropriety of thus and such for almost a full split-second before Kyle slung a haymaker. Ellington went flying back, wailing in agony.

Kyle scrambled after him as the other specters hollered in shock. The dandy was still trying to pick himself off the floor when Kyle kicked him in the side of the head and then proceeded to attack his stomach.

It couldn't have been more than a few seconds before the crowd of disaffected spirits were pulling Kyle off the beleaguered and bloody fop, his form leaking ectoplasm as Ellington's remaining flunkies lifted him off the floor.

His face rapidly healed, the pretty features as intact as they were when he had died.

The memory of that beating was going to sting for a while, though.

"I'll have you for that, Fitzpatrick!"

The dandy's veneer of civility and class disappeared as he went poltergeist. Kyle tried not to wince as Donna's shelving and decorations flew from their places and shattered against the floor.

Kyle steadied himself for whatever beating was coming his way. For some reason, the images of Eileen and Ramses were foremost in his mind. Possession hadn't helped him forget his troubles, smudging didn't ease his pain, but he knew for damn sure that an ass kicking would make him feel something different.

Even that weak solace was denied him as Steven Hager passed through the front door and then opened it for his living deputies to follow. Flashbulbs went off as the reporters followed like sharks in their wake . . .

This wasn't the first time Kyle had seen the inside of a cell. When he was alive he had found himself in a bar in Boston on St. Patrick's Day. His leprechaun impression hadn't gone over very well with the pub patrons. He found himself in the center of a brawl that left him with a cracked rib, a missing tooth in the back of his mouth, and a shiner worthy of being framed.

That was a few months before his death. Donna's scowl when she bailed him out was vicious, but he expected she would have more than a dirty look for him this time. He crossed a line.

"Fitzpatrick, do you think you could go even one day without making my job harder?"

He looked up at Sheriff Hager as he floated past the line of salt that served as bars for the ghost cells. The floors, ceiling, and walls in this part of the prison were insulated with salt as well. Kyle couldn't disapparate or run. He was stuck like a fly in a web.

"Oh, well, you know us proper roustabouts have an urge to cause mayhem. It's a sickness, really."

Kyle and Steven Hager had known each other for years, occasionally antagonistically, but as often as not socially. The ghost community accounted for the sheriff's appointment and dictated most of his policies. Kyle respected him, to be sure, but wasn't going to back down on account of the other ghost's badge. He'd apologize to Donna for her smashed dishes, but his reputation as a ne'er-do-well was at stake, and that aggression would not stand.

The police station was a fortified building that once was a National Guard armory before the military chose to stop funding the building, withdrawing and selling it to Sherman's Forest. It only seemed natural it was the best place to hold all manner of living and dead criminals. The front offices were fortified with bulletproof glass and salt lines around the perimeter, creating a maze only authorized personnel, whether living or dead, could navigate.

Roderick Ellington glowered at the Sheriff and his erstwhile opponent from his own salt cell across the way. "My barrister will have your badge for this, Constable. This is completely unjustified. I was attacked unjustly by that . . . less than a shade."

Steven deadpanned, "Be that as it may, Mr. Ellington, I've got you on trespassing and inciting a mob. You can sit quietly serving your time or I can hang up a remedial wind chime. I think I'd enjoy seeing both of your faces for that."

The poet looked aghast, his mouth upended in an offended sneer. Kyle tried to suppress a grin. The Sheriff was a lot of things, but he was above all else fair and never cruel. There weren't going to be any wind chimes ringing above the old fop's head, but he didn't know that.

"I'll remember that threat, sirrah!"

Steven waved a dismissive hand and crossed the hall to address Kyle in something more akin to privacy. "I know your sister won't sue me if I chime you, so better stow that laughter."

Kyle smirked. "Sorry, force of habit."

Steven pulled out a cigarette case, staring forlornly at the sticks of nicotine and carcinogens he would never be able to use again. This was the point in the evening where his deputies had gone home and he was going to start getting maudlin. Kyle had spent more than his fair share of nights in a salt cell idling away the hours with the sheriff.

"Died with half a pack on me. See the scuff marks from where I kept pulling them out of my pocket too fast? Yeah, I used to love having a puff and now I can only look at them. Life's a cruel joke, you know."

"And death's the punchline," Kyle said, supplying the back half of the old canard.

The cigarette pack disappeared back into Steven's pocket as he stared Kyle down with a pitying look. "Listen, I know what happened with your girlfriend and the dog. At least, what folks are saying happened. The ghost community won't take this sort of behavior very well. And you're not exactly a member in good standing as it is."

Kyle smirked. "We go way back. I was like this before I died. If old habits die hard, mine were dead, buried, and splattered across I-60."

The sheriff ran a hand through his hair. "Never say I didn't at least try to save you from yourself. Anyway, let's get you bailed out of here. Any idea where your sister is? She's not answering her phone and I sent a deputy by her business and she's not there either."

"That's because it's hanging on by a thread," Kyle chimed before looking out the window at the noonday sun. "She's with her new beau at the extrasensory deprivation place."

"New beau? Are you telling me Donna is cheating on her work-aholism?"

"Yeah, Leroy something or other. You'll know him by his exorcist's butt crack. But there's no hurry to go find them. At least I'm familiar with a salt cell. Better this than an impassable circle of reporters."

The sheriff laughed. "You've got more of a fool in you than I thought if you think the reporters aren't laying siege to this place right now."

Realizing he wasn't even safe from scrutiny in jail felt like a slap in the face to Kyle, a ghost of a feeling he hadn't experienced for real in a long time. He wondered how Eileen was doing, wondered if she was going to come out of the coma. Then he thought about the holes in the world.

He shivered, an utter, existential dread penetrating all of his senses.

17

NORMALLY, A VERITABLE ARMY OF ghostly protestors marched (or, rather, floated) outside the extrasensory deprivation clinic. Today, though, only a few bothered to show up, and they seemed noticeably bedraggled. Of the gaggle of Unenlightened who usually picketed the place alongside their spectral betters, only one preternaturally thin boy whose makeup seemed thrown on with no effort had shown up.

"Huh. Place is dead today," Donna said.

"Or not dead, to be more accurate," Leroy replied.

With her arm tucked into Leroy's crooked elbow, they took a deep breath and walked into the diminished scrum. A shallow trough of salt kept the protestors off the property itself, but they were a fixture of the sidewalk and parking lot.

"Hey! Hey! Here come some!" the slender Unenlightened cried out, pointing at Leroy and Donna as they approached.

"Stop discriminating against the dead!" yelled a shade who looked like she had burned out in the 1960s and never quite recovered.

The whole crowd gathered around them, placards raised high, to shout some obvious slogans at them. It wasn't a particularly popular cause, but undead discrimination groups always managed to gin up a few people for the extrasensory deprivation clinics. It was one of the few places where the vast majority of the population that comprised the dead could have a legitimate claim they were being discriminated against. ESD clinics, salt mines, and sage farms, Donna supposed.

"All right now," Leroy said, calmly but firmly, "the cops aren't here today, but you all know the rules. No molesting people coming in and out."

"We're allowed to be here, man!" the burnout moaned.

"Be annoying here as much as you want," Leroy said, "but don't block my path."

"Yeah?" she replied with a sneer. "What are you going to do if we don't move?"

Donna looked to Leroy. She'd spent some time with him lately and thought she knew what kind of a man he was, but hadn't seen him react to a situation like this before.

He reached into his pocket and flipped open his wallet, displaying his credentials.

"I am a licensed and bonded exorcist."

Before he could even complete his sentence, the shades were booing, hissing, and clearing a path for him. None of them wanted to deal with an exorcist. Their path was clear now, save for the unusually skinny ghostfucker. The boy stuck his pierced lower lip out defiantly.

"What did I just say?" Leroy asked.

Donna tugged on his sleeve. "Come on, we can go around him."

"Nah," the kid said, showing a surprising amount of spine, "you're going to have to go through me. I ain't scared of an exorcist. I ain't dead yet."

Leroy rolled up his sleeve. "You ready to be?"

A beat passed as Leroy stared into the kid's eyes. Leroy was a big guy, but the kid was . . . well, he seemed dangerous, the way a coke fiend was dangerous, or a punk who wanted to scrap at every concert. He didn't look like he could slug it out with Leroy, but he might pull a switchblade and needle him in the eye or neck before Leroy knew what was going on.

"Yeah, stand up to them, Colin!" one of the ghosts cried out.

The others cheered him on. Leroy didn't say a word. He stood stock still, and for a moment, Donna felt her stomach lurch. His whole appearance seemed to be saying, "Try me." Subtly, he pressed Donna behind him.

Colin spat on the ground. "You ain't worth it."

The kid stepped out of the way. Leroy let out a barely perceptible sigh of relief. He reached back to take Donna's hand, but she was already gone.

"Donna?"

"Excuse me," she said, tapping the little shit's shoulder.

Colin turned to her, shock playing out on his face as though she'd boiled his cat hairless in front of him. Perhaps the two men had accepted their chest-pounding display as complete, but she didn't give a shit about their macho decisions.

"You forgot this."

She raised her foot and wiped the yellowy gob of mucus she was balancing on the toe of her shoe onto Colin's pants. Without waiting for a response she turned her back to him and grabbed Leroy, pulling him after her.

"Did you see his face?" he asked, pointing back as she dragged him toward the door.

"Nope," she said.

When they stepped into the foyer Leroy grabbed her. "That was really hot."

She smiled.

"Welcome," a beatific voice intoned, forcing them to quickly pull apart from what was about to become a powerful and possibly wet public display of affection.

They turned around. The inside of the clinic was warm and welcoming, appointed with crushed leather and palms. Something about the protestors outside made her think it would be dull, sterile, and workmanlike, but it was quite the opposite.

"Hi," Leroy said, "two for Tate, please."

The receptionist punched up something on her computer. "Oh, yes, I remember. You said you wanted a tour and had some questions first, right?"

Leroy nodded. "If that's all right."

"It's more than all right. It's a bit flattering to meet someone who's interested in what we do here. With those jerks . . . pardon me, with those people outside."

"It's all right," Donna said, "they were jerkoffs to us to."

The receptionist attempted to cover her broad smile with her petite hand. Doubtless she was hired for her decorum in dealing not just with customers, but with the angry mobs that accumulated outside.

"You might come to regret this offer," Leroy said. "I could talk the legs off a donkey and still convince it to go for a walk afterwards."

The receptionist stepped around the desk and put a welcoming arm around him.

"Then you should fit right in around here. You should meet some of our technicians. Will you be joining us, Mrs. Tate?"

Donna blanched.

"It's, uh, Fitzpatrick, actually," Leroy said.

"Oh, yes, sorry."

"This could get technical. And dull," Leroy said. He turned to Donna. "Maybe you should head into the back and we can catch up after the appointment?"

Donna realized she didn't really have a whole lot of questions about the clinic, and Leroy seemed chomping at the bit to do some research. Her technician showed her to an antechamber where she disrobed before entering the extrasensory deprivation tank.

The room was lined with solid blocks of pink Himalayan salt. She worried briefly the bricks could fall over on her, but she had never heard of that happening to anybody, so they must have had a good system in place for preventing it. Soft muzak played in the room, some version of Chopin on mandolin or whalesong or something equally generic and inoffensive.

She sat down in the comfortable camp chair which had been set out for her. She breathed deep, relaxed, and waited.

There was no headache. No disorientation. She didn't feel woozy, didn't feel problems in her inner ear. There were no ghosts or shades or specters or ectoplasmic whorls, sure, but that was because the room was lined with salt.

She sighed. It seemed clear to her this was not connected to the phenomenon they had encountered at the Jackson house. Maybe Leroy could tease better information out of the experts, but she didn't think there was a ton to be learned here. Still, the day might not be a complete waste. People did pay good money for this treatment, after all. Leroy had paid good money for it. Maybe she could force herself to relax. Or was that an oxymoron?

She leaned back and let the ocean sounds wash over her. She smiled and let her stress melt away. Before she knew it, she snorted and opened her eyes. She had fallen asleep at some point. Her mouth was dry and scratchy. Her eyes were starting to weep as well.

Nobody had mentioned any of those side effects.

The technician had promised to gently knock when her time was up. Donna felt certain it had been longer than an hour. She didn't take quick naps; she zonked the hell out. Maybe she misjudged the time, but she was getting intensely uncomfortable. Even if she was in there less than an hour, it was time to leave. She stepped out of the salt chamber and into one of the clinic's corridors.

"Hello?" she called out.

There was no response. Wasn't somebody supposed to be here, keeping an eye on the time? This seemed more than unprofessional. It was downright dangerous. She grabbed her robe and fished her watch out of the pocket. It had easily been an hour and a half.

Pulling the robe on, she made her way through the dim lighting to the lobby. She could hear the low squawking of the TV in the lobby, but otherwise she could've heard a pin drop. She was understandably startled to find the lobby packed with people. All of the clinic patrons and staff had their eyes glued on the flickering screen. In fact, all of the protestors had come inside and were watching, too. That made Donna more confused and queasy than anything else.

She slowly pressed into the crowd, who let her in, until she found Leroy and wrapped her hand around his. He looked up in acknowledgement, but otherwise couldn't rip his eyes off the screen.

Sparrow Thames, looking ten times more haggard than usual, was shuffling through papers, phones, and mics to try to keep some semblance of order.

"Let's see that footage again," Sparrow said, but nothing happened. "Don? Can we get the footage?"

After another slight delay, the screen jumped to an image of a city, possibly in the Middle East. The streets were nearly deserted. A few people wandered about as if in a daze, but otherwise a neutron bomb could have gone off and the place wouldn't have seemed less empty.

"These images are coming to us straight from Istanbul. The scene is grotesque. Horrifying. Unthinkable. Though no physical damage was done to the streets the toll is . . . unimaginable. The phenomenon has struck northwestern Turkey, parts of southern Greece and Bulgaria, and, perhaps most disturbingly, ships on the Black Sea and Sea of Marmara."

"The phenomenon?" Donna asked, feeling her heart sink. She

turned to Leroy. "Are they talking about our phenomenon? It's in Europe now?"

"Istanbul is gone," Colin, the ghostfucker said, his voice like a mouse's squeak. "Every single ghost is . . . gone."

18

WORD OF ISTANBUL'S SPIRITUAL ANNIHILATION spread quickly. Kyle was enjoying the tranquility of his cell despite Ellington endlessly reciting verses and lyrics.

As far as Kyle could tell, he was composing a ballad to commemorate the loss of his lady love. It wasn't even strictly a terrible poem, and despite the older specter's arrogant nature, Kyle almost found himself sympathizing with him.

The thought of sympathizing with Roderick Ellington made him wish he could still vomit.

Steven Hager floated in and immediately his reverie evaporated as he saw the state of the sheriff. He barely had features. Kyle couldn't remember the last time he'd seen the details of anything through Steven's spirit, but right now he could see straight through to Ellington's cell.

"Steven," Kyle said his name hesitantly.

The sheriff's eyes stared ahead uncomprehendingly as he floated between the salt cells. He was barely holding it together and Kyle could tell he was on the verge of relapse.

"Constable? Are you feeling unwell?" Roderick Ellington had apparently taken a break from waxing lyrical when he saw Hager floating close to his cell. "Fitzpatrick, what is this?"

Kyle tried to think of anything that would rattle Steven Hager.

The realization hit him.

"He's seen it," Kyle said.

Ellington hesitated, practically recoiling in the cell to get away from the sheriff floating mere feet from him.

Kyle said, "Steven, listen, it's on the other side of town. It's not here."

The sheriff lazily rotated in the air, his eyes scanning all around. "What if it expands? My family . . ."

Kyle began to get agitated as he watched Hager sweep too close to the salt lines. A sympathetic fear coursed through him and the lightest edge of crimson began to appear at the edge of his vision.

"It isn't here," Kyle said. "It's not coming. Your family is safe!"

The sheriff cackled madly, his features rapidly deteriorating. "You don't know. Of course you don't know. Don't bother trying to run. You've fed it enough. Now it's coming."

With a scream he went full poltergeist before relapsing. A terrible shrieking sound and a gust of wind blew away the salt line to Kyle's cell. The crimson edge disappeared from his vision even as Ellington's dandy-like appearance became fuzzy and less coherent. Steven's emotionally unstable presence was gone.

"What the devil was that all about?" the poet asked.

Kyle grunted in pleasure, noting he was now free to leave the jailhouse. He floated ahead purposefully, cool and collected as he planned out his escape. He headed for the entrance to the cellblock before turning and looking back at his former sparring partner with a loud sigh.

"You're an asshole," Kyle said, "but it's not in me to leave anybody like this."

He concentrated on attempting to blow away the salt line in front of Ellington's cell but the other specter held up a threatening hand.

"Don't do me any favors."

"Isn't escaping punishment a pastime for the rich?"

Ellington gave a cold smile that radiated smugness. "You're assuming escape involves exiting a cell when, really, any meaningful notion of escape involves a barrister and obscene amounts of money. Fortunately, I have both. Run along. I'll see you behind bars again soon. Or, better yet, perhaps on the street."

The words chilled him to his core but Kyle gave the fop his best devil-may-care grin. "Oh, I'd love a repeat of the last time we met on the street. I could finish kicking your head in."

Kyle felt triumphant as flowery descriptions of his worthlessness followed him out of the cellblock.

Kyle was expecting to duck into closets or stand inside walls while he made his daring escape. He was expecting squads of deputies ready to apprehend him and send him back to his cell, but as he walked down the strictly defined pathways of the former armory, he was struck by how deserted the place seemed.

Normally deputies would have been hurrying back and forth, or at the very least, been sequestered in rooms filling out paperwork. Irresponsible sage burning was the number one cause of spiritual arrests in Sherman's Forest and was one of the talking points of Steven's last reelection campaign.

The silence permeating the station was maddening and Kyle thought back to the sheriff's episode. He had definitely witnessed the phenomenon, though his reaction was extreme. Maybe it was still in the building. The thought that it could have devoured all the officers popped into the ether of Kyle's head and he froze in his tracks.

What if he rounded a corner and was swallowed up, too?

Kyle gulped, an old habit from when he had saliva, and mustered his courage, forcing himself to move in an odd floating gait down the hall. He passed a few empty offices, paperwork spread across the floor as if whoever had been holding them had thrown them in a fit of rage before disapparating.

Kyle peeked before walking down each hallway, afraid he would see the anomaly squatting at the end like a spider waiting for a fly. Fortunately, the buzzing fluorescent lights and distant hum of the air conditioner were the only things that greeted him.

Had the Rapture the weirdoes like the Crucians preached about actually happened? Were he and Roderick Ellington, of all fucking people, the only entities left in the world? The thought was enough to fill him with morbid humor as he bitterly chuckled to himself. Wouldn't that have been a cruel cosmic trick?

His fears were allayed when he peeked around the last hallway between him and the lobby and saw one of Steven's breathing deputies, Julian Paulos. Julian was curled into a ball on his side, his arms wrapped around his knees, as he stared off into nothingness.

Kyle would have thought the man dead if not for the rise and fall of his chest. He approached gingerly, but it didn't matter. He didn't react to Kyle's presence in the slightest.

"Julian?"

The man's head snapped up and Kyle wanted to recoil at the sheer level of despair behind his brown eyes. Kyle had seen something like this once before, when an acquaintance of his, a ghost who had committed rape during an unlawful possession, had been forcibly regressed.

"I had family there, I don't . . ." Julian paused and took a long, shuddering breath. "I haven't heard from them."

Kyle didn't know what he was talking about. His family didn't hang out at the cop shop. Forgetting his precarious position, Kyle reached down and grabbed Julian's hand. "What happened? Where are the other cops? I need to know."

The man laughed bitterly. "It was here. A few of the specters lit out when the television said it was coming this way. I thought they were spineless wastes of ether until it actually showed up. It gobbled the rest of them right on up."

Kyle stood up and tried to resist the urge to run and find some hole he didn't have to come back out of until whatever dark storm was sweeping the world had broken. He left Julian Paulos in his fetal ball and went out into the lobby, passing directly through the door. Behind her bulletproof glass cage, the pretty secretary stared at the TV with her hands covering her mouth. He almost didn't want to follow her eyes, but like every other feeling warning him he shouldn't do something, he ignored it and raised his gaze to the screen.

Sparrow Thames's normally vulturine features were scrunched up in an expression of anxious terror, her once tidy hair spilling out in unruly curls.

The Jackson phenomenon was behind her, dominating the screen, swirling around the buildings like a hurricane or a tornado but there was no damage other than lack of spirits.

It had gobbled them all up.

What irony. How many specters had heaved a sigh of relief around the world today, knowing that Istanbul was a million miles away? But nobody was really safe. And Sherman's Forest had its own little homegrown anomaly. The red came charging to the edge of his vision and he looked away to prevent himself from relapsing. Sparrow's voice came in a near panic from the screen.

"The event appears to be expanding and all deceased citizens are urged to avoid the areas at the bottom of the screen at all costs."

The list of locations flashed across the bottom of the screen but Kyle didn't have time to take them in. He had to find Donna and her boy toy. They'd know what to do. That's why they'd gone on their date, right?

Kyle hurried out, making his way back to Donna's townhouse. He glanced down every street as he went, trying not to run headlong into a hole that devoured the dead.

19

LEROY AND DONNA WERE TENSE during the car ride home. The mood of the town was far worse. As they drove by the Milk Bar, it seemed to be hosting a funeral reception, but with the news from Istanbul, it didn't look like a single reveler was having fun. The whole thing was as somber as a court sentencing.

Leroy's shirt pocket had been buzzing intermittently since Donna caught up with him in the clinic lobby.

"Are you going to get that?" she asked.

He shook his head.

She said, "It could be important."

He shook his head again. "I already know who it is. It's everyone I called about this mess pumping me for information. They're going to couch it as concern, or professional courtesy, but mostly it's so they'll be prepared to go on TV."

Donna tried to plaster a smile on her face and rubbed his bicep. "What if it's Sparrow Thames asking *you* to come on TV?"

Leroy's face didn't crack. "She called a few times, too, I'm sure."

Donna's erstwhile smile collapsed in upon itself. She turned and stared back out the window. Fairly recently, Andy Warhol had said something about every ghost having fifteen minutes to haunt the world. Leroy, it seemed, was not interested in fame, though.

Donna's own phone went off. She looked at it, not recognizing the number. It wasn't local.

"Client?" Leroy asked.

"No, I don't think so. It's probably a telemarketer."

She gave Leroy a sidelong glance.

"Go ahead," he said. "My policy on taking calls doesn't have to be your policy."

Quirking her mouth, she shrugged and answered the phone. "Fitzpatrick."

"Donna." It was Spender.

"Not going to pretend to be in my basement or under my bed or—"

"Listen, I don't know if you've heard but, ah . . . it's bedlam out here."

Her finger was twirling, seemingly of its own accord. She looked over at it, realizing she was imitating what she would have done as a teenager with the cord of a landline phone. It was a nervous tick she hadn't employed in decades.

"Where are you?" she asked.

"Right now, um . . . Thailand. I think maybe I should come home but . . ."

As Spender trailed off, Donna realized how serious the situation was. Normally she could barely get a word in edgewise with her old business partner. Hearing him lapse into silence would've been the creepiest thing about the day if it hadn't already been for Istanbul and the veritable lynch mob out to get Kyle.

"What's the matter?" Donna said. "We've known each other for years. You know you can tell me anything."

Leroy raised his eyebrow but didn't say anything.

"All right," Spender said slowly, but then it all began pouring out of him. "I don't know if it's safe to come back. I was in Bangkok when it happened and I haven't left. Nobody's left. The news isn't saying anything. Nobody knows anything. Nobody knows if anything is safe."

"Safe? I don't understand. Can't you disapparate?"

Leroy shook his head and drew a series of curving lines through the air with his finger. Donna shook her head. She didn't understand.

"I know it looks instantaneous," Spender said. "You're living. You wouldn't understand."

"Hang on a second," she said, and tapped the mute button. "What am I not getting?"

Leroy said, "Sometimes they say it's like hopping on a train on a track or like following a tunnel. I don't know. It's never been closely studied. But the wormtrails might have a physical presence like ley lines. No one's really sure."

"So, for all the ghosts know, they might have to pass through Istanbul?" she asked.

He nodded.

She unmuted the phone. "Jack, couldn't you hop on a plane or something? I know, for you, it would be like taking a slow boat to China, but at least you would get here in one piece."

"It's not that simple. It's not just Istanbul or Sherman's Forest anymore. There are rumors about the phenomenon popping up everywhere. Little pockets, some no bigger than our office. This guy I met at the noodle shop said he swears he saw a hole in the world the size of Busan out in the middle of the Pacific. It could be anywhere, anytime. A plane could fly through it and then I'd be . . ."

Twice now, the normally garrulous Spender was unable to finish a sentence. Donna ran her hand through her hair, picking up a great lock of it and scratching at her scalp.

She said, "I know you're scared. But that's no way to exist. You can't be jumping at goblins and leprechauns that may or may not be around every corner. That's no way to be."

"I can't enjoy my existence knowing it could possibly end. How can you? Aren't you terrified? Doesn't it reach up and grab you by the stomach and guts and never let go?"

"I don't know."

"Donna," Leroy warned.

She looked up from the dashboard for the first time in minutes. They were outside her house.

"What?" she hissed in a tone harsher than she wanted it to be.

Leroy gestured. There was nobody there, really. That was quite a change from this afternoon when half the town was piled up outside her door.

"Shit," she said into the phone. "I've got to go. Stay safe, okay?"

Spender sounded like he had more to say, a lot more, a whole motherfuckton more, in fact, but she hung up on him.

"Where's the circus?" she asked.

"I don't know."

She tugged on the car door a few more times than was strictly necessary before it finally opened. She practically leapt out, shielding her eyes from the sun with her hand. Her heart was palpitating as she made a dead sprint for the door. The handle nearly came apart under her ministrations before she finally got the key in and got it open.

"Kyle!" she cried out.

No response. She hurried to the living room, checked the back porch, made a round of every room, including checking a few closets, all the while calling his name. Her heart nearly caught in her throat when she finally spotted an ectoplasmic hand in the upstairs bathroom.

"Everything all right?"

It was Mrs. Palladino, back, lounging lazily in the bathtub. Donna's heart went back to full throttle. A cold sweat broke out on her forehead. It was happening again, wasn't it? This was exactly how she had felt that day in the shop.

"Yes, fine, Mrs. Palladino. You haven't seen my brother, have you?"

"No, my love, I just got back a few minutes ago. Everything's such a fuss down in Ghosttown right now. I couldn't handle all the commotion."

Donna pulled the door closed behind her as she stepped out. Her temples were throbbing. She reached up and massaged them. A large, reassuring hand came down on her shoulder.

"Breathe," Leroy said.

"Why should I?"

"Because I don't want you to have a heart attack and die."

"Why not?"

"Because you can't fuck the dead. Or at least you shouldn't."

She looked up at him wryly. "You do know what I do for a living, don't you?"

"I can hear you, you know!" Mrs. Palladino called from inside the bathroom.

Leroy took her hand and led her back to the kitchen. "This was supposed to be a relaxing day."

"Well, I guess the universe doesn't want that for me. Sorry a million ghosts in Thrace had to unexist and now my brother is probably in the hands of that mob. It really messed up my day."

"You want me to wait here for him to come back or go searching? I figure you'd rather go searching, since you probably know all of his haunts."

Donna paused. Leroy was acting perfectly normal. His usual warm, kind self. But she could still sense there was something unspoken.

"You have to go, don't you?"

A smile gradually crossed his lips. "You never told me you were a futurologist."

She reached out and stroked his chin. "I'm not. I guess I'm starting to learn how to read you."

He shrugged. "Too bad. I could've used a futurologist on payroll. I would've paid you fifteen bucks an hour."

She snorted. "I won't get out of bed for less than thirty."

"Fair enough."

She folded her arms. "Where do you have to go?"

He said, "You want me to make you a list?"

"Okay."

"You want the short list or the long list?"

She patted his hand. "I know, I know. You've got to go. I'll take care of the business with my moron alone."

"I'll stay. I swear."

"I know you would. And that's what counts. But right now the world needs that genius exorcist I've been hogging all day."

They kissed and he departed. She looked around her messy place, messier now that Kyle had spent the night. She grabbed her car keys and then stopped.

"No," she said, "health first."

She put a kettle on the stove, concentrated on breathing slowly and meditated until the water boiled. She poured a cup of tea into her travel mug and then clambered behind the wheel. She spent the next two hours cruising around town, checking out the Skinner campus, Ghosttown, The Arrowhead, even the Milk Bar, which Kyle almost never frequented.

She didn't see Kyle or anyone who had seen him anywhere, and most of the specters were even less helpful than usual. The radio news was now calling the decimation of Istanbul the "Thracian Incident," about as Orwellian of a name as she could conceive of, but in Sherman's Forest all they could talk about was Jackson Manor. The dead were all in a tizzy about being at ground zero of what they all assumed Kyle had caused, or was at least connected to.

She was starting to get frustrated, but she didn't intend to let stress overwhelm her. Maybe she should have made Leroy stay and help after all. But no, that wasn't fair. She couldn't keep forcing him to help out with her dumb shit all the time.

She parked the car alongside a fire hydrant. Who gave a fuck at this point, right? She pressed her head down on the steering wheel. She'd been over every inch of the town. The only place he could be was gone, disappeared into that horrific phenomenon. Or he had gone back to her place while she was out. She raised her head slowly.

Will he have the wits to answer the phone if I call? I choose to believe . . . maybe?

She pulled out her cell and dialed her rarely used landline. It rang a few times. She thrilled when someone picked up.

"This better be you," Kyle said. "Do you have any idea how hard it is to get one of these things off the hook?"

"Where the *fuck* have you been?"

"Uh . . . jail."

"Jail? Are you kidding me?"

"No. Listen, do you have a gun?"

"A gun? No. What do you want a gun for?"

"I want to pay a guy a visit."

20

KYLE CAME UP WITH SOME terrible plans over the years, a few in life and many more in death. This, though, pushed the limits of what he thought he could accomplish. The thoughts buzzing around inside the ectoplasm that was his mind had made an unusual connection.

The event or anomaly (the dead had so many different names for it now and the media was throwing buzzwords all over the place to see what stuck) was swallowing ghosts and creating areas the dead couldn't enter. But he'd heard the concept before: artificial oases, free of spirits for people wanting the utmost privacy. The Ghost-Away guy was the only person he knew of who had the confidence to promote his product that way.

Kyle had suffered through too many of the man's ads to not remember his face or his name: Buster Beats. The image of that name flashing at the bottom of the television screen had etched itself in his mind.

Kyle snorted to himself. This had to be karmic punishment from the universe at large for his afterlife of misdeeds. He groaned to think his personal afterlife and maybe the fate of the world was left in the hands of a man who thought paying for cheap late-night infomercials was a good idea.

The only thing standing in his way was Donna giving him a look like she might call an exorcist on his ass.

"One more time so I can be sure I'm hearing correctly," she said, hovering on the border between rage and incredulous disbelief.

"Easy. Buster Beats is in Ganesh City, a simple drive from our humble little burg. We know he makes those Ghost-Away modules because he's a slimy man who is prejudiced against the living impaired. All of a sudden, anomalies that do the same thing as the modules are popping up like they're going out of style. So if we connect the dots, that sleazebag must be involved." Kyle threaded his hands together in preparation for his grand conclusion. "So I've drawn up a simple plan. Step 1: Find a gun. Step 2: Find Buster Beats and threaten to use the gun if he doesn't tell us what he knows. Step 3: Possible profits and movie rights."

Kyle flashed a nonchalant grin as Donna gave him a look that would've made a corpse shiver. She walked over to her kitchen island and dug through the small cupboard underneath until she produced a bottle of red wine. Kyle floated closer as she silently uncorked the bottle and poured herself half a glass, the red liquid sloshing like freshly spilled blood.

Donna sat the bottle back on the island and eyed the glass with a predatory gleam.

"Don't you have to chill that first?" Kyle asked as buoyantly as possible before she glared at him.

"I usually indulge your capering but, for once in your afterlife, shut . . . the hell . . . up."

Kyle's mouth snapped closed and he retreated a few feet, watching her like an antelope eyeing a lioness. With Ghosttown completely against him, he was running out of friends fast. Tommie Bones might stick by him for a while, but that would be delaying the inevitable. As much as he hated to admit it, Kyle needed Donna. And more than anything, he needed a solution to this crisis.

Donna took a sip of the wine, the red liquid accentuating her lips and bringing color back to her cheeks. Kyle knew his twin well enough to know she was thinking about what the next move was, running through all the possibilities in her head, grasping at whatever straws she could to convince him not to follow this plan.

She told him about the call from Spender. Kyle felt sorry for the man, and he could certainly sympathize with a fear of disapparating. Of course, Kyle's worry was relapse, not being swallowed whole. Either way he was worried, though he didn't want her to see it. The news was reporting more occurrences: a ghost village in the Iceland wilderness suddenly uninhabited, a hauntless restaurant in downtown L.A., the ghosts of prehistoric cave lions swallowed up in Morocco. And on and on it went.

He couldn't sit and do nothing anymore.

"Maybe Leroy has a gun," Donna said, looking straight ahead, not daring to look him in the eye, "or maybe he knows someone who will loan us one."

Kyle was struck by her eyes. He was reluctant to attribute it to Leroy's presence in her life, but she had lost weight recently. Overall she looked younger, but her eyes were drawn up with so many stress lines it canceled the effect. If she wasn't careful, she'd have half a head of gray within the year and worry herself into an early grave while she was at it.

That wasn't something Kyle had any intention of letting happen, and not for the first time (though, admittedly, it was something of a rarity) he thought outside his own existence.

"Let me take care of it by myself," Kyle said. "I just need a gun. I can threaten the ad man by myself, you can say you didn't know what I wanted it for or I forced you."

Donna downed the rest of her wine in one gulp. "Do you honestly think I'm not going to help you with this? Without me you'll end up in jail . . . again."

Kyle smiled and executed a mock bow. "Once again, my knack for flawless planning has slipped past your defenses and convinced you of the importance of my cause."

Donna hooked an index finger at him. "Don't get cute with me. I'm only agreeing to this because the world is falling apart. But get this through your transparent skull: I'm in charge."

Kyle was quiet. Donna often bitched and fumed, but it wasn't often she laid down the law with him. It was rarer still when he took her seriously.

Kyle played chicken with her emotions before raising both his hands in surrender. "Fine, fine, I'll take what I can get. Remember that time Mom said you were the brains behind our operation?"

"Not really." She waved a dismissive hand as she grabbed her landline from its cradle. "I always tried to be somewhere else when Mom and Dad wanted to feign interest in us."

Donna began dialing Leroy's number, vanishing down the hallway as Kyle stared after her. He could hear the muffled apologies as Donna interrupted whatever it was her new beau was up to.

The comment about their parents had struck a blow, although Kyle was not going to let Donna see it had gotten under his skin. He was atypical, perhaps, but he had always resented his parents for lounging on the beach in Mali during his formative years.

His great-grandparents were kind specters, and he'd never wanted for anything with them. They'd both even shown up at the funeral home when they'd brought his battered body in for him to view. He loved them, but had always felt a strange longing for his parents. In fact, the comment from his mother about Donna being the brains was one of his most treasured childhood memories.

Donna had never done anything so maudlin as frame a picture of their parents, but a stack of disorganized Polaroids on the table next to Donna's TV contained a photo of Mom and Dad. They looked so young in that photo. They still were, of course. The last time he had checked they were on a beach in Indonesia.

Neither one of them had bothered to call since his death. Even the Thracian Incident hadn't made them deign to check in. He supposed they'd start caring eventually, but at the rate the world was spiraling it was beginning to look like he'd be gone by then.

"Kyle?"

He swung around, quickly realizing he wasn't solid. He lifted a hand to his eyes and could see through it as clearly as a spotless window. He looked away from her, attempting to banish the unpleasant memories from his mind. She couldn't know he was scared. There were reputations to maintain and all that. It didn't take long before he was solid once more. He plastered on the cocky grin she hated so much before turning back around.

"Sorry, you caught me reminiscing about some of my old hauntings. Makes me emotional." He wiped a fake tear from his eye and was relieved when her grip on the phone tightened. "So? What did your beefy chunk of man meat say?"

Donna replaced the landline in the cradle, her lips tight. "He's got a pistol, a small one. We're going to go get it from him."

Kyle floated over, joy leaping through his being, almost attempting to hug his twin before he thought better of it. Then he saw the tears in Donna's eyes.

Kyle's eyes widened and he immediately threw away the mask he was using to hide his pain. "What happened?"

"I lied to him." The words hung like bitter curtains and suddenly Kyle thought his whole plan was a fool's errand. "I told him you were a fan of target shooting. Ever since you were a little kid you've liked to shoot, that you wanted to head up to Ganesh City and take your mind off everything. Told him it was for a little family time, that we didn't need help."

Donna gripped the kitchen counter so hard Kyle thought it would send cracks spiraling across its perfect white surface.

"Hey—" he started to say, but she cut him off. Through the salt and wetness of the tears running down Donna's cheeks he saw a streak of anger.

"If this goes south and I never see that man again, I'm done with you. You can handle your own business. I . . . I can't do this anymore." She took a shuddering sigh and looked away from him. "I love you, but I can't keep taking care of you forever."

The words got under his skin, there was no denying it. He knew he could have probably talked it out with her, reasoned with her, promised her he would shape up and be more responsible from there on out.

Instead he smiled benignly and shrugged. "If that's what you want. You always were the self-proclaimed wet blanket between the two of us, right?"

Kyle watched as Donna's face twitched, the movement almost natural now under all the stress, a part of her soul now.

Death might be good for her, actually, if it made her let go of some of that stress. Of course, that was only true if he fixed the phenomenon first.

"Let's go," she said.

Kyle followed her out of the townhouse.

The ride to Ganesh City was an exercise in stubbornness; anyone who knew either of the Fitzpatrick siblings were well aware they came by it naturally. When the family fell into conflict it was a textbook study of unstoppable forces meeting immovable objects.

Donna stared resolutely ahead in complete silence since the two of them had left her townhouse. The only break was when she had stopped to obtain the pistol from Leroy. Kyle hadn't followed her to the door, leaving her words with her boyfriend private.

Kyle didn't mind. He watched the trees and lights illuminating the highway, mile after mile of foliage and human civilization mixing into a hypnotic swirl. He only looked away when they passed the spot where he had died. The guard rail had long since been repaired, but he would have known the spot of gravel anywhere. It never failed to fill him with dread.

Kyle said, "There's a spot we're both pretty familiar with, huh?"

Donna didn't answer, continuing to stare forward as the Ganesh City skyline came into view, all pretty lines and brilliant lights.

Kyle didn't attempt to make any more conversation.

Buster Beats ran his business from a dilapidated strip mall in the city's East Side, where the rich graveyards and townhomes of the south gave way to shabby tenement housing and low-grade crematoria.

Ghost-Away 'R' Us was wedged between a Patricia's (Where Fun and Fantasy Meet) and a nail salon with bars protecting the already-broken windows.

"Well, at least if we hold him up here it won't look too out of the ordinary," Kyle said.

She continued not to speak to him as they sat casing the shady business. The lights were on inside but Kyle also wanted to be sure Buster was actually there. This was a flimsy enough plan as it was and he didn't want to be stuck with the scandal of threatening somebody's harmless secretary.

Donna pulled the gun out of her purse, a small pistol with the words "Sig Sauer" etched on the grip. Kyle didn't know much about guns but apparently this one was something Donna could fire comfortably as long as she was pointing it in the right direction.

Her hand trembled, barely keeping hold of the weapon. She looked at it like it was a poisonous snake, ready to rear back and strike before she had a chance to defend herself.

"I've never held a gun before," she said.

It was the first words she'd said to him since their fight at her townhouse.

"Never did when I was alive, either. Don't think I'll be starting now." As calm as he could make himself, he reached over and steadied Donna's hands, looking her in the eyes. "We aren't here to kill anyone. Just keep the safety on, okay?"

Donna still looked skeptical. Kyle thought she was going to call the whole thing off until a white truck trundled past them, the engine backfiring as it shut off. Buster Beats exited the vehicle and took a deep gulp of the night air before walking toward his business, keys in hand.

Donna hastily exited the car to follow, Kyle trailing in her wake as they hurried across the parking lot. They barely caught the door as it swung closed. A narrow hallway lit by two crackling lights led to a red door with peeling paint. Old posters of anti-drug campaigns and pro-living propaganda littered the walls, along with the occasional hole in the plaster. A few wooden chairs for prospective clients to wait in and a table with magazines at least three months old were the only real furnishings. A shadow moved under the red door and the distant tapping of footsteps sounded.

Kyle and Donna both moved down the hall as quietly as they could, a much easier feat for Kyle as he floated soundlessly above the faded tile.

"How are we going to do this?" Donna whispered as Kyle hovered at the edge of the office door.

"Just do what comes naturally."

He willed himself to vanish from sight, not a novice trick, but not impossible to master, either. Donna's bewildered expression was the last thing he saw before he passed through the door.

Buster Beats sat behind his desk in a third-rate affair of an office he had spruced up with fashionable plants and books to give him the veneer of professionalism. He was working on one of his modules, which he had pried open and scattered into a thousand pieces.

Kyle glanced around, looking for a distraction and settling on the shelves of books in the right corner of the room. He focused his rage, letting it bubble up to the surface.

A book flew off the shelf. Buster looked up, startled, the magnifying visor on his head making his brown eyes overlarge and comical. Kyle decided to crank it up a notch. The small lamplights began flickering, bright and dim, and the books began flying off the shelves in earnest now, one heavy encyclopedia putting a hole in the drywall.

Buster yelped and dove for cover, cowering under his desk. Kyle smiled to himself as he focused all his rage on the mahogany desk. He'd never lifted something so big before, but with the way he was feeling, he probably could have halted an elephant in its tracks. The desk shook, rattling against the floor as the lamp bulbs burst, sending shards of glass flying around the room and plunging them into darkness.

"I give! I give!" Buster screamed.

Kyle saw a pair of shaking hands appear from beneath the desk. Donna chose that moment to burst through the door, waving the pistol around and screaming like a madwoman. Kyle would have given her an A for effort if he weren't so worried she was going to accidentally pull the trigger and send their suspect off to his eternal reward.

"If this is about the boxes, our disclaimer is clearly spelled out in—" Buster hastily tried to explain as Donna shoved the gun in his face.

The older man cried out and squeezed his eyes shut, his breath escaping him like a deflating balloon.

"What do you know about the anomaly?" Donna asked.

Despite the seriousness of the situation, Kyle almost laughed at the sheer absurdity of Donna attempting to make a voice that sounded terrifying. To him, it sounded like the same voice she'd used to threaten to tell on him when they were children.

"What? I don't—" the balding salesman stammered as he held his hands up, his eyes shut so tightly Kyle thought his skin would rip from the tension.

"The Jackson anomaly," Donna repeated, her voice almost cracking as she wiggled the gun under the man's nose. "The one sucking up ghosts. You know what I'm talking about, right?"

The barrel against his nose caused Buster's eyes to flap open like he'd seen his mother parading around the streets naked. "I-I don't know. I mean, I've seen it on the news, but I don't know anything special."

Kyle decided it was time to bring the bad cop to the proceedings. He drifted into view of the huckster's face, his own features a mask of rotting sores and infected flesh, his insides dripping out through gigantic tears in his stomach, ectoplasmic intestines splattering against the floor.

"Stop lying!" Kyle's roar had all the echo of a pissed off poltergeist ready to bring down an entire building. "Stop lying! Your boxes make ghost no-go zones. The anomaly does the same thing. You expect me to believe it's a coincidence?"

Buster went limp in Donna's grasp, dropping from his knees to a prostrate position, face to the ground, tears staining the floor.

"It's not real!" Buster squealed out, his flesh breaking out in goose bumps. He glanced up at them, his eyes beet red. "There is no fourth physical component. All the boxes do is play a recording of wind chime music. It's below the range of human hearing so nobody gets wise. But you could replicate the same effect with your phone or a tape recorder. I just charge fifty bucks a pop. It's all fake." The man started sobbing again.

"Fuck me," Donna muttered, and Kyle shared the sentiment. They'd made complete fools of themselves and committed a felony to boot. But Beats didn't know he was safe.

"Please don't kill me! I thought I was safe being alive, as long as only the ghosts were disappearing!" He glanced between them, snot and tears mixing together and dripping in great globs onto the floor. "But if you kill me I could disappear, too. Forever. Here, take the money. Take it all. Here!"

Buster wildly tried to shove his wallet at the siblings. Donna took a step back, her face a mixture of revulsion and shame.

Kyle felt the cool tranquility of fury wash over him. He hadn't felt this real, this solid, since he was alive. He was barely aware when his fist lashed out and crashed against the fraudulent salesman's face, a mixture of blood and tooth chips spiraling through the air. Kyle hit Buster Beats again, barely hearing the man's cries for mercy.

He did hear Donna shouting his name and when she finally fired the gun into his belly he stared up at her in shock. Kyle's look was mirrored on her face, staring at him like he was a wretched thing or some kind of alien.

Staring like she didn't know him.

Kyle looked down on the whimpering huckster, crying in a heap before gesturing wordlessly at her. Both of them left the dirty strip mall silently.

21

DONNA DIDN'T LISTEN AS KYLE jabbered away, outlining his half-baked plans to dodge Steven for the night. Her suspicion was Steven—and the entire Sherman's Forest Sheriff's Department—would have more work than it could handle for the rest of the night. Possibly forever.

He would probably end up staying at Tommie Bones' place, and that was fine. As long as he avoided Ghosttown, he'd probably be all right. Frankly, he'd probably end up saged out of his mind, and while she didn't approve of that, she didn't see a point in fighting it anymore.

She found herself staring at the ceiling of her bedroom, the clock displaying three a.m. She sat up, rose, and wandered out into the hallway.

"Hey, Mrs. P.," she said, tightening her robe around her waist.

Mrs. Palladino looked up from the toilet where she was sitting, lost in her own thoughts. A wan smile crossed the specter's face.

"Hello, darling."

"What's on your mind?" Donna asked, entering and setting herself on the edge of the tub, opposite the apparition.

Mrs. Palladino shook her head. "Nothing you need concern yourself with, dear. You're young. And alive."

Despite her protestations, the old ghost's thoughts were easier to read than a children's book.

"You're thinking about leaving town?" Donna said. "I don't know that I've ever heard you mention leaving town before. Not even for a vacation."

"I never have," the spirit replied. "I've never been outside of Sherman's Forest before. Never saw a need to. Everyone I know and everything I like is here. I suppose I figured one day, sure. Go see the Pyramids or Machu Picchu. But I had all of eternity for that. Except now . . ."

"We don't know what happens beyond the phenomenon. We don't know that it's an end. Maybe it's like a different level of reality, a different plane of existence. Maybe it's better. Maybe it's a whole ghostly world where . . ."

She couldn't continue. Mrs. Palladino was staring at her, feigning politeness, but it was obvious she thought Donna's hastily thrown together theories were as impossible to believe as Donna herself found them.

"Maybe," Mrs. Palladino said magnanimously. "I've never had to grapple with the idea of an end before. Not the end to all this, I mean. The closest was when Vincent left me."

Donna traced her finger along the edge of the tub. She needed to clean it one of these days. She should have made Kyle do it, but that would have turned out the same as not doing it herself.

Donna said, "You never told me about your divorce."

The ghost actually smiled, broader than Donna had ever seen before. "Oh, we never got divorced. Forty-eight years we were together. I never had eyes for another man. Vincent didn't mind flirting but it was, you know, that harmless old man flirting. Like when the lifeguard or the girl at the grocery counter is so young it seems cute to her instead of dirty. But he never ran around on me. Worked every day of his life. After retirement, it was always chopping wood or pulling up weeds or something around the house. He never got complacent, that's the thing."

"Must've been nice."

Mrs. P.'s smile melted. "He had a stroke. Vincent always did love his salty foods. We'd discussed it and he preferred mercy to being spoon-fed and wheeled around all day. So I had the hospital dose him. Well, I did it, actually. You know they give you the choice to push the button yourself or have a tech do it."

"I've heard that."

"Well, afterwards we tried to make it work for a while but I was an old woman and he was a ghost. I couldn't keep up. And there was nothing holding us together, really. Not legally, anyway. One day I came home and he wasn't there and he didn't come back. I didn't mind. And when my time came I didn't really care to look him up."

"Really? I mean, I know it's tough when spouses go a few years apart, but you never even had the desire to find out what happened to him?"

She shrugged. "I guess he's in Maui or somewhere. I hope he found someone new. He was like that. Needed somebody in his life. I'm a loner, so I'm happy. I hope he's happy, too. It was nothing sad or depressing. It was . . ."

She made an anemic gesture with her hands, like an explosion that wasn't.

"I see," Donna said, though she really couldn't.

"That sort of thing ends, sure, but existence? The idea of going on and being bored, or watching everyone you care about forget you and move on to other things. We're brought up to worry about all that from day one, in our great-grandparents' arms. My Nana used to talk about what things were like before the Civil War. She was a nice old lady."

"Do you ever see her anymore?"

Mrs. Palladino shook her head. "She moved into one of those time capsule communities in Florida back in the seventies. I guess she missed antebellum life too much. Places like that, with all the hurricanes, most breathers—sorry, dear—most living people like you don't bother with. Ghosts can enact their fantasies."

"That almost sounds worse than an end to existence."

That comment set them both to ruminating. A curtain of silence descended, broken only by the distant hum of a few cicadas.

"Well," Mrs. Palladino said, rising from her customary spot, "I'm off. I never thought I'd say this, but . . . I'm off. Before this place is swallowed up."

"Oh, that won't be for . . ." Donna swallowed her own words. She stepped out into the hall and felt Mrs. P. breezily floating beside her. "Is it here already?"

Mrs. P. pointed. "The creep is slow. Right now it's about to the chandelier. Better tell your brother in case he tries to come back here."

"But," Donna said, flustered, and feeling the tears already falling from her eyes, "that means you can't come back."

"That's right."

"Then I'm never going to see you again."

Mrs. P. reached out and the normally chalk outlined ghost for once appeared to her as almost flesh-colored. She touched Donna's face, her hands firmer than Donna had ever felt.

"I could tell you that's not true, but it probably is. I'll miss you. I hope you'll think of me now and again, even if I never was much more than a nuisance in your life."

Donna took her hands, gingerly, not used to the specter being so close to solid with her.

"You weren't," Donna said.

Mrs. P. disapparated.

Donna asked, "Where are you going?"

It was too late. The specter was gone, off to climes unknown, never to be seen again.

Donna trudged downstairs and stuck her head in the dining room. The phenomenon was noticeable, but it was no longer sending her into paroxysms of pain and bewilderment. Perhaps all the time she'd spent at the Jackson house had inoculated her somewhat.

She set her teeth. The one thing she hadn't done—perhaps was deliberately avoiding doing—was returning to that unnatural place. Kyle's gambit in Ganesh City was foolish, insane even, perhaps, but now she was starting to understand his desperation. The Thracian Incident was like a leak breaking through a ceiling, sending cracks all throughout. The phenomenon was being reported in varying degrees all over the globe. But at the end of the day Donna still believed the source—the leak itself, to continue the metaphor—was Jackson Manor. If there was any stopping or slowing this business, it would have to happen there.

She grabbed a t-shirt, bra, and skirt out of the laundry, and slipped on a pair of flip-flops. She grabbed her keys from the hook, only glancing at the clock long enough to see it was 3:30. Her insomnia certainly wasn't going anywhere, and neither was the phenomenon.

As she put her keys in the car door a pair of trashcans across the street clattered. She glanced over to see a spectral raccoon hiding in one of them. She had forgotten about trash day tomorrow. Three redneck ghosts who made Tommie Bones seem positively dapper by comparison were circling the poor rodent. Well, maybe it wasn't a rodent, but she didn't know what the hell a raccoon was.

The whole affair was taking place catty-cornered to her and across the street, so she didn't interfere, but watched on for a moment. This sort of activity was unusual in her corner of town, and she wondered briefly if she should call Steven. Then she recalled there was a jailbreak, mass panic, and who knew what all else. This was probably spillover from that.

"Grab him!" one of the rednecks shouted.

The second passed right through the trashcan and snatched the raccoon up by the shoulders, holding it away from his body as it scratched in panic. Donna leaned over on the car roof, fascinated. Despite her job (or perhaps because of it) she never had cause to watch a whole lot of physical interaction between ghosts. The most she could recall was one client fighting to keep a somewhat ornery spectral dog on her lap.

Animals, she knew, were not smart or advanced enough to disapparate, and only did so under extreme emotional duress. Even then they usually only moved to their burrows and lairs. The raccoon, though it was obviously distressed, was not disappearing now. The ghost holding it floated up into the air, at least as high as the second level of Donna's house, then slowly, gingerly, moved toward her next-door neighbor's. All the while, the raccoon fretted and battered at him, and Donna almost hoped it was getting in some good scratches on his ectoplasmic form.

Though she couldn't see it, she knew the phenomenon was encroaching on her house, and therefore, most likely on her neighbor's. The redneck reluctantly approached as close as he dared.

"Come on, Rudy, toss it in there!" one of his friends shouted.

Donna clapped a hand over her mouth. She knew the ghosts weren't hiding their actions, but she certainly didn't want to call any attention to herself, especially in the town's current lawless state. She watched in mortified horror as the ghost of a human being used all of his strength to harm a tiny animal, and, as his friends had encouraged him, hurled it with all his might toward the phenomenon.

The raccoon let out an unholy screech as it tumbled, its chalk outline form flickering as it approached the phenomenon. It disappeared like a candle being snuffed out as soon as it struck the border of the phenomenon. Donna turned as the ghosts, still paying her no mind, welcomed their comrade back from his triumphant battle.

"What do you think?" Rudy asked, unnecessarily brushing off his spectral garments. "Did it shrink at all?"

"Yeah, maybe," one of his comrades said. "I couldn't swear but it was definitely, you know, shifting."

"Well, what are we waiting for, then?" the third specter asked, clapping his hands together. "Let's round us up some more varmints."

They disapparated, presumably off to hunt for some more helpless animals to sacrifice to the phenomenon. Donna leaned over and retched on her driveway.

22

KYLE VISITED THE FORESTS AND mountains north of Sherman's Forest a few times, mostly when he needed Tommie's help on his latest scheme. He knew he was going to wash into his friend's cabin sooner rather than later, but for the moment he was content to wander the hiking trails that threaded through the woods.

But instead of the serenity hiking usually brought, a single thought repeated like a steady drumbeat in his head. Kyle even thought his form got less solid with each repetition.

The thought was this: *Everything is pointless.*

During his escape from town, which was nerve-wracking despite remaining invisible, he'd caught some of what his former friends and neighbors were whispering in the alleyways and spiritual hangouts. The prevailing theories were the world had cracked, or something evil was trying to break through. Kyle only ever used the word "devil" as a pretty turn of phrase, but some people, like the Crucians, believe it's a literal being. For the first time ever he was terrified that might be true. The hole in the world had become an abyss.

Donna hadn't said farewell. They hadn't hugged, or done anything normal people did in a desperate situation. Even though they were never the type to express real emotion over banter, this time stung more than he could describe.

The holes were shifting and expanding, and they weren't stopping. For that matter, neither was Roderick as he rallied Ghosttown, calling for his ectoplasm.

Kyle suddenly noticed the cacophony of dead animals which filled the forest. Phantasmagorical squirrels chased each other through the trees while spectral owls called into the night. It was oddly comforting. Out here, away from the city, the simple dead were free to exist, doing what they'd done since they'd shuffled off the mortal coil.

Death was something everyone did, as natural as breathing, the second part of your eternity, the part where responsibilities were left behind for an afterlife of pleasure.

Kyle looked at his hand, clearly able to see the ground under him.

It was hard to keep from going to pieces when his whole damn worldview was crumbling down around him. No, not crumbling down. Being devoured by something alien.

He was so consumed by his musings he almost didn't notice the deer sprint past him. Kyle jumped when it bolted from the gulley to his left, crossing directly in front of his path barely a handbreadth away. It was like a dam breaking as a flood of possums, snakes, raccoons, and other animals came scurrying up the slope. Even a wraith-like bear sprinted as fast as it could past him.

The stampede headed farther up the mountains, none of them even pausing to look at Kyle as they passed. Spectral bugs flew and crawled to catch up with their compatriots.

Intellectually, Kyle knew what lay at the bottom of that gulley, but some part of his lizard brain wouldn't be able to rest until he confirmed it.

When he reached the edge of the gulley he stared down and saw the emptiness staring back. It swirled at the bottom of the ditch like a whirlpool, all red light and silence. A few spectral fireflies rapidly blinked in panic as they were caught in its slowly expanding event horizon.

Seeing something so antithetical to his wellness should have sent him scurrying off into gibbering madness but he'd seen too much and been through too much to care anymore.

Throw yourself in.

The thought came unbidden to him and he recoiled from the edge, wondering if the hole had come alive and whispered into his psyche. Maybe there really was a devil on the other side. Kyle shook his head, crouching at the edge of the slope. No, the thoughts were his own, not the hole's.

It had begun to fill the ravine, flowing like a creek reclaiming a dry riverbed. It lapped the edge of the gulley and Kyle felt it scrape across the bottom of his feet.

They may have been covered by spectral shoes, but it didn't really matter. Those shoes were nothing but memory attached to his soul. The hole barely lapped at him and Kyle recoiled immediately, clutching at himself as he scurried back up the embankment.

He remembered the feeling of pain, the memory of it. What had touched the bottom of his soul had reached inside his being and scraped away a small piece of who he was. It went much deeper than pain or death. It reached into the primal fear inside him and let him know if he ever fell into one of these, there was no way back.

The fear rose in him and he saw himself go practically translucent as he scrambled away from the edge.

23

UNABLE TO SHAKE THE MEMORY of the rednecks destroying that poor raccoon, Donna didn't realize she was driving in circles until her cell phone rang. Happy for the excuse, she pulled over and checked the number.

It wasn't even a complete number, just three digits. Some telemarketer in India or somewhere. She angrily flicked the big red button on the left side of her cell phone screen. She had more important things to deal with right now. Hell, didn't everybody?

But before she even put the phone back into her pocket it was ringing again. A little more angrily, she punched the "decline" button again. After the fourth time, though, she stopped being angry and got curious. Pulling up her web browser she saw the three-digit code wasn't India at all. It was Malaysia. Bangkok, in fact.

"Oh, shit," she muttered. "Spender! I completely forgot about him."

She stared at the phone for a full ten seconds, willing it to ring again.

"Sorry, Jack, sorry," she said, as though he could hear her.

As was customary, her phone steadfastly refused to ring now that she wanted it to. She pulled up her recent missed calls and tried to call back, but, naturally, a call to a weird three-digit non-number would not go through.

"Shit shit shit," she muttered.

Even though it was the middle of the night and she still had tons of shit to do, now this had happened. It would be weighing on her mind and she wouldn't be able to do anything else until it was taken care of. Finally, after what seemed like an eternity, the phone rang again. She answered it.

"Jack, is that you?"

"Fuck me. Where have you been? I've been ringing the phone off the hook at the office. It took me until now to dig up your cell, and then you ignore me on that, too!"

Spender sounded inordinately stressed. She hadn't heard him like that since he was alive and working on the heart attack which had taken his life. As a ghost he'd always been easy, breezy, lemon squeezy, if, admittedly, a bit of a spendthrift with what was (mostly) rightfully her money.

"Sorry, I haven't been at the office," she said.

"What? You? Since when?"

"Well, it's been—"

He cut her off. "That's great. I'm glad you're finally taking my advice and living your life. But this is an emergency and I need your help."

He certainly sounded like it.

"Anything," she said. "You know I'm here for you."

"All right. I need you to wire me eighty thousand dollars. Do you have a pen? I'm going to give you the address of a Western Union office."

She felt her gorge rising. If she'd been taking a drink at that moment she might have unironically done a Bugs Bunny-style spit take. She didn't want to scoff audibly into the phone, so she tried to swallow it.

Donna said, "I want to help you, but I don't have it."

"Fuck, I know it's not petty cash, but I know you have it. What about the condo? What about your savings? Can you borrow it?"

"Whoa, whoa, whoa. I'll do whatever I can to help you, but let's back it up a second. What do you need that kind of money for?"

"It's the going rate for a surrogate over here."

She didn't know the price for a surrogate in Bangkok off the top of her head, but she kept up with industry standards. On the rare occasions when she'd dealt with East Asia she recalled prices being around five hundred dollars, maybe a few thousand for a high-end place like Macao. Over ten thousand was extortionate for almost anything outside of taking an A-list celebrity for a weekend jaunt. She knew she could find out the truth before Jack could even gainsay her.

She grabbed a trade magazine from the back seat, went straight back to the index, and ran her finger down until she reached Thailand. Two hundred and fifty to four hundred dollars for a twenty-four-hour period. That was about what she was expecting.

"It is not," she said. "I'm looking at *Possession* right now and it's no more than four hundred. You want me to check *InFlesh*, too?"

"That's not what it is now."

She flipped over the broadsheet to check that it was the current issue. "This is this month's."

"Will you listen to me? It's not like that anymore."

The panic in his voice told her all she needed to know. Of course. She was being myopic. With the Thracian Incident, prices were probably through the roof. After what had happened to Lydia and Willie, which was surely happening elsewhere, and had no doubt been reported on by the media, surrogates would be able to charge whatever they wanted and surrogacy would be a bullish business. She briefly wondered if that meant she was about to make a fortune, but was immediately ashamed of having that thought.

"Sorry," she said. "I wasn't thinking. What do you need a surrogate for, though?"

"I need to get on a plane, now."

"I thought you were afraid to try that."

"I'm even more afraid to stay. It's getting to where you can't even walk around this city anymore without running into pockets of that red emptiness. I'm at the point where I'd possess someone without their permission if I could, but they won't let you on a plane if your paperwork's not in order."

"I know you. You wouldn't do that."

"I'm getting desperate here. I'll do anything. But I need to come home."

A nearby crash made her jump. She rolled down the window and peeked in every direction she could, but couldn't identify the source of the sound.

She was starting to worry she'd parked too long. The streets of Sherman's Forest were not exactly homey and uplifting right now. The police presence was oppressive. Steven Hager had deputized half the town to smash in the heads of the other half. And the other half were smashing windows, all because of the phenomenon, which was everywhere.

"I've got to warn you, Jack, it's not really any better here."

"Will you get up off a buck? I know it's a lot to ask, but we're talking about my existence here. I will pay you back, every dime, I swear. But I need this right now."

She closed her eyes and pinched her temples. "All right. I don't know how, but I'll get the money."

His voice suddenly took on the most panicked tone she'd ever heard from him. "Oh, fuck! It's here!"

The phone hissed, an unpleasant, shrieking sound, so loud she had to yank it away from her ear in pain. As she did so, it tumbled from her grip, falling (of course) out the window and clattering to the street. She popped her door open and fetched it to see her screen was spiderwebbed with cracks.

Damn it. She'd been meaning to get a case for her phone but, of course, never had. Hoping she wouldn't shred up her ear, she gingerly put the phone back in place. There was no dial tone, at least, which was positive.

"Jack?" she whispered, her mouth dry, her voice hoarse. There was no response. "It's okay, call me back to let me know you got somewhere safe."

She waited another few seconds. She reached down to push the red button.

"*Salam?*" a voice, clearly not Spender's, said.

"Uh, hi," she replied, "is this the operator? I think my call was dropped."

"Hey, I'm sorry, lady," the man replied in lightly accented English.

"I am not the operator. I was walking by and the pay phone was hanging. One of those things appeared here, I'm sorry to say. Your friend is gone."

"Thank you," she whispered.

As she ran her thumb across the screen, she absently forgot it had cracked and left a bloody thumbprint there. It was more than what was left of Jack Spender.

24

TOMMIE BONES' CABIN WAS AT the edge of the woods, close to where the slope started to rise and head upwards to the towering peaks of the Dragon's Backbone. A cold creek ran close by, the water crystal clear as it bubbled up straight out of the mountains.

Kyle smelled hints of sage long before he spotted Tommie sitting on the cabin porch, warm candles burning in the window as the dead mountain man rocked in his chair, staring at the darkening countryside and coughing occasionally.

Tommie had obviously been smudging for a while. Kyle could barely make out the details of his friend, but strangely, Tommie wore his death wounds, obvious in the light reflected by the candles. Trying to flash fry a turkey in gasoline had seemed like another one of his harebrained schemes until the explosion killed him in the most gruesome manner imaginable.

He stopped in mid-air when he saw the charred remnants of Tommie's lips turned down in a disapproving scowl at spotting his friend. In the candlelight, Kyle thought his eyes were burning like miniature suns.

A deep and melodious groan escaped the mountain man's lips. "Shouldn't have come up here. I've seen it out there in the deep woods, eating up everything that can't run. Gonna wash over this place soon, too, I think." Tommie took a deep mournful hit of sage, his form fuzzing like static on a TV screen. His eyes fixed onto Kyle's like searchlights. "Been talking to folks. Need you to be honest with me. They said you started all this. Is that true?"

Kyle pursed his lips, memories of Ramses and Eileen flashing through his mind. He shook his head. "I just found the first one. I didn't start anything."

Tommie stood up and Kyle involuntarily flinched. He didn't know why Tommie was choosing not to hide his grotesquerie of burns today—perhaps with the nearness of the phenomenon he simply couldn't—but the display was truly repulsive. Nevertheless, Kyle held still as Tommie stared deeply into his face through melted eyeballs.

Finally, as though coming to the solution to a math problem, Tommie smiled and clapped him on both shoulders simultaneously. "I'm fucking with you. But the hornets' nest is sure riled about this, that's for sure." He gestured over his shoulder back to the cabin. "Well, come on, let's get inside, smoke some sage, and forget the world until it comes for us."

Kyle gratefully followed his friend, ready to lose himself in sage. Having not experienced pain since his death, he didn't know if sage would make the soles of his feet feel better, but he certainly hoped so.

Both spirits smudged well into the early morning hours, telling tales of love and war, the sage vapors carried away by the late-night wind. Kyle was barely aware through his high that the breeze had stopped and silence had claimed the woods. Still, at the back of his soul, Kyle knew something was out of place. Despite the world being on the verge of madness, Kyle could feel some intrinsic danger creeping up on him and his friend.

"You really saw it?" Tommie asked suddenly, though they had avoided the subject all night.

"Yeah, I saw it. I even touched it." Kyle stared over his shoulder, that nagging feeling of something heavy descending on them both like a blanket growing more intense with each passing second.

"The world's coming to a damn end for us. End of the road."

Kyle wondered how hard Tommie was maintaining his high. He usually only sounded this depressed after a few days' worth. Kyle wanted to open up with his friend, but even with the world turned upside down he couldn't. All he could think about was maintaining his reputation.

"Come on, Bones, it isn't that bad. This shit is like solar flares or something, right? It'll pass and they'll make the TV announcements." Kyle did his best imitation of the president. "'We'll be on guard next time. We'll be better prepared. The spirits lost will always be remembered!'"

He laughed as he puffed out his chest and made mocking hand gestures but Tommie, usually so full of life for a dead man, continued to stare at him in morose despair. Even as Kyle laughed he couldn't shake the feeling of paranoia, that a monster was closing in on him.

Tommie put the sage down. "It's coming. To devour everything beautiful."

Kyle felt a chill, the memory of fear creeping into him. He saw the same fear reflected in his friend's eyes.

Suddenly, the woods behind Tommie's cabin were swallowed by a darkness so complete the forest might not have been there. It flowed through the creek beside the cabin and caused the spectral fish to try to beach themselves in the dirt to escape.

Kyle scrambled away as the phenomenon advanced, swallowing half the cabin. Tommie barely moved, cocking his head over his shoulder at the advancing hole in the world and barely reacting.

Kyle panicked, trying to keep his mind calm as red began to appear at the edge of his vision. He couldn't disappear, couldn't go back to that roadside. Not without at least making peace with Donna first.

"Bones! Run! Come on!"

The hole inched closer and Tommie looked at him with that sorrowful half-grin of burned flesh and exposed teeth. "No can do on this one. Ruckus raising is over for me. Don't feel like running if I can't come back."

He took a puff of the sage and sighed deeply, reveling in the pleasure. He fixed Kyle with one last gaze. "It doesn't really matter in the end. There are no safe places left." The hole was at the edge of his chair. "Maybe I'll see you soon."

The ghost of the mountain man rocked back in his chair.

Kyle screamed, "Bones!"

The chair rocked forward again, empty this time.

25

IT WAS THE MIDDLE OF the night as Donna drove through Sherman's Forest and the town was acting . . . strangely. Ghosttown was empty of the usual revelers indulging in sage at this time of night. Meanwhile the streets were thick with the living.

Sheriff Hager had his hands more than full keeping the peace. Donna saw more than a few shiny badges, indicating Steven had gone on a veritable spree of deputizing. But if it kept the looters from emptying her agency's register and the rioters from smashing her windows, she could accept it.

The strangest thing of all, though, revealed itself as she passed the community rec center. There was a line out the door, all living people like her. She was eager to get to Jackson Manor, but her curiosity was piqued. She rolled down her window and whistled sharply.

A kid at the back of the line turned to look at her. His face was weirdly familiar, and by his shocked expression, he obviously recognized her, too. Maybe he'd been a client once? Well, not important. It would come to her.

"Hey, what's going on?"

The kid looked embarrassed, but realizing she didn't recognize him, answered tentatively.

"It's an Amediums Anonymous meeting," he said.

Hearing his voice, she realized who he was: Colin, the Unenlightened kid from the clinic earlier. Colin flipped his collar up to cover his face and hurried off in the opposite direction, abandoning his spot in the line as though he hadn't been waiting to get in. What would he be doing trying to get into an AA meeting, though? For that matter, what were all these people doing here?

Like a congenital heart defect or deafness, something like one in a thousand children was born without ghostsense. And, like being blinded by cataracts or losing your hearing in an explosion, severe trauma could cause some people to lose it in adulthood as well. Donna wasn't sure of the exact numbers. It had never been something she'd studied closely. She'd donated to amediumship charities on occasion, of course, but it was no closer to her heart than any other cause.

Which meant there was a line out the door to a support group for a disability that made up a tiny percentage of the population. Shaking her head at the strangeness of it all, Donna was about to pull the car out of park when an older lady emerged from the main entrance of the community center.

The woman wore thick sunglasses and carried a white cane, sure signs she was blind. Over her heart she wore an overlarge white button depicting a spectral character with a red circle around it and a slash through it. Just as the white cane signaled her lack of vision to the world, this badge was her wearing her amediumship on her sleeve. Likely in her case the two conditions were connected. Severe nerve or brain damage could cause either or both.

"Can I have your attention, please?" the lady called out in a commanding voice.

The people in the line, who were chattering in excitement, fell compliantly silent.

"Thank you," the woman said after a moment, shifting her cane to the other hand. "I want to say a few things. Everyone is, of course, welcome at our meeting. We are open to the public. But this is a support group for the disabled. We are not kooks. We do not believe the earth is flat any more than we believe there is no such thing as ghosts. If you are looking for a place to discuss conspiracy theories, please do so in your own homes. Or another public place. But the room is reserved for those with concerns about genuine amediumship."

People in the crowd started to slink away in shame, realizing they'd been acting like children. The show now seemingly over,

Donna prepared to head out herself.

"Bullshit!"

The crowd, almost as one, turned to look at a long-haired man who came bursting up the rec center steps. He was nearly at the front of the line, which meant he had probably come down here much earlier. Donna swallowed a gasp in her throat as she was afraid for a moment the man was going to hit the blind woman. But he stopped a few steps from the top.

"I'm sorry, sir, but—" the AA group facilitator (or whatever she was) started to say.

"You can stuff your sorries up your ass, lady. You knew. You people knew! You knew the dead were going to disappear and you didn't do anything to stop it! Do you know how many families will be ripped apart, how many lovers separated because of your arrogance?"

The blind woman was shaking her head, her mouth working as if dumbfounded by the big man's ignorance.

"We don't . . . we're not—"

"Why don't you leave her alone, Jimmy?" one of what was presumably the long-haired man's friends asked. "They don't know anything. They don't have ghostsense."

The orderly line had turned into a mewling crowd and Donna could not spot the next person who spoke.

"That's bullshit about them believing in ghosts," someone in the thick mass of people piped up. "I've read dozens of their websites asserting the ghosts were always a hoax."

"How could that even be true?" someone else asked.

"Ghosts could be a mass delusion," the unseen speaker was quick to reply, based on his literal minutes of research online, "or worse, a government plot."

"Sir, madam," the blind woman said, holding up her free hand to call for some semblance of sanity and order. "Please, those sorts of fringe views represent a very tiny segment of people suffering from a very real disorder."

The crowd looked like it was about to tear itself apart. Steven Hager, looking so haggard he might as well have been drawn on the scene with a pencil, was starting to drift away from Ghosttown and toward the near-riot at the rec center. Realizing she had more than overstayed her welcome, Donna put the SUV in gear and headed onward to her original destination.

Donna slowed the SUV to a crawl. As much as she had gotten used to the lack of ghostsense from her vacation at the Jackson house, she still knew it could be dangerous passing into a pocket of the nothing. She didn't want to go swerving off the road from being disoriented.

She inched the SUV slowly toward the edge of the effect. Sniffing the air, she could sort of smell the border between the regular, paranormal world and the strange, empty redness which had so recently sprung into non-existence. Before crossing that line, though, she glanced around.

There was a sort of a demilitarized zone here. The supernal animals did not even approach. She was reminded of Tommie Bones' reaction when he first brought her up here, and his weird fit that prevented him from approaching the manor. Now she was much farther out and the last specter she'd seen was a chalk outline stag darting across the road about a mile back.

She reached into the back seat and pulled forward a brown paper grocery bag full of cheap, dollar store amethysts. Unlike Leroy, she'd never had any formal exorcism training outside of required Paranormal Studies classes in high school, but she knew amethyst was the preferred crystal for amplifying ghostly energy. She gritted her teeth. This felt like an utterly hopeless task.

She turned back until she spotted a lone ghostly squirrel chittering up in a tree. As though she were tossing nuts to a live animal, she dropped an amethyst. The squirrel's ears rose and it continued chittering. She turned the SUV back toward the Jackson place and slowly let the machine crawl forward. The squirrel eventually floated down toward the crystal she'd left. She dropped another then pulled forward again.

Tentatively, the squirrel followed along as she dropped crystals like breadcrumbs. It seemed reluctant, as though sensing she had ulterior motives, but not willing to ignore the crystals and their healthy ectoplasm amplifying effects.

"Come on, little friend," she whispered, "if it can push out, maybe we can push back."

The ghostly squirrel followed her for the better part of half a mile, but at that point, even the crystals could not force it to take another step. It seemed torn, but, after a hard-fought internal battle, it turned and darted back to nominal safety.

Donna took careful measure of the area. She didn't sense any difference. True, a squirrel was a tiny splotch of ghostly energy, but it was energy nonetheless. The redneck assholes at her home were sacrificing animals to the phenomenon. She didn't know if that would have an effect or not, but she was hoping there might be a different solution.

Perhaps the ghosts could band together and, instead of being overtaken by the effect, they might use all of their combined energy to push it back. Maybe all the ghosts in the world could push it all the way back. But so far she saw nothing to support her hypothesis.

"Okay," she muttered. "Let's try something else."

She took the SUV on a lazy circuit around the perimeter of the phenomenon, dropping crystals as she went. If the amethysts really amplified ghostly energy, maybe they could set up a network of dikes, like the seawater ones in Holland, and hold the phenomenon back. Maybe fixing the problem in Sherman's Forest, where it had all started, would have a multiplicative effect on the rest of the world. They could avoid future Thracian incidents.

When she'd laid out her first "dike" she stopped the vehicle again to gauge any changes. She didn't feel anything terribly different. Maybe the wind was different. She closed her eyes and tried to reach out with her sixth sense, but all she could really feel was the cold absence of any spectral beings on the Jackson Manor grounds or in the demilitarized zone surrounding it.

Her ghostsense was terribly unrefined. It wasn't something she normally thought about at all. It was funny that she dealt every day with specters, but never really worked on developing her mediumship abilities. She should've asked for Leroy's help, maybe, but she was sick of always leaning on him all the time.

Crawling along at ten miles per hour she crossed the threshold of the phenomenon and slowly approached the house. The first time she had come here, the place was a strange but pleasant little Air B&B to her. She'd had no idea of the utter banality which made the place so unusual and, frankly, terrifying. Now she was coming here for about the exact opposite of a vacation, if such a thing existed, and the entire premises was like a sponge, thick with all of her anxiety and worry.

The structure loomed over her imagination like all her failures: her childlessness, her reprobate brother, her business failing, all of it. It was a lone, silent testament to that which could be without the warm embrace of death to look forward to. It was like an empty, nihilistic tomb. A strange, esoteric monument, Crucian, almost, in philosophy. A way of remembering the dead with whom you could no longer interact.

She shut off the headlights and breathed deeply, trying to calm the throbbing in her head. She could feel every heartbeat in her left ear. There were only a few hours of darkness left in which to work, so she forced herself to calm down.

Reaching into the grocery sack, she pulled out a small, handheld fan. She sniffed at the air, but didn't smell any sage on it. Nevertheless, she turned on the fan and stepped out of the car, trying to blow away any smoke that might have inadvertently been smudging the area. This all felt hopeless and, perhaps worse, pointless.

No lights were on in the house but there were still some ambient sources: alarm clocks with lighted numbers, a blinking "Ready" light on an appliance here or there, and so forth. Donna blew a puff of air between her teeth. She picked up the false rock on the ground where the owners had left the key for her last time. She slipped it out and, before entering the house, patted the doorjamb thoroughly, searching for perhaps a set of wind chimes.

There were, of course, none to be found so she stepped into the yawning chasm. The place was empty in the purest, most deliberate sense. Not a sound could be heard, and so far she had found not the slightest reason why a ghost would avoid this place. Nor had she found any way to make it more hospitable to the spectral kind, not with amethysts or anything else.

This whole exercise was in vain. Did she really think that an ill-placed pile of salt somewhere in Jackson Manor caused Istanbul to disappear? Well, slow and deliberate had always served her before, so she'd continue, obstinately perhaps, on her course. Even knowing it was in vain, she flipped the switches in the fuse box. The last of the ambient light disappeared.

She crouched down and clutched her head in her hands.

"Hello?" she cried out.

She was greeted with nothing more than the echoes of her own words forming a chorus of "hellos" back at her.

"Please?" she asked with a whisper.

The place was an existential nightmare. It was empty beyond empty. It was the start of a brand new and unfathomable life where death was the end and not a new beginning. What did that mean? Only your actions on Earth counted? Did even they? Would parents have to start paying attention to their children, not abandoning their lives to hedonism? Would mad cults like the Crucians hold sway, promising futures that could never be delivered or even confirmed?

"Please, somebody be here," she whispered, a warm tear sliding down her face.

A hand came down on her shoulder.

26

KYLE DRIFTED BACK TOWARD TOWN, Tommie's melting face silhouetted against that yawning maw as present as if he were still looking at it. He was beginning to get used to the red rings around his vision. The threat of regression became so constant in recent days it no longer frightened him. The world had flipped upside down the past few days. The immutable truths of the world became desperate hopes. The thought of a blissful nothing wrapping him up in endless sleep comforted him, even though he had no idea if that was what waited for him on the other side.

Kyle stuck to the scrublands and prairie that separated the forested mountains from the town. He wasn't sure he cared anymore if he was spotted by some car or ghostly hitchhiker. Everybody already thought the worst of him, and with more holes appearing and shifting by the hour, people would be looking for someone to blame. Kyle wasn't exactly sure he didn't blame himself.

He didn't know where to go. He had burned his bridge with Donna. Their worse than awkward ride back from threatening Buster Beats with a gun made that fact abundantly clear.

Despair became his constant companion. One shitty thing about being a ghost was negative emotions lingering while happy ones barely made an impression.

Maybe Tommie Bones had the right idea letting himself be swallowed up by the phenomenon. If the whole damn world was going pear-shaped, and it was going to happen sooner rather than later anyway, then maybe it was better to go out on his own terms.

He thought about Eileen, wondering if he should visit her again. Getting in would be hard. Her overprotective grandmother would see to that. He couldn't blame her, really. His reputation was bleak and Eileen saw Ramses vanish, never to return. Kyle could see how some people couldn't handle a reality like that.

One where the end of life was the final end.

Kyle drifted into a shitty neighborhood on Gateway Lane. Most of the shops were closed down long ago, the never-ending jungle of capitalism devouring them and making way for newer shops and franchises farther south.

Only living bums and ghosts with no places to go occupied this part of town anymore. Kyle hated to do it, but he knew he could lie low in a rat's nest somewhere on Gateway Lane.

He shook his hands. It wasn't a permanent solution, of course. He didn't think there were permanent solutions anymore.

His thoughts were interrupted by a steadily ringing bell. He looked up from the pavement and found a man standing on the street, a large brass bell in his hand and a cardboard sign proclaiming, "Repent Before the Judgment".

A Crucian. It was bizarre to see one in real life, like spotting a polar bear ambling down a city street. Any thoughts of trying to avoid the man were stymied when he looked straight at Kyle, giving him a welcoming smile and gesturing him forward. Kyle hesitated a moment. If the man hadn't parked directly in front of an alleyway that Kyle knew for a fact contained some places to squat, he would have turned around and walked the other way.

Instead, he sighed to himself and shuffled forward.

The Crucian spoke up as Kyle got within arm's reach, eyes shifting to make sure this wasn't some kind of guerilla worship service.

"Hello, may I—"

Kyle held up a hand and immediately tried to pass through the man, rude though that might have been. He was way past worrying about manners. "Heard it all before, buddy. Not interested in whatever you're peddling."

The man smiled warmly and held out a handful of sage brush. "I was just offering a gift."

Once again, Kyle glanced around, wondering if he was the victim of some sick joke. Warily, he took the sage with a muttered,

"Thanks."

"Don't mention it," the man replied. He spoke with a twang identifying him as a pilgrim from the south, one of the Carolinas maybe. He looked Kyle up and down. "I don't usually ask this of souls but would you like to talk? Sit a spell maybe?"

Kyle immediately wanted to run, get away from the man. He'd always been raised to believe religion was for kooks and degenerates. But then the thought of the holes chewing away at the world came back to his mind, eliciting a weary chuckle from him.

Hell, without Tommie, Eileen, or Donna, what did he have to lose? A little religion couldn't hurt at this point. Kyle found himself nodding and easing himself to the ground as the street preacher mimicked the motion. The man wiped a huge bead of sweat from his forehead and he stared up into the night.

"Lovely evening," the man said. "I hope a few more out there will take the time to enjoy it."

Kyle placed the sage on the ground next to him and stared suspiciously. "Okay, man, what's your angle? When's the hellfire, brimstone, and judgment going to come?"

The man chuckled wearily. "You're a wary soul, Mr. Fitzpatrick. I don't blame you, but you've got me all wrong. I only spread the Good News to those who want to hear it." He gave Kyle a knowing smile. "And I don't think you want to hear it."

Kyle looked away sheepishly before that innate suspicion crept back into him. "How'd you know my name?"

"Yeah, that was rude to use yours without giving mine." The man offered his hand. "Floyd Alan."

Kyle didn't take it and Floyd withdrew it after an awkward pause. The world-weary warmth was gone, replaced by a man who'd been on the frontlines for too long and seen their efforts to change the world blow away like a puff of smoke.

"How'd you know my name?" Kyle repeated.

"You're the most famous ghost in town, if not the world. I've heard the talk about you and the house where this started. The things they say."

Floyd clucked his tongue like a disapproving great-grandmother. Kyle felt on edge, ready to run if this man tried to trap him. He was still terrified to disapparate, but he was still considering it. He might have been alone, might have been thinking of ending it, but he was going to go on his terms, not anybody else's.

"What do you want from me?"

"Nothing. I thought you could use the sage. It's getting pretty rough out there. People like me have been preparing for Judgment Day all our lives. Now it's here and, well, it's your kind being judged, not mine." Kyle immediately opened his mouth to tell the man off, but Floyd held up a hand. "No need to argue. It's personal belief, not fact. Everybody has to believe in something, right?"

Floyd sighed and Kyle briefly wondered if the man was having some kind of crisis of faith.

"I never thought I believed in anything, except my own awesomeness," Kyle admitted, "but then I was never faced with the unknown before."

"I know it sounds like my beliefs are ridiculous but I do believe a man came back from the dead in the flesh. A lot of people focus on how weird that sounds, but He had a lot of good things to say."

Kyle stood up, gritting his teeth and trying not to laugh in the poor man's face. He knew a con job when he heard one.

"You could have put more effort into it, Floyd. See you around."

He was about to turn and leave when the street preacher's words hit him. "Where are you going to run to now? Back to your sister? Or to a friend? It's all going to be swallowed up before too long. Sure you may make it, might even make it to the very end, the last ghost in all the world."

Kyle turned and gave a devil's grin, shaking in his thoughts but maintaining his image. "I like the sound of that, actually. Kyle Fitzpatrick: The Last Ghost. Good ending for a guy like me."

Floyd stared at him, long and hard. Silence remained between the two of them and, though he stared back defiantly, Kyle would have rather looked at the inside of a cell or into the maw of one of the holes rather than Floyd Alan's gaze.

"Bullshit," Floyd said simply.

"What?" Kyle managed to mutter, momentarily at a loss.

"Bullshit," Floyd repeated again. "You put on a good front, but that's all it is. You're terrified of whatever's on the other side, be it God or nothing or something else we can't even conceive of. You're afraid to go it alone."

Kyle wanted to protest, wanted to tell him to stick his middle finger up his ass and spin, but in the end bitterly whispered, "No one is going to care if a hole swallows me."

"Then what are you waiting for?"

Kyle grinned wickedly and thought about possessing the schmuck. See how high and mighty he was when he was the one facing oblivion. But as soon as he thought it, he disregarded the idea, feeling shame. Willie Chang's visage came to his mind. He wasn't like that, even facing the end.

"I figured you'd at least say you'd miss me. Or your imaginary god would. Or something."

Floyd grunted as he reached down to pick up his discarded sign. He then looked off toward the mountains. "My outlook on the world is different from yours. It has to be. I'm still alive. My parents are still alive too, if you can believe it."

Kyle balked. "What? They'd have to be ancient. In like their sixties or something."

"Crucians live that long sometimes. But everyone has a limit, of course. They were considering overdosing on their meds to start their eternal existence. That was before all of this, of course. Now they're quaking with fear of what's coming and wishing they'd actually gotten out and done something with their lives. It's a hell of a thing, finding out we've only got one life. You know, I don't have any siblings. When they're gone, I'll be the only one who misses them."

The missionary began to walk down the street and Kyle was happy to let him go. Floyd called back over his shoulder, "In the end, it's the living that are going to remember the dead. If I were you, I'd make peace with those who'll remember you fondly."

Then he was gone and Kyle was left alone on the street, his rat's nest and a few more days of safety waiting. The dark alley was inviting, seeming to whisper into Kyle's ear, *Come on in, stay for a spell, let me take away all the things you don't want to face.*

Instead, Kyle looked away and began walking down the street. He had to find Donna. Had to make amends. Had to be responsible for once in his misbegotten existence.

A ghost came sprinting down the street, looking over his shoulder as he ran, practically barreling into Kyle, who braced himself and caught the guy. "Whoa, man!"

The ghost an elderly man dressed in rags, a homeless guy, and by the looks of things, his spirit had remained itinerant in death.

"Please don't. Please don't." The ghost's voice came out as a musty groan, like an old rocking chair that could no longer support any weight.

"Easy, old timer, easy. I'm not going to hurt you." Kyle looked up and down the street, wondering what had frightened the old ghost this much, a sinking feeling in his gut whispering the most likely option. "Is the phenomenon headed this way?"

Somehow, the truth was even worse.

"No. I mean, not exactly. It's our own kind. The rich ones are rounding up sods like us and . . . sticking us in the holes." The old man's form flickered and Kyle reached out with a steadying hand. If he relapsed now there was no telling where he would end up. The man's babbling never ceased. "It shrinks them, for a while. These yokels were throwing squirrels and shit in, then one of them got too close when it expanded . . . like the fucking hole was full or something."

Kyle looked around, his momentary feeling of peace and purpose extinguished. Phantom images of ghostly mobs coming around the corner to feed one another to the holes came to his mind and frightened him.

"Okay, listen. Listen!" Kyle practically had to shout to get the old spirit's attention. "Down the street, maybe a quarter mile, there is an alleyway. I think I remember there being cots and some essentials to lay low. Use it while you can. And . . . take this."

He handed the old timer the sprig of sage Floyd had given him. He wasn't sure he was swearing off the stuff permanently, but it seemed like a good idea to stay sober, at least through the crisis. The ghost looked at him with wide eyes, small lice spirits scooting through the tangles of his unkempt hair and beard. For a moment, Kyle was sure the man would break down in a fit of gratitude, phantom tears filling his eyes. Then he remembered this was the real fucking world, and no good deed goes unpunished.

"You're that Kyle Fitzgerald from the news, aren't you? They want you the most."

The old man licked his chops. Kyle shut his lips tight, already knowing the old ghost was sure of his guess.

He rushed off, checking over his shoulder every two seconds.

27

"YOU'RE REAL."

Donna nearly jumped out of her skin from the touch of the other woman's palm on her shoulder. Her voice, by contrast, was gentle and soothing, almost heartbreakingly so. "Are you going to kill me?" Donna whispered, her throat parched.

The woman snatched her hand away. Donna turned slowly and was surprised at how young she was, barely in her teens.

The teenager had an embarrassed look on her face. No, she wasn't going to kill Donna. Or mug her, either. Donna could immediately tell she was a gentle soul. Too many years as an agent had given her a razor-quick capacity to gauge a person's trustworthiness, and she instantly, if perhaps a bit foolhardily, didn't think the girl was a threat.

"I'm sorry," the girl said. "I didn't mean to startle you. You surprised me. I wasn't expecting to find anyone here."

"Me either," Donna agreed. "The ghosts have all . . . well, you know. And nobody living can approach this place without getting hit by a wave of nausea."

The girl's eyes were wide and shining.

"There are ghosts here?" the girl asked, her voice dropping almost to a whisper.

"Well, not anymore, obviously," Donna said, nervously patting her hips and taking a few steps around the room.

"Obviously why?" the girl asked, sounding heartbroken.

Donna furrowed her brow and looked the girl up and down. "The . . . event," she said. "The phenomenon. The Thracian thing. Except it didn't really start in Istanbul. It really started here. Or, I mean, maybe that's self-centered of me to think I was the first person to discover it. Obviously it could have started somewhere else first. Antarctica, for all I know, but . . ."

Donna let her words slow to a trickle like that from a broken faucet. The little girl's eyes were wet with unshed tears.

"What's, ah . . . what's your name, honey?"

"Bonnie," the little girl responded, wiping her face with her fist as though she had an itch, but really wiping the snot leaking from her nose. It was a child's gesture.

Donna's heart sank into her gut. "Bonnie Jackson?"

The little girl's eyes twinkled, an edge of long-unused mischievousness showing itself. "How do you know that?"

"Well, this is your house, isn't it?"

Bonnie walked over to a table supporting a desk lamp. She placed her hands, palm down, on the table, as though it were the only thing in the world holding her up.

"Well, it used to be. My family sold the house years ago. My dad, when he could be bothered to talk to me, told me it had bad bones. But I think we all knew about the . . . what did you call it? Phenomenon?"

Donna was glad she hadn't used the more common term. Who wanted to find out their family was a namesake for some kind of existential disease?

"Yeah," Bonnie said. "I guess we all knew about the phenomenon. We never talked about it, of course. Everybody kept pretending my Gee-Ga was off gallivanting around somewhere. Fucking liars, pardon my French."

"It's all right," Donna said, feeling like it wasn't her place. Sure, maybe she was nominally the adult, but this was the girl who had really discovered the phenomenon. And they were in her house. Donna didn't begrudge her a single dirty word in the dictionary.

Bonnie jumped up and sat on the table. She was so tiny, her legs dangled off it. Donna couldn't help but think if she was the one to sit there, it would have collapsed under her weight. But there sat Bonnie Jackson, her legs kicking like she was on the side of a swimming pool.

"So who are you?" Bonnie asked.

"My name's Donna Fitzpatrick."

Bonnie perked up a little at that. "Well, now I know why you're here. Blood is thicker than water, they sometimes say. I guess we're both dealing with family curses."

Donna sighed, wanting to protest that her brother was not a curse, but the words sounded hollow even before they came out.

"Yeah, I guess so," she agreed.

"So what have you figured out so far?" Bonnie asked.

Donna shrugged and launched into a recounting of the past few weeks of her life. She was shocked at how easily it slid out of her, diarrhea of the mouth to stand in stark contrast to her usual digestive sufferings.

Bonnie nodded along with the story for the most part, offering only the occasional interjection. She sounded less like a child trying to feign knowledge of matters beyond her ken and more like a fellow traveler, a scientist who'd already conducted all the same experiments and come to the same conclusions.

By the time Donna was finished, she understood Bonnie had been pondering these matters for years, while she herself was a rank amateur.

"I guess you know all of this already," Donna said.

"Well, I didn't know Ghost-Away was fake. I liked that part, even if you seemed embarrassed about it."

"Well, yeah."

Bonnie took a long, deep breath, like someone three times her age might. "Yeah, I wasn't willing to give up on my Gee-Ga. Sorry, my great-grandmother. But it seemed like I was the only one who wasn't. I've been over this house with a fine-tooth comb. And I must've read every book in the library on metaphysics, quantum theory, and parapsychology. Twice."

Donna chuckled. "Well, you're doing better than me, then. I don't even know what most of those words mean."

Bonnie narrowed her eyes. That was more like the gesture of a teenage girl. "Don't patronize me."

Donna put on a serious expression. "I'm not. I mean, I won't anymore. I really want to know . . . what do you think is causing all of this?"

Bonnie sighed like someone about to launch into a story she was ridiculed for telling a dozen times before. "You've heard of multiverse theory?"

"Sure," Donna said.

"That's good. No need to waste everybody's time explaining it, then. So picture one of many possible worlds, except in this one ghosts don't exist."

"Don't exist period?" Donna asked.

Bonnie said, "Actually, could we turn the lights back on? Maybe it's easier to show you."

Nodding, Donna picked her way to the fuse box and restored power to the place. When she returned to the foyer, Bonnie was tentatively picking up a poker from the fireplace. Donna raised her eyebrow but the teenager waved off her concerns. Aside from the scuffs of their feet, the floor, like the desk, was covered with dust. Bonnie drew two interlocking circles in the dust.

"A Venn diagram?" Donna asked.

Bonnie nodded. "All right," she said, pointing at the right circle, "so this is our world."

"And this is the one without ghosts?" Donna guessed, pointing at the left.

Bonnie continued without pausing. "And this is the house we're standing in," she said, pointing at the intersection.

"The perfectly fine house," Donna agreed.

"Perhaps. But perhaps in No Ghost World it's haunted. Like, dreadfully haunted, positively thick with restless spirits. So if the house represents a borderland, something that exists in both dimensions, then that might explain our problem. When our ghostly world peeks through into theirs, they see ghosts who, to their logic, don't exist."

"And by contrast," Donna said, "we're seeing their nothing when we should be seeing our dearly departed friends."

Bonnie shrugged. It sounded ludicrous, sure, but it was closer to a working theory than anything Donna had gotten from the media or anywhere else.

Donna said, "So all we have to do is . . . what, burn down the house?"

"I don't think the physical structure of the house has anything to do with it."

"Right," Donna agreed, getting excited again, "but we could plug the hole or close the door or whatever you call it. In all your research, did you find anything? Is there a way?"

"There is," Bonnie said.

Donna couldn't contain herself. She rushed up to her new young friend and grabbed her shoulders. "Well, let's do it! What is there, a formula? What do we need, exorcists? Crystals?"

Bonnie looked far too somber to actually have a solution. "Actually," she said quietly, "I already did it. About three years ago."

Donna shook her head. "But that doesn't make any sense. You must've done something wrong. Left the ritual incomplete."

"The reason I came by here tonight was to double check. That's it, right there. The epicenter of the phenomenon."

The girl pointed at what looked like a perfectly ordinary spot on the wall. There was nothing special about it. No discoloration. No gaping portal to a confusing alternate reality. Not even a speck of mold to make it stand out. Just a spot on the wall.

Donna walked over and scratched at the paint. "Here?"

"About three inches to the left, but, yes, right about there."

"You're telling me something no bigger than ... what, my thumb ... caused all this devastation?"

"Actually, it was no bigger than a pinprick when I first found it. I figure when it took my great-grandmother it was microscopic. And now it's ... well, bigger than the city of Istanbul, at least, I guess."

Donna grunted. "Take a penny and double it every day for a month. How much do you have?"

"I dunno. A couple bucks?" Bonnie said.

"Over five million. We let it go. We let it go and let it go until it got completely out of hand. But you said it's not here anymore?"

"Nope. The hole is plugged. The door is shut. The bridge is out. Our worlds are separate again."

"I don't understand."

"Imagine you take an ice cube," Bonnie said, "and you drop it into a glass of water. They're both the same, basically. H_2O. The same structure, following different laws. The ice will make the water cool for a while but after a time, the water will melt the ice."

"Okay," Donna said, "I think I understand. The other universe has different physical laws. Laws that preclude the existence of ghosts. Once our universe is exposed to them it has to ... adjust itself to account for them. But our laws will reassert themselves. It's a waiting game. We have to wait for the ice cube to melt."

A sad look crossed Bonnie's face. "No. The universe is going to keep adjusting until there are no ghosts. We're the ice cube."

Donna covered her mouth and muffled a scream. She hoped it was pent-up tension, but judging by the look on Bonnie's face, it may have been the terror of coming to grips with a horror the teenager had accepted years ago. She assumed the disaster would result in some shuffling around, some ghosts lost, maybe some areas where they couldn't go anymore. But the extinction of all spirits? It was too horrible to imagine.

Donna said, "We can stop it, though, right? Can't we change . . . the laws of physics?"

"I don't think so. The Crucians and some other weird sects believe in a being with that power. But if He exists then He wants this. Wants our world like this."

"Perfectly normal," Donna spat. "What do we do now?"

"Me? I'm going to go home, to my new home, Dad's apartment, I mean, and study. I have a test in the morning. Life goes on, you know, even if death doesn't."

"That's a very mature attitude, I guess. I don't know how I'm supposed to go on as though the world weren't ending."

Bonnie scratched behind her ear. "Well, there's one thing that eats away at me. Every day. And that's not getting to tell my Gee-Ga how I felt about her before she disappeared. You know that falling out you had with your brother?"

"Yeah."

"Go make it right while you still can. Maybe we can't stop the world from ending, but we can make things right with our loved ones before it does."

The girl with the wisdom of an elder was right. There was no stopping the phenomenon. It was as inexorable as the tides now. And soon it would sweep Kyle away. She hurried off to find him before it was too late.

28

KYLE RETURNED TO DONNA'S HOUSING complex but hadn't found any trace of her. There was something melancholic about the place at this time of night. The new buildings were bathed in shadows from a broken streetlight nearby, and most of the interior lights were snuffed out.

He'd tried to call her, but all he got was an automated message, as though her phone were damaged or something. He couldn't think of where else Donna could be. He'd already checked her office but the overrated dating service was empty.

Where did Leroy live? Or work? Kyle suddenly wished he'd paid better attention when Joe Exorcist was giving his big spiel.

He let himself into her townhouse again and scoured the whole place. Even that annoying Palladino chick wasn't there to tell him where Donna had gone.

She wasn't here and, in all likelihood, he wasn't going to be able to find her anytime soon.

He supposed he could look Leroy up, or his business anyway. If they were at the exorcist's house he had about as much chance of finding them as he did piecing his body back together.

Walking the grim sidewalks, he stopped only once, when he spotted a person still awake inside. The man looked at him quizzically through the window, and Kyle lost all his nerve, hurrying on and hoping he hadn't been recognized.

"Kyle? Kyle Fitzpatrick?"

He tensed, trying to keep calm. No use panicking and apparating himself straight into a hole's yawning mouth. Maybe he could talk himself out of this.

The lady was standing in the parking lot, two bags of groceries in her hands. In other words: still alive. He recognized her. Angela Abbott, the neighbor woman who'd been in Donna's place a few scant days ago. It might as well have been a century.

"Angela, right? I'm sorry if I don't have a lot of time to talk right now but have you seen—"

The woman walked straight toward him, quick enough Kyle was worried she would pass right through him. Her groceries tumbled to the ground, eggs splattering against the cement and fruit bouncing down the sidewalk and rolling toward the street.

"Oh my. Oh dear." The woman placed her hands on Kyle's chest. "All the spirits are gone from this place. I haven't—"

He groaned lightly, coughing in his throat to let the crazy woman know he was distinctly uncomfortable with her hands wandering across his chest.

Angela seemed to come back to herself. The older woman blushed in embarrassment and stepped away.

"Not going to at least buy me dinner first?"

"Sorry," she muttered

Kyle could see she wasn't mad, more thankful than anything.

"Mind if I ask why you were copping a feel?" Kyle tried to keep his question as chipper as possible. He didn't want Angela to see how much her reaction had bothered him.

"It was an . . . an . . ." the medium seemed to be searching for the right words, "extreme reaction. It's . . . well, you're the first ghost I've seen in ages."

Kyle looked around, expecting to be able to point out a dead rat, flies, maybe even a bird that had come sweeping through from the outside of the condominium.

There was nothing.

"That's . . . ominous," Kyle said.

"I've been feeling sick lately. There are certain spots around here, out of the way places you see, like down by my trashcan or in the laundry room where I can't feel anything. It makes me worry. If ghosts leave this town, what good is a medium?"

What she was describing made Kyle's guts twist in fear. He knew quite well what was hiding in the trash and laundry room. Other ghosts were fleeing the area or swallowed up already. Or maybe . . . taken? If things kept going the way they were, he was going to go the way of the dodo. Of course there might not be any dodos left anymore, either. A hole could have taken them as easily as they'd taken the spirits in Sherman's Forest.

Angela started gathering her spilled groceries up. The eggs were ruined.

"Do you need any help with that?"

She was a scant shell now, the eccentricities and nervous tics Kyle noticed on their first meeting having dulled entirely. Angela looked up at him.

"Thanks for the offer, but I'm fine. I shouldn't have gotten so excited. Those were going to be breakfast."

Kyle watched as the medium reluctantly picked everything else up, discarding the eggs. Kyle scratched the back of his neck.

"Do you know where Donna went?"

"Sorry, I haven't seen her in a while. But I can tell you you're not the first one to come around asking about her. They were people I didn't recognize. Expensive clothes, though."

Kyle's thoughts shifted to Eileen's family in their gigantic house. Some of them were still living.

"What did you tell them?"

"The truth! That I haven't seen her." She gave Kyle a conspiratorial wink. "But maybe . . . just maybe . . . I did get a good read on her aura before she left. Before it stopped."

Kyle wasn't following for a moment. A good medium should have been able to follow a friend's aura like a hunter tracking a deer. Some mediums, the kind that got on TV, could even do it with strangers. Angela was weird, and chattered like a spectral mockingbird, but she seemed to be legit otherwise. How was it she could feel nothing unless . . .

Kyle asked, "She's inside of one of those holes right now, isn't she?"

Angela shrugged, a motion clearer than a nod in this case. "You know your sister better than I."

Kyle did know Donna. Better than he liked, in some ways. He thought about what she would have done with the situation presented to her. Donna's dogged determination to find answers.

"She's at that horrible house," he said.

Angela shrugged, though Kyle thought he could see the barest hint of a smile on her face. It was hard to say if she knew where Donna was all along and enjoyed playing with him or was glad she was able to help him figure it out.

"Best be heading that way, then," he said.

He couldn't get near the house, but he could go that way and see if he could see Donna's car. Maybe call out to her. Or meet her on her way back into town. It seemed like a long shot, but worth a try. When he turned to bid the strange medium goodbye, Kyle could see the tears in her eyes.

"What's the matter?" he asked, unable to hide the genuine concern in his voice.

"I hope that whatever happens, this all ends soon. I don't know if I could keep going in a perfectly normal world."

Kyle nodded, any words to reassure her it wouldn't come to that feeling like sweet lies in his mind.

The house was south of here and he would have to pick his way carefully to avoid the hole's widening maw.

He must've come a mile south through a complete wasteland, devoid of anything spectral, before he encountered his first fellow spirit. The ghost barely looked up, but when he did his eyes widened.

It had been a while since Kyle felt true dread. Drifting through the afterlife on smart-ass wit and a general sense of carelessness left him pretty much immune to such feelings. Seeing the recognition on the spirit's face gave him the feeling of his stomach dropping.

"Hey . . . hey! You're Kyle Fitzpatrick!"

Kyle shook his head and even though he felt stupid doing it, he tried to change his voice.

"No, no, you've got me confused with someone else. That dirty reprobate has—"

"Spare me the bullshit. Roderick Ellington is offering a mint for you."

Kyle briefly considered disapparating, but still couldn't bring himself to do it. Instead, he immediately took off, floating as fast as he could toward the woods.

Behind him, he heard the echoing calls.

"He's over here! It's him!"

29

CEMETERIES, OF ALL THINGS, WERE on Donna's mind. The places were neither fish nor fowl. Wealthy ghosts might pay to have a monument erected to their earthly body, but then hardly ever visit it. And the living had no need of such reminders that rich people could find stupid ways to waste anything, even land. Donna wondered briefly if cemeteries might make a resurgence when the phenomenon consumed everything. Would people care to "visit" their dead relatives?

Mostly, though, she was thinking about them because Ghosttown was about as abandoned as a cemetery.

The phenomenon hadn't passed through here, or if it had, it had done so in patches. A few spectral rats and bugs proved it hadn't consumed the whole neighborhood. So where was everyone?

She passed by the community center again as well. Now that it was nearly dawn, the crowd had dissipated. A handful of people were gathered around a trashcan fire, listening to Jimmy, the long-haired ghost denier she saw earlier, pontificating about something stupid, no doubt.

She shook her head and drove on. As she approached her neighborhood, she spotted something strange in the distance, toward the 18-Point Stag Country Club. Not seeing much point in fighting it, she turned the car. She began to feel more and more as though she'd passed into a post-apocalyptic urban wasteland.

Trashcan fires were almost as regular as street signs. Ghosts, reduced to mere chalk outlines in most cases, were chasing after spectral animals like lunatics. Everyone seemed desperate and on edge.

She started to have a sinking feeling as she approached the country club and realized she was seeing fewer and fewer living people and more and more ghosts. So this was where all the specters had gone. In fact, it was starting to look like Burning Man for the dead out here, complete with what appeared to be a great wooden effigy at the center of the crowd.

She'd never seen so many ghosts in one place. Nor had she seen more than one or two in all her life that looked as drawn and worn out as nearly every person in this crowd did. The chatter was constant and the effect it had on her mind, even having never done much to develop her ghostsense, was particularly negative. She felt suffused with ugly emotions. Every ghost in town was in this crowd, and every ghost in the crowd was full of worry, fear, trepidation, terror, and most of all, uncertainty. They were a great sea of raw nerves.

A spectral figure passed right through her car.

"Hey!" she shouted.

The figure, a man who'd once been young, but now seemed old and haggard, turned and fixed her with a stare.

"What do you want, lady?"

Her lower lip quivered. She wanted to light him up, but he seemed so wretched she couldn't.

"Could you move along?" she asked, giving the universal "move along" gesture which police officers had perfected so well over the centuries.

"Ain't that what we're all worried about?" he asked.

Before she could respond, he disapparated.

In her line of work she'd met many rude ghosts, and many, like that one, had disapparated on her for various reasons. It didn't mean much. It was about the equivalent of angrily hanging up a telephone. Except that wasn't the case anymore, was it? A disapparating specter could end up in a hole in the world and disappear himself. There was no safety in rudeness anymore, she supposed.

As the crowd stretched out before her she began to realize she wasn't going to be able to reach the country club's parking lot without plowing through a virtual football field of specters. Though a car passing through an ectoplasmic organism would do very little damage, it would hurt a lot of feelings, and if there was one thing she didn't need right now it was the poltergeist powers of an angry mob of ghosts directed at her. Ghosts out-and-out killing a breather was a rare occurrence, but given the frayed nerves on display here tonight she wouldn't be surprised if they ripped her apart like a rag doll.

She brought the car to an idle and simply stopped in the middle of the street. It wasn't as though there were any other cars approaching. She considered leaving her car in the middle of the street like that overnight, and it occurred to her decisions like that were what led to Sherman's Forest's current state. It was decision after decision like that. Something was astray, and others led themselves astray along with it. Crowds were here so cars were abandoned there. Looting, fires, vandalism all followed. The place was turning into a nightmarescape.

Now that she was closer, she tried to make out what the great wooden statue was. Initially she had taken it for an effigy, but now she saw that wasn't right. It wasn't in the shape of a man, or any animal really. It was almost like a scaffold.

With typical spectral craftsmanship, the scaffolding was poorly constructed and slapdash. But it did the job of raising a platform above the milling crowd. A figure appeared on the platform. He was foppish, with an Edgar Allan Poe-type look to him. Donna had met Poe at a book signing once, but he'd had his head screwed on pretty straight. This man looked perfectly demented. She'd seen him before somewhere, she realized.

Roderick Ellington.

"My friends, my friends!" Ellington called out. "We all know why we're here. We want a solution to this nightmarish problem which has overtaken our fair town. Well, tonight I believe I may have it for you."

Ellington turned to face the opposite direction. Donna realized the crowd came to something of a cusp. They were milling all around the golf course, but they went no farther than a certain invisible line drawn in the sand. An edge of the phenomenon, she realized.

Ellington floated off the scaffold and hung in mid-air a few feet from it.

"Release the mechanism, if you would, gentlemen!" he called down below.

A few specters, struggling to become material enough to work a catch and a lever, triggered something in the wooden construct. Almost like a baseball pitching machine, or a clay pigeon trap, the scaffold shot forward.

The platform where Ellington was standing a moment before snapped out and into what Donna assumed was another hole in the world. Slowly, as though coming down off a post-coital high, the scaffold returned to its original position. Donna realized with a sinking feeling this was an execution device. The concept was completely foreign in the ghost world, and though executions did sometimes take place amongst the living, they were usually festive, jolly affairs, where people got to free their loved ones from cancer or other earthly woes. This was something new, though. The dead would be cast into the red outer darkness to be disposed of. And mob justice would determine who.

"You've all seen," Ellington announced, "what effect our sacrifices of the simple and dumb animals has had on this vituperative phenomenon. Squirrels, rats, and the like. When we give specters to it, it shrinks!"

The crowd cheered, the most miserable cheer Donna had heard in her entire life. Ellington, though, was enjoying his moment in the sun.

"How much more do you expect it will be affected by accepting the mind of a thinking animal? How much more could we reduce this pernicious anomaly's effect by feeding it a man's ghost?"

Donna took a step back. This wasn't a mob. This was a lynch mob. The ghosts must be getting desperate if they'd been reduced to this. She eyed her car. It wasn't terribly far away, but she would have to walk back through a half dozen specters to get there.

"Do we have any volunteers?" Ellington continued. "It might not seem particularly salubrious, but there is something to be said for sacrificing oneself for others. It's so rare that such matters are genuinely put to the test, of course. Have we a good, stout lad who will do his bit for the greater good?"

The mob grew silent. Her car seemed very inviting now. The specters were so focused on Ellington they hadn't noticed her, but that could change in a heartbeat. She got on her hands and knees and began to crawl, hoping to stay below the attention of the crowd, toward her vehicle. It wasn't terribly far away. Maybe if she could avoid . . .

"Hey, lady!"

She looked up. She was smack dab in the middle of a tall, thin specter, glaring down at Donna with anger in her eyes.

"What do you think you're doing?"

"Sorry," Donna said. "I'm just trying to—"

"This isn't for you. Why don't you get the hell out of here?"

She rose. She took a breath and pressed through the crowd.

"That's all right," Ellington was saying, "because, believe it or not, we don't need a volunteer yet. We have someone deserving of this sacrifice."

No, no, no. Donna didn't want to hear it. But she couldn't un-hear it now. As she broke through the crowd to reach her car she looked up. A gang of not less than half a dozen burly ghosts were grasping Kyle around his every limb and orifice and floating him up to the top of the scaffolding. The crowd jeered and booed. After becoming an instant celebrity ("Just add hate!") they recognized him on sight.

"You all know the harbinger of this doom which has come upon us," Ellington announced, "Kyle Fitzpatrick. I'm surprised you don't disapparate, Fitzpatrick. Run, like you have from every trial, every responsibility all your existence."

"I can't," Kyle said. "Nobody can. There are too many holes in the world. It's not safe."

"And whose fault is that?"

For an instant, Ellington flashed almost solid, burning with hate and embarrassment, a cocktail of all the worst and most potent emotions. He really didn't like Kyle, which was convenient, she supposed. It was that combination of a need for a scapegoat and unlucky coincidence which brought Kyle to this point.

"I didn't have anything to do with it and you know it," Kyle spat out.

"Do I? Do I really? I don't know anything except what I can see with my eyes and hear with my ears. None of us do. And we all saw you, first on the scene to one of these events. What did you do to cause it?"

Gritting her teeth, Donna stepped onto the hood of her car. Grimacing and cursing herself, she took another unbalanced step onto the roof.

"Hey! Ellington!" she yelled.

The crowd all turned to look at her. Oh, this was a bad idea.

They would tear her to bits and pieces. Well, everybody had to become a ghost sometime. She just wouldn't get to enjoy it very long.

"This is what you people do now?" Donna asked, addressing the crowd as much as Ellington. "Human sacrifice? After all the years I've had to endure all the snide remarks, all the under-breath comments about how I wouldn't be civilized until I'd been dead for a few decades? But it all gets tossed into the trash as soon as you get scared, huh?"

Ellington chuckled, a smarmy noise, but not absolutely effective in belittling her.

"How typical to this point. Another of the Fitzpatrick siblings dissembling. Well, madam, let me assure you the carapace of civilization with which we have sheathed ourselves has gone nowhere. Not out of fear. And let me reassure you we are not merely afraid for no good reason. This . . ."—he gestured at the imminent hole in the world which lay beyond the scaffolding's reach—". . . represents an existential threat to our kind. And yet we have not become any less than we were, have we? We have not diminished. We have come together as a community, nay, a family, resolved to find a solution to this situation."

Donna said, "If you're no different than you were, then you'll respect the rule of law. Turn him over to Sheriff Hager. Let the law deal with it."

Ellington turned and looked down into the crowd.

Oh, shit, Donna thought.

Much to her chagrin, Steven rose up out of the crowd. He held his Smokey the Bear hat over his crotch somewhat contritely, but he wasn't exactly rushing to shut the situation down.

"I'm sorry," Steven said, seemingly addressing her and not the crowd. "You know I'm dedicated to law and order. That's not a campaign slogan. I've been doing this as long as you've been alive. But I've seen things tonight no ghost should ever see. You don't understand the magnitude of the problem. You're alive. You don't understand."

"I understand the difference between a lynch mob and a court of law!" Donna shrieked, immediately cursing herself for how shrill she knew she sounded.

Ellington held up his hands. "Very well! Even as time presses in on us, his inexorable finger moving ever towards our damnation, we shall remain as fair as custom and our reputations demand. Let us hear evidence. Let us decide. Even though Armageddon presseth upon us, let us be a fair and civilized people. A jury of this calumnious blackguard's peers shall rate him."

Ellington gestured at the audience. Oh, great. An angry mob lifting its thumbs or jabbing them down. Like the famous judgments of the Roman Colosseum.

"Let's hear all his crimes. Marie! Where are you?"

A stiff, tight figure floated from out of the crowd to the top of the platform, though clearly she was in a position of some honor. She was more put-together and colorized than the rest of the crowd. Donna had never seen the woman before.

"Whither sayest thou against this cur, unworthy of the title 'man,' Kyle Fitzpatrick?" Marie said. "He destroyed my great-granddaughter's mind. And killed her dog."

30

KYLE HEARD THE CHARGES, UNDERSTOOD them, and cracked a wide, cavalier grin. He felt the end coming for him and for everyone. Tommie Bones was right. When all was said and done there was nowhere to run.

Donna, his indomitable sister, red hair askew and with a look of fury in her eyes, stood atop her SUV like a burning beacon in the dead sea. Roderick Ellington and Marie stood as prosecutors before an angry god. The roiling redness of the hole in the world was storming and hungry for him.

It didn't matter, they'd caught him. It was an odd feeling, knowing all that counted from this moment on was how he acquitted himself in his final moments.

"I destroyed nothing. The dog, Ramses, fell into the hole," Kyle said, hovering over the platform, Donna far below him, and the dead staring daggers into him. "You're right about one thing, though, Ellington. My sister can't understand. But neither can I. I can barely look at the fucking thing. And neither can the rest of you. It defies understanding."

The phenomenon edged closer, lapping at the base of the scaffolding. The ghosts beyond stepped back and even Roderick Ellington looked uneasy. Marie was all dignity, barely moving and avoiding eye contact with both Kyle and the anomaly behind her.

Kyle could see he had zero chance. He could disapparate of

course. Maybe he wouldn't relapse. Maybe he wouldn't pass through the phenomenon as he went. Maybe he'd buy a few precious days of existence. Certainly he'd deny the lynch mob the pleasure of destroying him. But he didn't want Donna's last memories of him to be of him running. For some reason, that seemed to matter now.

He was going to make it up to her.

He was also going to make sure the cowards who put him here knew what he thought about them.

"What, nothing to say? Of course not. Why say anything else? We all know you've made up your minds. What's a little eternal destruction of the soul between friends?" Kyle said, wagging a finger at the assembled haunts. "No take backs, exchanges, or refunds."

Maybe shame passed through them, maybe guilt, but the army of ghosts roiled with anger. The scaffolding shook and Roderick hastily held up his hands, admonishing the ghosts to calm themselves.

"Friends, friends!"

Kyle smiled, expecting the contraption to collapse and everything to be over. Donna would see him defiant, going with dignity. He smiled. He never thought he'd see the day when he could be called dignified.

Donna always surprised him. Whenever he thought he had her figured out she went and did something unexpected. While the ghosts roiled with anger, Donna hurried through them, uncaring of whose toes she stepped on, who she walked through. She mounted the scaffolding and Kyle watched her, deciding maybe she had more in common with him than he'd initially thought. He was nearly joyous when he found himself calm enough, solid enough, for her to embrace.

"You never did know when to shut up," she whispered in his ear.

The pure joy of the moment worked against him. Donna nearly tumbled through him as intangibility returned. The dangerously shoddy scaffolding swayed, and for a moment he thought Donna would plummet to the ground, smack dab in the middle of the phenomenon.

Focusing like he'd never done before, he reached out and grabbed her, getting a good solid hold of her scruff.

"I got you," he whispered.

The scaffolding stopped swaying after a second.

"I'm going to get you out of here." She said it with such certainty Kyle almost believed her.

"Always the control freak."

"Madam, step away from the condemned," said Ellington.

Kyle dearly wanted to grab the pompous ass and run headlong into the hole. But he knew Ellington would activate the execution device before he even got close.

Donna scowled at the poet. Kyle could see the other ghosts beginning to grow anxious. It wasn't a good sign. Already they were shouting to kill her and throw them both in.

"You're a coward, whatever you think he's done wrong. This won't make things better." Donna seemed to pull herself up higher. Even though she was shorter than the dead Poe wannabe, she seemed to tower over him. "It won't save you."

She was on a tirade now, though. Nothing would stop her. She looked at the assembled crowd. "What happens when it doesn't go away? What happens when it comes again? How many of your own are you willing to feed it?"

Kyle admired her. When he was alive she'd always covered for him, protected him.

"Donna," Kyle said.

Donna ignored him, intent on taking on the whole mob with nothing but moxie.

"And you," she rounded on Roderick with fury. "You spineless waste of ectoplasm. Tear me apart, see if I—"

"Donna!" Kyle shouted. The world rattled and everyone, his sister included, finally noticed him. He took a deep breath, closing his eyes and gathering his thoughts. It was hard to stay calm.

"I'll do it," Kyle said. "I'll volunteer to go into the hole. No need for a show trial."

He said it with such clarity it put a smile on his face when he saw Ellington's mask of bewilderment. Donna, on the other hand, looked like a mad ball of fear, anger, and, yes, a bit of respect.

"No," she said. "No, you don't have to do this!"

He walked forward and hugged her tightly. "I'm sorry. Sorry for everything I put you through. I'm sorry for having you chase me all over the place, cover for me."

"Shut up, shut up, just—"

He felt Donna's body twitch, wracked with quiet sobs, yet still carrying herself with quiet dignity.

Kyle broke the embrace. Donna's eyes were wet. She was barely holding it together.

"You're really going to do it, aren't you?" Kyle couldn't meet her eyes. "You can run, apparate away. Don't worry about your pride."

"It's all over the place," Kyle said quietly, not daring to look behind him. "It's going to eat everything. At least remember me well."

"All right," Ellington said, causing Kyle to twitch and Donna to shoot a glare of undisguised loathing, "we've allowed all the time propriety demands. It's time."

Though he retained his usual snooty air, Kyle could tell the poet was panicking. He could feel it behind him, sending chills through his soul.

He put on a brave face but Kyle was feeling anything but brave. Defiant, for sure, but defiant and afraid. Standing on the platform, he looked at Donna.

"Release it!" Ellington cried.

Somewhere gears rumbled.

"Kyle, I can't . . . I don't—"

"Live your life. Marry Joe Exorcist and have wonderful, fat babies." He didn't want to look at what was behind him. He was so afraid. He wanted sage and home.

"Fuck you," she laughed and cried.

The platform started to move. Kyle held his head high, but he trembled, the memories of tears made trails down his face.

"Please don't leave me alone," he barely whispered.

"I'm here, little brother, I'm here." Donna held him close as the platform moved. He was surprised to feel so solid.

Coldness and the sense of nothing stroked his back. He remembered what he wanted to say. "Donna, I love—"

31

EARLY MORNING LIGHT STREAMED IN through the wall-length plate glass window. Somehow, almost miraculously, the agency survived the many nights of looting which followed the event. That surprised Donna. She would have thought the prominent "Fitzpatrick" on the sign would have acted like a homing target for smash-and-grabbers.

Then again, the same wave of hysteria that drove people to petty crime also instilled them all with a healthy sense of superstition and paranoia. It was as likely they were terrified to smash the Fitz sign in light of Kyle's supposed connection to the phenomenon.

In the background, the television blared. She always liked to have a little noise in the background when she did menial labor.

". . . one month since Silence Night, and five weeks since the Thracian Incident which preceded it," the ever-chipper Sparrow Thames was saying while attempting to sound grim and heavy with gravitas. She continued, "Here's a look back at some of the reporting from that chaotic period."

Donna glanced up at the screen. Kyle's face whizzed by along with a kaleidoscope of other images. The media made zero effort to clear his name. He was gone now, of course, so it hardly seemed to matter if they spoke ill of the gone, but it irked Donna like sand in her shoe.

She put her fists on her hips and stared at the sign.

"Spender/Fitzpatrick Surrogacy Agency." Of course, from the inside, it was reversed. She still remembered the day they'd bought the sign. And the day before when they'd argued over what to call the agency. She'd argued for alphabetical order. Spender naturally preferred seniority, and as he had both that and more money invested in the business, he won out. Thinking of Spender made her heart ache again.

"Thanks for being with us today, Dr. Rausch," Sparrow was saying on the TV. "The scientific and paranormal communities have had a few weeks now to examine the data. What can you tell us today you couldn't tell us before about Silence Night?"

A gray-bearded, bespectacled academic type sat across from her. He was hefty, but the strangest thing about him was he wore a patch over one eye. Two months ago, Donna would have wondered what had caused that. But in the wake of the phenomenon, there were countless thousands of bizarre accidents. Driverless vehicles crashing into things. Factories ceasing production for lack of knowledge. The brain drain since the loss of the ghosts was enormous. Something horrible happened to Rausch, she had no doubt, and yet it was now just another in a long list of "Let me tell you about what happened to me on Silence Night" anecdotes.

She glanced at the razor blade in her hand. Somehow, she always believed this day would never come. She stepped forward and began to scrape the corner of the last "K" in her name off the window.

She'd always thought she wouldn't be doing this job for a long, long time. Long enough for the constipation and whatever it foretold—heart disease, bowel cancer, whatever—to kill her and make her a happy ghost, anyway. Then she'd planned to spend a few years as Spender had, acting like the senior partner, no longer working herself into the ground, hiring on a new agent to take her place, maybe. Then someday sell it to the junior partner, whoever they turned out to be.

"Thanks for having me, Sparrow," Rausch was saying. "Unfortunately, we know very little new. A Crucian might describe this as an 'Act of God.'"

They both chuckled mindlessly. As a kneejerk reaction, people still belittled the strange sect, but Donna recently read its membership had risen astronomically in the last month. For perhaps the first time ever, people wanted answers about what happened after they died. Donna tried to ignore it, but the broadcast had sucked her in.

"Seriously, though, Doctor," Sparrow prompted.

Rausch said, "The one good piece of news I can tell you is this appears to be a localized phenomenon. Inasmuch as our friends in the paranormal studies community can tell, the phenomenon, the absence of spiritual activity, ceases somewhere in our atmosphere."

"Yes, I've heard about this," Sparrow said, "the airplane ghosts."

"Just so," Rausch agreed. "Of the few ghosts who happened to be traveling by air on Silence Night, the ones with the presence of mind to take refuge upwards rather than returning to earth are still up there. I imagine it must be a miserable existence, flittering among the clouds like that. But, yes, multiple airlines have reported ghostly hitch-hikers hopping aboard planes as they reach cruising altitude. So far, mostly they've been seeking to pass on messages to their loved ones and, frankly, seek a little companionship. Who can blame them?"

"There's also the story of Lucas Tremblay aboard the ISS."

"Yes, that's right. Although Lieutenant Commander Tremblay was not the first astronaut to die in outer space, he has, due to circumstances, been the first to remain there. From all reports, he's proven himself to be quite an asset."

"Yes," Sparrow agreed, "everything I've heard is that he's proving a ghost can still do anything a living person can."

"Indeed. Of course, now I fear he may be in a lonely position, as the last of his kind in regular contact with us."

"We will, of course, be having more on Commander Tremblay when we have our exclusive interview with him later in this broadcast. But, Dr. Rausch, back to our original discussion, what caused the phenomenon?"

"Yes, I suppose that's what I am here for, aren't I, Sparrow? Well, there are any number of theories and, frankly, we don't have any way of knowing for sure with our current technology. We were able to monitor the spectral world rather well up until the event. But with it completely disappearing out from under us, it's difficult to learn from what isn't there, if you follow my meaning."

"Setting aside outlandish theories like the so-called 'God' you mentioned earlier, what do you think?"

Rausch nodded, shifted in his chair, and seemed to be jonesing for something. By the look of him, Donna guessed, a pipe of tobacco.

"The so-called mushroom theory is rather popular. The general principle is the spiritual phenomena was not native to our planet. Something inherent in either the Earth, or possibly our civilization (ley lines, or some such) caused spiritual phenomena to mushroom outward, so to speak. Their regression in this past year was simply a return to normality. The ley lines receding, perhaps.

"There's also the bad actor concept. Perhaps an alien intelligence—alien in the sense of either extraterrestrial or outside of our sphere of knowledge—desired to wipe out our spiritual brethren."

"A demon, you mean?" Sparrow suggested.

"We could call it that. Hypothetically. At this point I can't really fault anyone's theory, even the wild ones, considering the dearth of evidence."

"What do *you* think happened, Doctor?"

Rausch paused, acting a bit taken aback, although certainly he must have expected the question. Purely theatrics for the viewing audience.

He said, "I may be biased on account of my profession, but I'm a man who believes in natural law. The laws of physics, for instance. What goes up must come down. The laws of thermodynamics. And so forth. Our co-existence with ghosts throughout history has simply been a part of the natural order of things. But I can conceive of a world without a spiritual counterpoint. A reality where ghosts simply don't exist, and that's their natural law. We in the scientific community, of course, have largely accepted the many worlds theory."

"You'll have to slow down," Sparrow chuckled.

"Of course." He pulled a penny out of his pocket. "A minor wager. The loser gets the winner a cup of coffee. Agreed?"

She said, "Yes."

"Call it."

"Heads."

He flipped it, caught it, slammed it on the back of his hand, and peered at it.

"Tails," he said. "That coin flip is now a part of our collective reality. But the many worlds theory posits the world where this landed heads and I owe you a cup of coffee will continue. There is another me and another you.

"What I think has never been considered before is the possible intersection of various universes. If two such worlds collided, say at a single point. A sort of a hole or a portal. Take, for instance, these two sheets of paper. Similar, no doubt, but with different lines of text on it written by me."

He held up a notebook, thumbed two pages, and pressed a pencil point between both sheets at once.

"This pinprick now connects the two pages. And if these are worlds with individual laws, well, perhaps those laws could bleed through into each other. One could imagine a house, say, in the world where ghosts do not exist, suddenly becoming haunted, not by spirits from our world, but by the laws of our world overwriting the laws of theirs."

"Fuck me," Donna breathed.

She had heard almost this exact explanation once before, from Bonnie Jackson in her ancestral home. And with that thought, all of Donna's memories of the awful place came rushing back to her. She'd taken great pains to dismiss the apparent capacity of that damned house to prey upon her thoughts. But it never really left her. The place was constantly there, hiding in the dark recesses of her brain.

"In this theory," Sparrow said, sounding desperately like she was trying to understand, "the entire Earth has, uh, I don't know, intersected with another dimension?"

Rausch shook his head. "I wouldn't think that would be necessary. Have you ever had a cup of hot cocoa on a snowy day?"

Now that was something Sparrow understood. "Of course!"

"By ingesting a little bit of liquid, a cup or so, your entire body warms up. I would think it's like that. Another dimension's natural laws have warmed up, so to speak, ours."

"Scary," Sparrow said.

As though chastened by the television figures, Donna shivered.

"Of course," Rausch said, chuckling, at last, "it could also be something completely different."

She shook her head and turned back to her work. Her "work." Her "work" at present consisted of tearing down the edifice of everything she'd done with her life up until now. Where would she go from here? What was she supposed to do?

She supposed she'd have to find someone to take over for her after she died. But who the hell would want to do that? Then again, there would be money in it. Or there would have been, if the ghost surrogacy agency business hadn't up and disappeared like a fart in the wind. She'd have to find a new line of work altogether, of course. But then what? Maybe she'd have to hand it down to her kids, if she ever had any. That would keep the money in the family, after all, which seemed important all of a sudden.

She supposed she'd better work on having kids, then. Leaving three quarters of a "K" unremoved, she wiped her hands off and headed back toward the storage room. The room was filled with cardboard boxes full of personalized pens, key chains, and calendars (supposedly to help advertise the business) as well as the usual detritus of any office: pencil sharpeners, staple removers, file folders, and the like.

Leroy was going through her files. Actually, he was supposed to be packing them in boxes, but instead he was leaning against her filing cabinet, reading one of the files, shaking his head, and laughing. He nearly jumped out of his skin when she came in.

"I wasn't doing anything I wasn't supposed to," he said.

"I can see that. Whose file were you reading?"

He held up his hands. "I wouldn't, baby. I know that stuff is like, confidential and covered by HIPAA and all those laws and whatnot and you could get in big trouble for—"

"No, it's not."

"Huh?"

She smiled wryly. "Where do you think I work? We're matchmakers, not doctors. There's no law against reading our files. I mean, it is a little skeevy . . ."

Rubbing his hands excitedly, he opened the file and put it down on a ping pong table which both she and Spender had sworn up and down they would use daily in order to justify purchasing it.

"Okay, skeevy I'll take," he said. "Did you read this? Look at this shit. This kid was seven years old when he died. You know, one of those tragic child leukemia blah blah blah. The girl was forty-five. I mean, I say 'girl' but really, she's a woman. Three kids, twice divorced. I mean, I get it, the kid died in the sixties so he's, like, in his sixties or something, technically, but can you imagine boinking the ghost of a seven-year-old? I mean, that makes her a pedophile, right? Technically?"

Donna crossed her arms and shook her head, but couldn't keep the smile off her face.

"I guess you're talking about Rory St. Andrews and Amanda Milch. And I don't have to read it. They were one of the first couples that walked through the door. Spender was still out getting paint for the sign."

Leroy closed up the file folder. He seemed to have sobered up a bit. She knew why it seemed funny. A lot of times this business seemed funny. Real funny. People who shouldn't have been in love, but were.

Like her and Leroy, come to think of it. What did they even have in common? But they got along so well. That was the thing. Despite being so ground down into the dirt by it, despite all the ghostfuckers and halfway-pedophiles who walked through the door, at the end of the day she was making love connections. She was bringing people who cared about each other together and that was the closest thing to meaningful work she could imagine.

Now she couldn't do it anymore. What kind of skillset did she have anyway? A knack for telling which ghosts and breathers would work together? Half of that equation didn't even exist anymore. She had no idea if her soft skills would even vaguely translate into another field.

"I'm sorry, baby. I didn't mean to make fun."

She smiled wistfully. "It's not making fun. It is fun. I remember laughing at some of these people the same as you. You know what I did when they were really ridiculous?"

He shook his head. She plopped down on an old stack of ghost interest periodicals. She supposed she wouldn't be needing those anymore, either.

"I used to tell them our first meeting would be in a week. I had no reason to put people off. Most people I could do on a walk-in basis. Maybe, worst-case scenario, if I was completely swamped, I would tell them to come back first thing in the morning. I didn't care. I'd come in whenever. But you give those people a week, the real jokers, and they'd never come back. And if they did come back? I'd do them for free. They deserved it. Because just because you look goofy together doesn't mean you're not in love. And love is a . . . it's a sacred thing."

He crouched down, took her hand and looked in her eyes. "What'd you need from back here?"

She put her hand under her chin, thinking back. Then she remembered. "You ever think about having kids?"

Leroy scratched the back of his neck. "I don't know. Who'd take care of them now?"

"I guess . . . the parents would have to."

"So, us, in other words."

She smiled. "Yeah, I guess so."

He shook his head. "That sounds miserable. But I guess it's the way things are going to have to be from now on. So . . . yes?"

"Yes, what?"

"Yes, I'll have kids with you?"

"That sounded like a question. Only, not the right question."

"Oh," he said, finally understanding, "You wanted to hear *that* question."

"Yes."

"Well, I'm not going to do it because you asked me to. It would cheapen the whole thing. I'm going to do it because I want to."

Leroy got down on one knee and reached into his back pocket. Donna's hand went over her mouth in surprise. "You didn't. Did you?"

He drew out of his pocket . . . a set of keys. "No," he said, "I didn't get a ring yet. But how perfect would that have been if I had?"

She shoved his shoulder. Then she paused and thought about it. "Did you say 'yet'?"

He shrugged. "Don't read too much into it, Fitz's sister."

Although he had always called her that occasionally, he immediately regretted doing it this time. She held out her hand and helped him to his feet.

"Fitz's sister," she said. "I'm glad I got to be that."

"Yeah," Leroy agreed, "I'm sorry I didn't get to know him better. We didn't have enough time apparently. What was he like?"

"Exhausting. Annoying. Crude. A fucking child sometimes. But in the end . . . brave."

Leroy lowered his bulk down onto one of the file boxes. She winced, hoping it wouldn't crumple, but apparently it was full and held him up.

He said. "You've never told me about what happened that night."

"And you've never pushed the issue, either. And I appreciate that."

"I'm pushing now. I want to know."

She supposed she owed him that much. "It was horrible. All the haunts in Sherman's Forest turned on him like a mob. They tossed him into one of those holes in the world. I got to hug him before he

215

went. He told me he loved me."

"That's good."

"Yeah, I guess."

"And that all happened on Silence Night?"

Unexpectedly, she burst out crying. Leroy looked mortified and jumped to his feet. She held out her hands to ward him off, but he took her into his arms anyway.

"That's all right," he said. "I'm sorry I pushed."

"No, no," she said, wiping her nose on her hand and wishing she hadn't. "I'm pissed off about it. They really believed putting ghosts in the phenomenon would make it shrink. I don't know where the idea came from. I think it moved and they wanted to see some pattern in the movement and that was it, you know?

"After they put Kyle in it, it didn't go away. Of course. You already know that. It was the night the dead went silent. The funny thing is they'd all been ready to tear me apart. They were ready to kill me, even knowing death is like a sentence for the end of your own existence now. They were still going to kill me."

"So what happened?"

She snapped her fingers. "It went out like a light. All that anger. As soon as Kyle was gone they . . . they all looked at me like they realized they'd fucked up. You remember Steven Hager, the sheriff?"

"Vaguely."

She was sneering now and didn't like how it made her sound, but she couldn't hold it back either.

"He actually came up and touched my shoulder and tried to comfort me. Of all people. The one who wouldn't rein in an angry mob. But then I guess they realized their mistake. The hole in the world didn't recede. It lunged forward like a wave. That asshole ringleader Roderick Ellington? He disappeared screaming. And that Unenlightened girl's great-grandmother? She stood there like a statue, like her dignity couldn't submit to this. They were all . . . swept away. I was looking into Hager's face as it washed over him. It was like he was pleading, begging me for forgiveness."

"Did you give it?"

"I didn't have time. I still don't know if I would or I wouldn't have. I don't like what that says about me."

He took her hand. "It says you have conflicted feelings about a lynch mob that tried to kill you. You're hardly a monster."

"What was Silence Night like for you?"

He shook his head. "I wasn't even around any ghosts at the time, which is kind of ironic, considering my profession. I was buttoned up in the library with about fifteen other 'cists, and we were all debating and discussing and trying to figure out how to fix everything. When we finally realized the library poltergeists weren't throwing books around anymore, it was all over. Had been for hours. We'd completely missed it, too busy trying to solve it."

"And how are you feeling?" she asked, hoping she didn't seem like a nag for asking all the time.

To all appearances, Leroy was a big, strong, unflappable teddy bear. But being a psychic medium necessitated being in touch with your deepest emotions, and Leroy had been a potent medium. He'd lost something truly exceptional.

"I had this surgery when I was a kid. Appendix out, you know. They said I'd never miss it. That the appendix was a useless organ, a vestigial thing from a different time in our evolutionary history. But I felt its absence when it was gone."

His hand went to his navel, and his fingers danced along his belly. She took it away from there and held it.

"It got better, though, didn't it?"

"It got better," he agreed, "but sometimes I can still feel it missing."

"I felt the same way when I had my wisdom teeth out. I thought I would never get over the irritation. Every meal I had to clean out those weird little gaps in my gums. I almost wished I had left them in, because it was better than the feeling of having a different mouth, being a different person. But you know what? Now I don't even remember what it was like to have them in."

He stared down at the ground. "If I'm not a medium, if I'm not an exorcist, what am I?"

"You're a kind, big-hearted—"

"Don't bullshit me."

She smiled weakly.

"All right," she said. "All right. I know it's not like having your tonsils out or your appendix. A part of you is missing. My brother was a huge part of my life. I'll never see him again. I don't have a job anymore. I know it's not the same for you. A surrogacy agency is a paycheck. I mean, I did it well, I worked hard at it, but being an exorcist is who you are. Were. It was a calling for you. But as for who you are, you're a good man. You're kind and decent. People respect you. Even my brother respected you, and he didn't respect anybody, believe me. And . . . you're my boyfriend. And we'll figure it out together."

"Okay," he said. "I think I can work with that."

"Come on. Let's finish packing up all the old memories in this place. Once I'm out of my lease that'll be, I don't know, something."

Leroy went back to packing up the files. She stepped back out into the lobby. Sparrow was back on the television, interviewing the astronaut who'd miraculously survived the phenomenon that devastated the rest of the world's spectral community. At least things worked out for him. There was hope, she supposed, and that was something. She scraped furiously at the window until it was clean, and by the time she was done, Leroy had finished loading up the moving van and came to find her.

She glanced one last time at their slogan. "We don't believe in unhappy endings." Well, maybe so. Maybe so. She walked, arm-in-arm with the love of her life, out of her shop for the last time.

EPILOGUE

LIEUTENANT COMMANDER LUCAS TREMBLAY floated inside the space station, staring out into the void. Below him, he was told the planet Earth still spun in its celestial dance around the sun, but all he could see was a redness, somehow darker than the void of space around it.

As far as he knew, he was the last ghost, a terrible title and one he would have gladly done anything to forsake. It'd been hell staring off into the void, knowing Gracie was down there. His wife had given birth days after he'd arrived. Commander Southard had shocked him by opening his bottle of Aberlour 16, best damn scotch there was, for celebratory drinks. They'd had to enjoy them with sippy cups, but it had still been the best damn thing anyone had ever done for him, except for Gracie agreeing to be his beautiful bride.

Then he'd died.

It hadn't been pleasant. He'd basically spent the last moments of his life clawing at his throat as his blood boiled inside his chest. Then he'd found himself back on the station, watching as his body curlicued away into the void, never to be recovered, despite the urgent attempts of his crewmates. Now he was stuck, twirling around the green and blue orb that was the planet, presumably forever.

He'd called his wife every day. She'd sobbed and vowed they would be together, that she was fine with using a surrogate. In short, all the cliché empty promises spouses made to each other when a marriage ended prematurely.

It wasn't the other man, the living one, that made Tremblay give up hope. No, it was when the hole, the void, the nothing, whatever it was had finally eaten the world and he could no longer even hear the transmissions of the living within it.

He'd been told Earth was still there, still spinning somewhere in that emptiness, but he couldn't see it, couldn't hear it.

Even if he persisted to a ripe old age, Lucas Tremblay would never be able to have a conversation with his daughter.

"Staring at it won't make it go away." Commander Southard's soulful eyes were full of pity. Nobody ever looked at him anymore. They always had to pity him, too.

"I guess you're right," Tremblay responded, pushing off and pulling himself toward the US Orbital Segment.

The rest of the astronauts on the ISS were alive, though in the zero-gravity environment they all moved in about the same fashion. Before he'd realized what an absolute outcast he was, he'd joked that it put them on equal footing: the ghost spaceman and the living hangers-on, floating around inside a tin can speeding through the empty abyss.

But then he'd started to notice the sideways glances. Conversations would end when he entered the room, even mundane ones. No one could look him in the face anymore. Once he'd even caught Dries cursing him when he thought he couldn't hear. And worst of all was the pity. The pity was never-ending.

It was like this for the past few weeks. Once the Earth was taken from his sight they'd begun describing the blues and greens of the living world below for him, a routine that had quickly worn out its welcome. Probably they thought they were doing him a kindness, but it felt like the exact opposite. He didn't need to be reminded of the fact he could never go back or that he was the last ghost in existence.

Dying wasn't just an inconvenience like puberty or menopause anymore. If anything, it felt like he'd lost everything when he'd died.

When he came onto the USOS, Jennings looked up at him with a smile which instantly faded. The last time she'd smiled like that, it was because she'd been operating his e-mail for him. It took precision to operate the instruments up here and methodical focus to repair anything and those were skills Tremblay no longer possessed.

He hadn't learned how to focus and become solid enough to manipulate anything, and even if he could, he couldn't do it for long.

So Jennings read his mail for him. Pity, once again couched as kindness. At least she had up until a few days ago. She had gone off on a gushing tirade, thinking it would bring him joy to hear about his daughter, about how she was growing. Then she turned the screen for him to see a photograph. Except, to him, it wasn't a photograph of anything except the red emptiness. His vision had gone red and he'd forgotten he was dead. They'd found him back in the airlock, silently suffocating as he relapsed.

This time Jennings remained silent, returning to her work. Commander Southard appeared a moment later, apparently tailing him. Southard made Tremblay a lot of promises about finding a place for him and keeping him useful, but the truth was depressing, obviously. He was nothing more than a burden, even if none of them had the guts to acknowledge it to his face.

He needed to get away.

"Permission to go for a spacewalk? I want to make sure everything's still shipshape. I can save . . ."—he glanced at the duty roster and grimaced in distaste—". . . Dries from having to do a safety inspection."

Commander Southard looked taken aback for a moment. He opened his mouth, clearly about to say no because no one could be spared to help him into a suit. But Southard's expression turned bleak as he seemed to recall Tremblay would need no protection from the vacuum. He gave a slow nod, holding his hands out in a gesture of solidarity.

"Yeah, of course."

Something thrilled inside Tremblay. For the first time since his death, perhaps, he didn't feel completely useless. Maybe with some lateral thinking he could be a useful member of the crew again. Maybe, since safety wasn't an issue, the most useful member. That was in the distance, of course, but for now he could at least do something.

Then Southard smashed it all.

"You don't have to worry so much about the inspection. I'll still send Dries out later. But feel free to get some space . . . er, well, privacy. Just be careful, okay?"

So much for that. Tremblay was sick of everyone walking on eggshells around him. And the thought of facing it for the rest of time was unbearable. Sometimes the only respite was to get away from it all.

Screw Southard. And Dries, and Jennings, and all the rest of them. He'd prove himself one way or another. He was still an astronaut, damn it, a world class athlete and a top tier mathematician. He phased through the bulkhead of the station, leaving the crew behind and emerging into the vast stillness of the cosmos.

He'd always felt oddly comfortable in the vacuum of space. The quiet allowed him access to his thoughts, a place where he could sit and contemplate the mysteries of the universe. It was harder to do that now. Even though he couldn't breathe he felt like hyperventilating every time he looked down and saw the gaping rupture where his home used to be spinning through space.

Lieutenant Commander Tremblay sat on the edge of forever and contemplated the thought of drifting through space for the rest of eternity.

He might have sat there for hours. Without communications in the constant blackness that betrayed no measure of time, it was hard to tell. It might have been hours or it might have been a few seconds. Either way, it was astounding to him when he heard a noise. It was like a pop, or shifting sand, then a slow steady whistling like wind through a keyhole.

Lieutenant Commander Tremblay turned and saw a wall of red nothingness, expanding out in all directions from the Earth below, beginning to devour the space station.

Acknowledgments

Thank you to C.V. Hunt, Andersen Prunty, and the entire crew at Grindhouse Press for taking a chance on a couple of roustabouts who broke all the rules while calling no man "Mister."

Our gratitude goes out to Rachel Grundon for her invaluable lessons on mediumship, with our apologies for the liberties we took on the subject matter. We'd also like to thank Donna Fitzpatrick and Steven Hager for letting us use their names in vain.

We would like to thank a few mentors, friends, and peers: Brian Keene, Mary San Giovanni, Bob Ford, Kelli Owen, Somer Canon, Wesley Southard, Mike Lombardo, Linda Addison, and a long list of others. Stephen would like to point out that Wile E. included Kelli Owen in that list, not him.

Wile E. would like to thank his wife, Emily, who has stayed with him through the worst and has ridden with him through the best, has labored over and beta-read everything, and who has helpfully told him when he needed a good kick in the pants.

Stephen would like to thank his partner, Amy, for exorcising all the bad from his life.

Stephen Kozeniewski (pronounced "causin' ooze key") lives in Pennsylvania, the birthplace of the modern zombie. During his time as a Field Artillery officer, he served for three years in Oklahoma and one in Iraq, where, due to what he assumes was a clerical error, he was awarded the Bronze Star. He is also a classically trained linguist, which sounds much more impressive than saying his bachelor's degree is in German.

Wile E. Young is from Texas, where he grew up surrounded by stories of ghosts and monsters. During his writing career he has managed to both have a price put on his head and publish his southern themed horror stories, both terrifying and bizarre. He obtained his bachelor's degree in History, which provided no advantage or benefit during his years as an aviation specialist and I.T. guru.

Other Grindhouse Press Titles

#666__*Satanic Summer* by Andersen Prunty

#062__*Savage Mountain* by John Quick

#061__*Cocksucker* by Lucas Milliron

#060__*Luciferin* by J. Peter W.

#059__*The Fucking Zombie Apocalypse* by Bryan Smith

#058__*True Crime* by Samantha Kolesnik

#057__*The Cycle* by John Wayne Comunale

#056__*A Voice So Soft* by Patrick Lacey

#055__*Merciless* by Bryan Smith

#054__*The Long Shadows of October* by Kristopher Triana

#053__*House of Blood* by Bryan Smith

#052__*The Freakshow* by Bryan Smith

#051__*Dirty Rotten Hippies and Other Stories* by Bryan Smith

#050__*Rites of Extinction* by Matt Serafini

#049__*Saint Sadist* by Lucas Mangum

#048__*Neon Dies at Dawn* by Andersen Prunty

#047__*Halloween Fiend* by C.V. Hunt

#046__*Limbs: A Love Story* by Tim Meyer

#045__*As Seen On T.V.* by John Wayne Comunale

#044__*Where Stars Won't Shine* by Patrick Lacey

#043__*Kinfolk* by Matt Kurtz

#042__*Kill For Satan!* by Bryan Smith

#041__*Dead Stripper Storage* by Bryan Smith

#040__*Triple Axe* by Scott Cole

#039__*Scummer* by John Wayne Comunale

#038__*Cockblock* by C.V. Hunt

#037__*Irrationalia* by Andersen Prunty

#036__*Full Brutal* by Kristopher Triana

#035__*Office Mutant* by Pete Risley

#034__*Death Pacts and Left-Hand Paths* by John Wayne
          Comunale

#033__*Home Is Where the Horror Is* by C.V. Hunt

#032__*This Town Needs A Monster* by Andersen Prunty

#031__*The Fetishists* by A.S. Coomer

#030__*Ritualistic Human Sacrifice* by C.V. Hunt

#029__*The Atrocity Vendor* by Nick Cato

#028__*Burn Down the House and Everyone In It* by Zachary T. Owen

#027__*Misery and Death and Everything Depressing* by C.V. Hunt

#026__*Naked Friends* by Justin Grimbol

#025__*Ghost Chant* by Gina Ranalli

#024__*Hearers of the Constant Hum* by William Pauley III

#023__*Hell's Waiting Room* by C.V. Hunt

#022__*Creep House: Horror Stories* by Andersen Prunty

#021__*Other People's Shit* by C.V. Hunt

#020__*The Party Lords* by Justin Grimbol

#019__*Sociopaths In Love* by Andersen Prunty

#018__*The Last Porno Theater* by Nick Cato

#017__*Zombieville* by C.V. Hunt

#016__*Samurai Vs. Robo-Dick* by Steve Lowe

#015__*The Warm Glow of Happy Homes* by Andersen Prunty

#014__*How To Kill Yourself* by C.V. Hunt

#013__*Bury the Children in the Yard: Horror Stories* by Andersen Prunty

#012__*Return to Devil Town (Vampires in Devil Town Book Three)* by Wayne Hixon

#011__*Pray You Die Alone: Horror Stories* by Andersen Prunty

#010__*King of the Perverts* by Steve Lowe

#009__*Sunruined: Horror Stories* by Andersen Prunty

#008__*Bright Black Moon (Vampires in Devil Town Book Two)* by Wayne Hixon

#007__*Hi I'm a Social Disease: Horror Stories* by Andersen Prunty

#006__*A Life On Fire* by Chris Bowsman

#005__*The Sorrow King* by Andersen Prunty

#004__*The Brothers Crunk* by William Pauley III

#003__*The Horribles* by Nathaniel Lambert

#002__*Vampires in Devil Town* by Wayne Hixon

#001__*House of Fallen Trees* by Gina Ranalli

#000__*Morning is Dead* by Andersen Prunty